continued . . .

MORE BIG RAVES FOR
BIG TROUBLE

"VERY FUNNY . . . SATIRICAL SOCIOLOGY WOR-
THY OF TOM WOLFE. 'A.' "   —*Entertainment Weekly*

"A screwball thriller that reads like a fast-paced screen-
play."   —*USA Today*

"Following the age-old advice to 'write what you know,'
the Pulitzer Prize–winning columnist has produced a novel
involving nuclear bombs, Russian gangsters, giant pythons,
tree-dwelling street people, and teenagers . . . Throw in a
poison toad and a robber blinded by dark panty hose, and
this is about as funny as a book can be."
                            —*The Christian Science Monitor*

"Hilarious . . . Dave Barry is not just an amusing social
observer; he's a novelist of genuine skill . . . he could
become the most important American humorist since Mark
Twain."   —*Fort Lauderdale Sun-Sentinel*

"It'll make you laugh. Out loud. Many, many times."
                            —*The San Diego Union-Tribune*

"Let's face it, Florida is almost as funny as New Jersey,
and any novel in which the mean guy goes insane from the
toxins of a giant toad fills a gentle reader with . . . warmth."
                                      —*Los Angeles Times*

"A satirical romp through Miami's wacky, criminally infest-
ed mean streets . . . a madcap mockery of urban life."
                                        —Ridley Peterson

"Barry has found new life for his comic bag of tricks . . . a
ridiculous and often hilarious farce. [*Big Trouble*] is an
engaging thriller."   —*Chicago Tribune*

"A very funny . . . poison-tipped valentine to Miami."
                        —*The Atlanta Journal-Constitution*

TITLES BY DAVE BARRY

Tricky Business

DAVE BARRY

BERKLEY BOOKS, NEW YORK

TRICKY BUSINESS

A Berkley Book / published by arrangement with
the author

PRINTING HISTORY
G. P. Putnam's Sons hardcover edition / September 2002
Berkley mass-market edition / October 2003

ISBN: 0-425-19274-1

BERKLEY®
Berkley Books are published by The Berkley Publishing Group,
a division of Penguin Group (USA) Inc.,
375 Hudson Street, New York, New York 10014.
BERKLEY and the "B" design
are trademarks belonging to Penguin Group (USA) Inc.

PRINTED IN THE UNITED STATES OF AMERICA

10 9 8 7 6 5 4 3 2 1

THIS BOOK IS DEDICATED TO THE PEOPLE OF SOUTH FLORIDA,
FOR BEING SO CONSISTENTLY WEIRD.

ACKNOWLEDGMENTS AND WARNING

I'm going to start with the same warning I put in my first novel, *Big Trouble*, only this time I'll be more explicit and use a larger typeface:

THIS BOOK CONTAINS SOME BAD WORDS.

I stress this because when *Big Trouble* was published, even though it had a warning at the beginning, I got mail from people who were upset about the language. I wrote them back and explained that, yes, it did have some unsavory language, but that was because the story involved some unsavory characters, and that is the way they talk. Characters like these don't say: "I am going to blow your goshdarned head off, you rascal!" They just don't.

So let me stress that:

THIS BOOK CONTAINS SOME BAD WORDS.

Or, to put it another way:

IF YOU DO NOT WISH TO SEE BAD WORDS, PLEASE DO NOT READ THIS BOOK. THANK YOU.

Next, I'd like to thank some people. I'll start with my editor at Putnam, Neil Nyren, who somehow remains eerily calm when the book deadline has long since passed, and the book cover has been printed, and the catalog copy for the book has been written, and yet Neil has not yet received what the publishing industry refers to, technically, as "the book."

I also thank my suave and urbane agent, Al Hart, who regularly assures me that, not to worry, the book will get done, and, all evidence to the contrary, I *believe* him, because that is how suave and urbane he is.

I thank Judi Smith, my wonderful staff and research department, who is efficient to the point of being prescient, and who never runs from the room, screaming, which is certainly what *I* would do, if I worked for me.

I also thank the people who provided technical guidance when I was writing the book, particularly Jeff Berkowitz, Alan Greer, Patricia Seitz, Ben Stavis, and Rob Stavis. By "provided technical guidance," I mean they listened thoughtfully to some of my earlier plot concepts, and then they politely explained to me that I was an idiot. I especially thank my friend Gene Weingarten, who is insane but who also gave me a huge shove in the right direction when I really needed it.

I thank Gene Singletary, who took the trouble to get me the phone numbers of a couple of people who I bet would have given me some really useful information if I had called them. Gene is also the finest caterer I have ever met.

I thank my writer friends, particularly Jeff Arch, Paul Levine, and Ridley Pearson, for their moral support.

I thank my two wonderful children, Rob and Sophie, although I forbid Sophie from reading this book, assuming that she learns to read.

Finally, and most of all, I thank my wife, Michelle, a sportswriter who works in the very same room where I work. When two people can be on deadline so many times in the same room and still want to eat dinner together at the end of the day, you know that's love.

Tricky Business

One

THE CAPTAIN PUNCHED IN A NUMBER AND HELD
the phone to his ear. He looked out over Biscayne Bay,
which was choppy, toward the sky over the Atlantic, which
was dark.

"What," said a voice in the phone.

"It's me," said the captain.

"Yeah?"

"Have you looked out the window?" said the captain.

"What about it?"

"It's getting worse," said the captain. "It's a tropical
storm now. Tropical Storm Hector. They're forecasting . . ."

"I don't give a rat's ass what they're forecasting. I don't
care if it's Hurricane Shaquille O'Neal, you understand? I
told you that last night."

"I know," said the captain, "but I'm just wondering if
we could do this another . . ."

"*No.* It's set up for tonight. We do it on the night it's set
up for, like always."

The captain took a deep breath. "The thing is," he said, "these winds, it's gonna be rough out there. Somebody could fall, a customer could get hurt."

"That's why we got insurance. Plus, weather like this, probably won't be no customers."

"That's where you're wrong," said the captain. "If we go out, we got customers. These people, they're *crazy*. They don't care about weather, they don't care about *anything*. They just want to get out there."

"Then we're giving them what they want."

"I don't like it," said the captain. "I mean, it's my ship; I'm responsible."

"Number one, it ain't your boat. Number two, you wanna keep working, you do what I tell you."

The captain gripped the phone, but said nothing.

"Besides," said the voice, "that's a big boat."

And the captain thought: *So was the* Titanic.

WALLY HARTLEY AWOKE TO THE SOUND OF HIS mother's knock, followed by the sound of his mother's voice through the bedroom door.

"Wally," she said, "it's your mother."

She always told him this, as if somehow, during the night, he might have forgotten.

"Hi Mom," he said, trying not to sound tired and annoyed, both of which he was. He looked at the clock radio. It was 8:15 A.M. Wally had gone to bed at 5 A.M.

The door opened. Wally squinted his eyes against the light, saw his mom in the doorway. She was dressed and had fixed her hair, as if she had somewhere to go, which she never did, unless you counted the supermarket. She'd gotten up, as always, at 5:30.

"Did you want some waffles?" she asked.

"No thanks, Mom," he said, as he had every morning

since he had, in shame and desperation, at age 29—29, *for God's sake*—moved back in with his mother. Wally did not eat breakfast, but he had given up on trying to explain this to his mother. She'd gotten it into her head that she would make waffles for her son. She was not one to give up easily.

"Are you sure?" she asked.

"I'm sure, Mom," he said. "Thanks."

Wally waited for her to tell him that she had made some fresh.

"I made some fresh," she said.

"Mom, thanks, but really, no."

Now it was time for her to tell him that she hated to see them go to waste.

"I hate to see them go to waste," she said.

"I'm sorry, Mom," said Wally, because it would do no good to yell, IF YOU DON'T WANT TO WASTE THE DAMN WAFFLES, THEN DON'T *MAKE* THE DAMN WAFFLES.

"OK," she said. "I'll save them for later, in case." And she would. She would wrap them in aluminum foil and put them in the refrigerator. Later today, when she was cleaning the kitchen for the fourth time, she would take them out of the refrigerator, throw them away, fold the aluminum foil (she had pieces of aluminum foil dating back to the first Bush administration), and save it in a drawer, for tomorrow's waffles.

"I'm sorry, Mom," said Wally, again.

She sniffed the air in his room. Wally hated that, his mom sniffing his room, his b.o.

"It smells musty in here," she said. Everything always smelled musty to his mother; everything looked dirty. Show her Michelangelo's *David,* and she'd want to get after it with some Spic and Span.

"It's fine, Mom," he said.

"I'm gonna vacuum in here," she said. She vacuumed

his room every day. Some days she vacuumed it twice. She also did his laundry and straightened up his belongings. She *folded his underwear*. Wally had to keep his pot in his car, or she'd find it.

"Mom, you don't need to clean my room," he said.

"It has a musty smell," she said. "I'm gonna vacuum."

Wally lay back on his bed and closed his eyes, hoping his mom would close the door, let him drift back to sleep. But no, she'd been up for more than two hours, and she'd had two cups of coffee, and there was nobody else for her to talk to, and Regis did not come on for another hour. It was time for the weather report.

"Bob Soper said there's a storm coming," she said. Bob Soper was a Miami TV weatherman, her favorite. She'd seen him at the Publix supermarket on Miami Beach once, at the deli counter, and she'd said hello, and—as she always said when recounting this historic event—he couldn't have been nicer. This was one of the highlights of her life since her husband, Wally's father, had died.

"Tropical Storm Hector," she said. "Bob Soper said it could be fifty-five-mile-an-hour winds. Very rough seas, he said."

"Huh," said Wally, keeping his eyes closed.

"So the boat won't go out, right?" she said. "You won't go out in that?"

"I dunno, Mom," Wally said. "Probably not. I have to call. But not now. I'm gonna sleep some more now, OK? I got in kind of late." He turned his body away from the light, from his mother's silhouette.

"Fifty-five miles an hour," she said. "They won't go out in that."

Wally said nothing.

"I saw him at Publix that time," she said. "Bob Soper."

Wally said nothing.

"He was at the deli, waiting just like everybody else," she said. "He couldn't have been nicer."

Wally said nothing.

"He got the honey-baked ham, a half pound," she said. "Boar's Head."

Wally said nothing. Ten seconds passed; he could feel her standing there.

"I just thought you might want some waffles," she said.

Another ten seconds.

"I'm definitely gonna vacuum in here," she said, and closed the door.

Wally, now totally awake, rolled onto his back, stared at the ceiling, and thought, as he did pretty much every waking minute that he spent in his mother's house, *I have got to get out of here.* He willed his brain to think about *how* he was going to get out of there, and his brain, having been through this many times, responded with: despair.

Wally was broke. His only assets, other than his clothes, were his guitar, an Ernie Ball Music Man Axis worth maybe $800 if he sold it, which he never would; and his car, a 1986 Nissan Sentra that ran but was probably not salable, as its body was riddled with some kind of car leprosy. As a professional musician, Wally was currently making $50 a day, playing with the band on the ship, but that was only on days that the ship went out, and that money was usually gone within hours for the necessities of Wally's life: food, gas, a cell phone, and pot.

Wally was more than $5,000 in debt to three credit-card companies; he did not know the exact amount, because he threw the statements away without opening them. Wally had gotten the credit cards a few months earlier when he'd gotten his first-ever real day job, a short-lived attempt to leave the gig-to-gig life of the bar musician. He'd gotten the job through his fiancée, Amanda, who had grown tired of paying most of the rent on the apartment they shared. Amanda had also grown tired of the band lifestyle.

"No offense," she'd said one night, "but I don't want to spend the rest of my life sitting at the bar getting hit on by creeps and listening to you play 'Brown Eyed Girl.' "

"I thought you liked 'Brown Eyed Girl,' " Wally said.

"I did," she said, "the first three million times."

"You think we need some new songs?" he said.

"I think you need a new job," she said. Lately this had become the theme of many of their conversations.

"You're almost thirty years old," Amanda said. "How're we supposed to get married on what you make? How're we supposed to raise a family if you're out all night all the time? Do you even *want* to get married?"

"Of course I want to get married," said Wally, who was not one million percent sure, but also was not stupid enough to express any reservations now. "But the band, I mean, those guys are my best friends. We've been through a lot."

"You've been through a lot of pot, is what you've been through," she said. This had also become a theme. She used to happily partake in the doobie-passing back when they started dating, when she liked the idea that her guy was a musician, an *artist*. But she didn't smoke weed anymore, didn't even drink beer. When she came to gigs, which she did less and less often, she drank Perrier and looked bored.

"What do you want me to do?" Wally asked her. He really meant it. She was changing, and he wasn't, and he didn't want to lose her, and it scared him that he didn't know what she wanted anymore.

"Do you love me?" she asked.

"Yes," he said. "Of course I love you." *I do love her. That's the truth. I love her, and I don't want to lose her.*

"Then talk to Tom about the job," she said.

"OK," said Wally. "I'll talk to Tom."

Tom was Tom Recker, Amanda's new boss, who was starting a new company and was hiring. He'd hired Amanda away from her job as a secretary in a law firm to be his administrative assistant. As far as Wally could tell, administrative assistant was the same thing as secretary, but with more syllables.

Recker was 26 and had an MBA from Wharton, which he would let you know if you gave him an opening. He lifted weights and Rollerbladed and—although he did not tell people this—believed he looked like Keanu Reeves. His company was called Recker International; he was financing the start-up (Amanda confided this to Wally) with $3 million he got from his father. .

Wally's job interview consisted mostly of a lengthy explanation by Recker of what a great concept Recker International was. It had to do with investments, but Wally really didn't understand it because every other sentence Recker said had "paradigm" in it. Later on, Wally looked "paradigm" up in the dictionary, but that had not helped.

The actual interview part of the interview had been brief.

"So," Recker said. "Mandy tells me you play the guitar."

"Yeah," said Wally, thinking, *Mandy?*

"She says you're in a band," said Recker.

"Yeah," said Wally.

"What kind of music do you play?" asked Recker.

"Mostly covers," said Wally, "but we try to . . ."

Recker interrupted. "I used to fool around with the guitar," he said.

"Huh," said Wally. Sometimes it seemed like everybody he met used to fool around with the guitar.

"Tell you the truth, I wasn't bad," said Recker, making an air-guitar move that told Wally, in an instant, that

Recker had been bad. "I wish I'd kept up with it, but I'm trying to run a business here. Not much time for fun, I'm afraid. Somebody's got to be the grown-up."

Right, with Daddy's money, thought Wally.

"You have any business experience, Wally?" asked Recker.

"Well," said Wally, "I handle the bookings for the band."

Recker laughed out loud at that—a hearty, Wharton-man laugh.

"That's not *exactly* the kind of experience I'm looking for," he said, still chuckling at the thought—*bookings for the band!*—"but I'm going to take a chance on you." He leaned forward and pressed his fingertips together, a 26-year-old Rollerblader talking to Wally like he was Wally's dad. "Mandy tells me you're a fast learner and a self-starter. Is that true, Wally? Would you call yourself a self-starter?"

"Yes, Tom, I would," said Wally, who, as Amanda well knew, rarely started anything, including breakfast, before 1 P.M.

"Welcome to the Recker International team," said Recker, reaching across his new desk to give Wally a manly handshake.

"Thanks," said Wally.

"Hey," said Recker, still shaking Wally's hand, gripping it a little too hard, "maybe you can bring your guitar and entertain us at the Christmas party, ha ha."

"Ha ha," said Wally. *Asshole.*

And so Wally quit his band and joined Recker International, where his job title was assistant systems technician. What this meant was that he unpacked desktop computers and then helped the systems technician try, with sporadic success, to hook these up into a network. As far as Wally could tell, it didn't really matter whether the computers worked or not, because the other members of the Recker International team seemed to have no clear idea what they were doing. There was much wandering from cubicle to cubicle, long meetings about designing the website, and a lot of talk about stock options. He never saw anybody do anything that seemed like actual work.

Except for Amanda. She was working all the time, many nights late, sometimes really late. He asked her what was going on, and she said a lot of things, and he asked her what kind of things, and she said complicated business financial stuff that she was too tired to talk about. He said he thought Recker was taking advantage of her, and she got mad and said she *wanted* to be part of this, this was *important,* this was going to be *big,* and Wally should be grateful to be part of a company run by somebody like Tommy, because he had *vision.*

And Wally thought, *Tommy?*

One night, out of loneliness, Wally went to a bar where his ex-bandmates were playing. Wally was pleased to note that the guitar player they'd replaced him with wasn't particularly good.

During the breaks, his old bandmates sat at his table and gave him a hard time about being a corporate sellout. He gave them a hard time about being stoner bar-band losers. Two breaks and some beers later, he told them what was going on with Amanda. They listened sympathetically— these were Wally's oldest and best friends—then assured him that Amanda's new boss was definitely porking her. Wally understood that they were just busting his balls. But when he left the bar, he drove to the Recker International offices.

He let himself in with his security card and closed the door quietly. It was dark in the lobby and in the main cubicle area. Recker's office door was closed; there was light shining through the bottom crack. Wally could hear talking in there, then silence for a while, then more talking. He decided the talking was a good sign. He thought about leaving, but instead went to a corner cubicle and sat down. He was there almost an hour, not really thinking about anything, suspended in a pure state of waiting.

Finally, Recker's office door opened. Amanda walked out, holding her purse. Recker was behind her. They were both fully dressed. Recker was holding some papers.

They'd been working.

"Thanks for tonight," Recker said. "See you tomorrow."

"OK," said Amanda.

"I'm afraid it's gonna be another long one," Recker said. "We got that stupid brokerage thing to deal with."

"I'll be here," said Amanda, and turned toward the lobby.

She was working late on financial stuff, just like she said, you jealous moron. You faithless jerk. You don't deserve her.

Wally shrunk down in the chair, praying they wouldn't notice him, off in the corner, in the dark. Amanda took a few steps.

"Hey, Mandy," said Recker.

She stopped. Wally's heart stopped.

"Come here," said Recker.

And she turned and went to him, and in a second they were locked together, mouth on mouth, and Wally knew this was not the first time. Recker reached down and pulled Amanda's skirt up over her hips, and she moaned. Wally moaned, too, but they didn't hear him, as they slid to the floor, groping each other frantically. Nor did they see Wally stand up, take a step toward them, then turn and walk out of the office, eyes burning, trying to get his mind around the fact that he had no fiancée, and no job, and nowhere to live.

A few hours later, he showed up at his mom's house, the house he grew up in, with all his stuff, which wasn't much, piled randomly into his Sentra. It was still dark, but his mom was up already.

"Mom," he said, "I need to stay here for a while."

His mom looked at him for a moment.

"I'll make you some waffles," she said.

ARNOLD PULLMAN, AGE 83, LOOKED OUT THE BIG dining-room window in the Beaux Arts Senior Living Center, which Arnold always referred to as the Old Farts Senile Dying Center.

"Doesn't look so bad to me," he said. "A little rain maybe."

"Arnie," said Phil Hoffman, age 81, "are you blind? It's a goddamn hurricane out there."

Phil was Arnie's best friend—only friend, really—at the retirement home. They'd met when they were assigned to sit together in the dining room, at a table for four. The other two seats were filled by a man named Harold Tutter, age 77, who could not remember anything for more than fifteen seconds; and a very hostile woman, known to Phil and Arnie only as the Old Bat, who believed that everybody was trying to steal her food.

"It's not a hurricane," said Arnie. "It's a tropical storm, Hector. How bad can it be, with a name like Hector?"

"I don't like the names they use these days," said Phil. "I liked it better when it was just girls. Donna, that was a good hurricane name. 1960."

"Christ, 1960," said Arnie. And for a moment, he and Phil reflected on 1960, when they were young bucks at the height of their physical powers, capable of taking a dump in under an hour.

During the silence, Harold Tutter looked up from his oatmeal, turned to Phil, and extended his hand. "I'm Harold Tutter," he said.

"A pleasure to meet you, Harold," said Phil, shaking Tutter's hand. "I'm the Hunchback of Notre Dame."

"The pleasure is mine, Mr. Dame," said Tutter, turning back to his oatmeal.

"It's a little rain, is all," said Arnie, looking out the window again.

"If you're thinking the boat is going out in this," said Phil, "you're nuts." He reached to get a Sweet'n Low packet from the container in the middle of the table. Seeing his hand move her way, the Old Bat hissed and covered her bowl with both arms.

"I don't *want* your food," Phil told her. "Prunes, for Chrissakes. I'd rather eat my socks."

The Old Bat gathered her prunes closer to herself, ready to fight for them.

"They call them dried plums now," said Arnie.

"What?" said Phil.

"Prunes," said Arnie. "I saw an article. They call them dried plums now."

"Why?" said Phil.

"Public relations," said Arnie. "People today, they don't want prunes. So now they call them dried plums."

"They can't do that," said Phil. "Prunes are . . . *prunes*."

"I'm Harold Tutter," said Tutter, extending his hand to Phil.

"Jesus," said Phil.

"Good to meet you," said Tutter, turning back to his oatmeal.

"But do you know where they come from?" said Arnie.

"What?" said Phil.

"Prunes," said Arnie.

Phil thought about it.

"Prune trees," he said.

"Nope," said Arnie. "From plums. There's no prune trees."

"You sure about that?" said Phil. "Because I'm pretty sure I saw trees somewhere that were prune trees."

"Yeah?" said Arnie. "Where?"

Phil thought some more. "*National Geographic,*" he said.

"Harold Tutter," said Tutter, extending his hand to Phil.

"Good for you," said Phil. "May I present my girlfriend, the Wicked Witch of the West." He gestured toward the Old Bat.

"It's a pleasure, Miss West," said Tutter. He reached his hand toward the Old Bat, who recoiled, yanking her bowl toward her so that her prunes fell into her lap. Tutter returned to his oatmeal.

"I used to get *National Geographic,*" said Arnie. "Marge always said it was so I could look at the titties." Marge was Arnie's wife of 53 years. She had died when Arnie was 79, and four months later his children had moved him into the Old Farts Senile Dying Center.

"I remember," said Phil. "They always had some article in there, some primitive tribe, the Ubongi People of the Amazon, or whatever, and there'd always be pictures in there, the Ubongi women pounding roots with their ta-tas hanging out."

"Well," said Arnie, "Marge always claimed I was pounding *my* root."

Now Phil and Arnie were laughing, in that old-man way that was 60 percent laugh, 40 percent cough. This caused a stir in the dining room, where there was rarely any sound other than the clink of silverware and the occasional dry echoing *braap* of an elderly fart. Heads turned toward their table. The Beaux Arts assistant day manager, Dexter Harpwell, a taut man who ran a taut ship, scurried over.

"What seems to be the trouble?" he said.

"No trouble, officer," said Arnie.

"What happened here?" said Harpwell, spying the Old Bat's prune-covered lap. He grabbed a napkin and leaned over to wipe her off. "Here, let's get you cl*OOOW!*"

As the Old Bat sank her teeth into Harpwell's flesh, he jerked his hand out of her mouth. With it came her dentures, which flew across the table, landing in Tutter's oatmeal. Tutter regarded them for a moment, picked them out of his bowl, set them aside, and resumed eating.

"Watch out," said Phil, to Harpwell. "She bites."

Harpwell, clutching his hand, glared at Phil and Arnie.

"May I remind you gentlemen," he said, "that disturbing other residents is a Conduct Violation."

"We didn't disturb her," said Phil.

"She's already disturbed," said Arnie.

Harpwell turned away, looking for a dining-room attendant. "Nestor!" he called. "Get over here and clean her up."

The attendant, a large Jamaican man, approached the Old Bat.

"Darlin'," he said, "you messed up that pretty dress." Gently, he began to clean her off. She made no move to stop him.

Harpwell turned back to Arnie and Phil.

"I don't want to see any more of this kind of outburst," he said. "If I do, I'm going to have to take disciplinary action."

"Golly," said Arnie, "will it go on our permanent record?"

"Can we still go to the prom?" asked Phil.

"I'm Harold Tutter," said Tutter, extending his hand to Harpwell. Harpwell, ignoring him, gave Arnie and Phil one last glare, then walked tautly away.

"My pleasure," said Tutter, returning to his oatmeal.

"Talk about a guy who needs some prunes," said Phil.

"Dried plums," said Arnie. "Hey, Nestor."

The attendant looked up from the Old Bat.

"We're gonna need your taxi service tonight," said Arnie.

"Tonight?" said Nestor. "You want to go out on the boat in this weather?"

"My point exactly," said Phil.

"A little rain, is all," said Arnie.

"Man, I bet that boat won't even go out in this," said Nestor.

"Well, if it does," said Arnie, "you'll take us, right?"

Arnie and Phil had a deal with Nestor: On nights when they wanted to go to the ship, he drove them. When the ship returned, he picked them up, brought them back to Beaux Arts, and sneaked them in through a service door. Arnie and Phil paid for this service by giving Nestor all the pills that they were handed at mealtimes by the pill man, who walked from table to table dispensing vast quantities of medication. On a normal day, the pill man gave a total of 17 pills to Arnie and 23 to Phil. Neither man had any idea what most of the pills did. One day they'd decided simply not to take them. Not only did they not die, they both felt better, and more alert, than they had in years. From then on, they slipped their pills to Nestor in return for various favors, the main one being transportation to the ship. Nestor sold the pills to various parties in his neighborhood, where he was known as The Doctor. He was saving up for a Lexus.

"OK," Nestor said. "If the boat goes, I take you."

"Not me, you won't," said Phil. "I'm too young to die."

"Die, schmie," said Arnie. "A big boat like that, this weather is nothing. A little rain. Besides, you got something better to do? You wanna spend your night here, running away from Mrs. Krugerman?"

Phil winced. Mrs. Krugerman was an 80-year-old woman who had the hots for him. He could usually maintain his distance from her, because she used a walker and moved slowly. But she never stopped coming.

"Another thing," said Arnie. "You know what the entertainment is here tonight? The broad that sings the show tunes."

"No," said Phil. "The one that killed Mrs. Fenwick?"

"Same one," said Arnie.

Two weeks earlier, the woman who sang show tunes, a Mrs. Bendocker, had performed a medley from *The Sound of Music,* and during her big finale, "Climb Every Mountain," while she was shrieking out the high notes for ". . . till you find your dreeeeeeeeeam," Mrs. Fenwick, who was sitting in the front row, had emitted a *gack* and keeled over, dead as a doornail. A lawsuit had already been filed.

"I can't believe they're bringing her back," said Phil.

"Point is," said Arnie, "you stay here tonight, you could die anyway."

Phil looked around the dining room at his fellow Beaux Arts patrons, some eating, some sleeping, some staring and drooling. None were talking.

"OK," he said. "I'll go."

"Regular time?" Arnie said to Nestor.

"OK," said Nestor. "But you people are crazy."

"We're off our medication," said Phil.

"I'm Harold Tutter," said Tutter, extending his hand.

AT A SMALL MARINA IN THE BAHAMAS, TWO men, one large and one small, shrugged their way through the gusting rain toward a cabin cruiser tied to the dock.

When they reached the boat, the large man, whose name was Frank, cupped his mouth and shouted, "Hey! Anybody here?"

There was no response.

"Maybe he's not here," said the smaller man, whose name was Juan.

"Oh, he's here, all right," said Frank. "He just likes

watching us get wet." He shouted at the boat again: "TARK! OPEN UP!"

Still no response. Frank and Juan stood still in the rain for thirty seconds, a minute. Frank looked around, found a boat hook. He picked it up and clanged the metal end against the boat hull.

Instantly, the aft cabin door burst open, and a lean, weathered man emerged, wearing only cutoff shorts, holding a knife.

"You touch my boat again," he said, "I'll cut off your goddamn hand."

"And good morning to *you*, Tark," said Frank. "You gonna invite us in outta the rain?"

"Nope," said Tark, then, looking at Juan: "I just got rid of the smell from last time you was on."

"Fuck you," said Juan.

Tark ignored him, looked back at Frank. "You're way early."

"We just want to make sure you know it's still on for tonight," said Frank. "We don't want you thinking this weather's gonna stop the operation."

"Weather don't bother me," said Tark. "I ain't the pussy who pukes every time we hit the Gulf Stream." He was back to looking at Juan, who did in fact puke the last time they hit the Gulf Stream.

"You want to see who's a pussy?" said Juan. "Put down the blade, get off the boat, we find out who's a pussy." Juan had boxed some, professional.

"You afraid of a knife, Pancho?" said Tark. "I thought spics liked knives."

Juan made a move to climb onto the boat. Frank put a large restraining hand on his shoulder. "Boys, boys," he said. "Can't we all just get along?"

"Not with that prick," said Juan.

"No," agreed Tark.

"I didn't think so," said Frank. "But we have to get along for a little while. Big job tonight. After that, we get back, everything's put away nice, *then* you boys can kill each other, OK?"

"I'm ready," said Tark, staring at Juan.

"Anytime, asshole," said Juan, staring back.

"That's the spirit!" said Frank. "Kumbaya. We'll be back at six."

"I'll be here," said Tark.

"If you need us," said Frank, "we're at the inn."

"I won't need you," said Tark. "Fact is, I could do this whole thing without you. You and puking Pancho just get in the way out there."

"Ah, but we'd miss *you,* Tark," said Frank. "Your smiling face, your sparkling wit."

"Bite me," said Tark.

"See?" said Frank. "Sparkling. Bye for now, Tark."

Frank and Juan turned and headed back toward the village. When they'd gone about twenty yards, Juan said, "I *hate* that prick. Why do we gotta use him? Why can't we use some other boat? Plenty of boats around here."

"Tell you the truth," said Frank, "I don't know why we use him. I just do what they tell me, and they tell me, use Tark."

Juan shook his head. "I don't trust him."

"Me either," said Frank. "That's why we watch each other's back tonight, right?"

"OK," said Juan. Then: "I *hate* that prick."

Back on the boat, still holding the knife, Tark watched the two men recede in the rain. A voice spoke to him from inside the cabin.

"That's the guys?" it said.

"That's them," said Tark.

"Big one looks like a handful," said the voice.

"He won't be no problem," said Tark. "Rough seas like

this, a boat can jerk around a lot, 'specially if you steer it wrong. I'll make it easy."

"What about the little one?" said the voice.

Tark, looking down at his knife, said, "You leave the spic to me."

FAY BENTON WAS STARTLED FROM SLEEP BY A

27-pound weight thumping down on her abdomen.

"Bear!" said the weight. "Bear! Bear!"

"OK, honey," said Fay. "But first Mommy has to go potty."

She sat up, wrapped her arms around her daughter, Estelle, age two, got out of bed, and went into the bathroom. She set Estelle gently on the floor and sat on the toilet.

"Mommy potty," said Estelle.

"That's right," said Fay. "Mommy's going potty."

"Peepee," said Estelle, hearing the tinkle.

"Peepee," agreed Fay.

"It smells like smoke in here," said Fay's mother, appearing in the doorway.

"Mother, do you *mind*?" said Fay, pushing the door closed.

"Bear!" said Estelle. "Bear! Bear! Bear!"

"In a minute, honey," said Fay. "Mommy's going potty."

"Peepee," said Estelle.

"Have you been smoking?" said Fay's mother, through the door. "Because I smell smoke."

"No, I haven't been smoking," said Fay. "The people on the boat smoke, and it gets in my clothes." She wiped, flushed, stood.

"Bye-bye, peepee!" said Estelle, waving to the swirling water.

"That secondhand smoke can kill you," said Fay's mother.

"Bear!" said Estelle. "Bear! Bear! Bear! Bear! Bear!"

"OK, honey," said Fay. "We'll go see the bear." She opened the bathroom door.

"You look terrible," her mother said.

"Thanks, Mom," said Fay. "I got to sleep at two-thirty."

"Bear!" said Estelle. "Bear! Bear! Bear!"

"You need to get out of that job," said her mother. "You're gonna kill yourself."

"Bear!" said Estelle.

"OK, honey," said Fay. She picked up Estelle and carried her into the living room, where she turned on the TV and VCR and shoved in a videotape of *Bear in the Big Blue House,* which Estelle watched a minimum of five times a day. Estelle stood directly in front of the TV set, perhaps six inches away, waiting. When the bear appeared, she said, "Bear!"

"She shouldn't stand so close," said Fay's mother. "Those cathode radiations, you can get brain cancer."

Fay went into the kitchen, filled a small Winnie-the-Pooh bowl with Froot Loops, brought it back and set it on the coffee table. She picked up Estelle and set her down next to the table.

"Fwoops!" said Estelle, spying the cereal. She reached into the bowl, carefully selected a purple Froot Loop, and put it into her mouth. When she had swallowed, she began selecting another.

"That cereal is nothing but chemicals," her mother said. "Those things can kill you."

"Mom, I'm really, really tired," said Fay. "Let me just get some coffee, OK?"

She headed back to the kitchen, trailed by her mother, who said, "Your hair smells like cigarettes. You need to get off that boat."

"Mom," said Fay, "like I told you, I'll get out of this as

soon as I can. I really, really appreciate you staying here with Estelle all these nights. I'm hoping the boat thing is only another few days. I don't like it any more than you."

"I don't see why Todd can't take the baby at night if you have to work," said Fay's mother.

"He won't."

"Why not?"

"Because he's an asshole."

"There's no need for that language," said her mother.

"OK," said Fay, "he's a shithead."

"Fay!" said her mother.

"OK, then," said Fay, "he's a dickwad."

"DIT wad!" said Estelle, toddling into the kitchen. "DIT wad!"

"Now look what you've done," said Fay's mother.

"Go watch Bear, honey," said Fay. "Bear is on TV!"

"Bear!" said Estelle, toddling back out.

"Todd is that baby's father," said Fay's mother. "He has a responsibility."

"If he had any responsibility," said Fay, spooning coffee into the Mister Coffee filter, "I'd still be married to him. Truth is, I don't even know where he lives right now. With some bimbo, probably. I'm not gonna leave Estelle with him."

"Is that caffeinated?" said her mother. "That caffeine can give you a heart attack."

"Mom, *please*," said Fay.

"Anyway," said her mother, "you won't need me tonight, because that boat isn't going out in this weather."

Fay looked out the window. "I have to call in and check," she said.

"It won't go out," said her mother. "It's a tropical storm out there. Tropical Storm Hector. Bob Soper said it could be fifty-five-mile-per-hour winds.

"Well, I still have to call."

"Well, it shouldn't go out. Winds like that, you could get killed."

Estelle toddled in, holding out her empty Winnie-the-Pooh bowl with both hands.

"Fwoops!" she said.

"OK, honey," said Fay, reaching for the Froot Loops box.

"Pure chemicals," said her mother. "You should give her fruit." She bent down to Estelle, and, in the hideously unnatural high-pitched voice that many older people use when addressing babies, said: "Gramma give Estelle some nice prunes!"

"DIT wad!" said Estelle.

Two

THE *EXTRAVAGANZA OF THE SEAS* WAS A 198-foot, 5,000-ton cash machine, an ugly, top-heavy tub with 205 slot machines and 29 gaming tables in two big rooms glowing with cheesy neon, reeking of stale smoke and beer-breath curses. The ship's sole function was to carry gamblers three miles from the Florida coast each night, take as much of their money as possible, then return them to land four hours later, so they could go find more money.

Gambling cruises are a big business, especially in South Florida, where more than two dozen ships take roughly 8,000 customers out nightly. Nobody really knows how much money these ships make; it's a cash business, which means it's easy to prevent nosy outfits such as the United States government from finding out where it all comes from, and where it all goes.

There are many mysteries in the gambling-cruise business, besides the profits. The identities of the real owners of the ships are often hidden via dummy corporations and

silent partnerships. And since the gambling takes place un-
regulated, in international waters, nobody has any idea
how honest the games are. If you were a gambler, you
might *suspect* that the roulette wheel was rigged, or the
blackjack deck was stacked, or your chances of hitting a
jackpot on the slot machine were about as good as if you'd
been throwing your coins directly overboard. But who are
you going to complain to? Seagulls? There's no state gambling commission out there in the Gulf Stream.

Of course, none of this keeps the gamblers from coming. Gamblers need action, even when the odds suck. And
so they return to the ships, night after night—the slot-
machine ladies, clutching their plastic cups of quarters; the
shouting, hard-drinking craps-table crowd; the roulette ad-
dicts, who truly believe, all evidence to the contrary, that
there is something lucky about their birthdates; the blackjack loners, with their foolproof systems that don't work—
all of them eager to resume the inexorable process of
transferring their cash to whoever owns the ship.

In the case of the *Extravaganza of the Seas,* the owner
of record was a man named Bobby Kemp, who was usually
described in the newspaper as a millionaire entrepreneur.
Kemp liked the look of that, *entrepreneur,* although he personally could not pronounce it.

Pretty much the entire reason that he wound up as the
owner of the *Extravaganza of the Seas* was that he'd
wanted to impress a date who had big tits. This happened
after he'd made his fortune. He was a rags-to-riches story,
the son of a white-trash welfare mother and a disappeared
alcoholic father, a high-school dropout who'd been scrap-
ing by in the field of freelance auto-body repair and insurance fraud when he got his first big entrepreneurial break.
This was the federal law requiring all new cars to be
equipped, at considerable expense, with air bags, to protect

motorists who were too stupid, lazy, or drunk to go to the trouble of buckling their seat belts.

This meant that whenever a car hit something hard enough that its air bags deployed, those bags had to be replaced. A new bag from the factory could cost $1,000 or more. But Bobby Kemp had realized that he did not need to pay the factory: He could get air bags for free! All he had to do was remove them from unattended cars. This enabled him to sell them to customers for as little as $500, and still make an excellent profit.

In short order, Kemp was the unofficial air-bag king of Miami-Dade County. Demand was so great for his bargain air bags that he could no longer steal them fast enough. And so, again using his entrepreneurial brain, he came up with the idea of replacing deployed air bags with . . . *pretend* air bags. He simply repacked the customer's old air-bag canister with whatever random trash he had around the shop—wadded-up newspaper, McDonald's bags, whatever—sealed the canister back up, and reinstalled it in the car, as good as new, except that it no longer contained an actual air bag.

Business continued to boom, and soon Kemp was employing a staff of illegal immigrants, paid a sub-minimum wage, to do the actual work. Occasionally, this led to quality-control problems, most notably when one of his workers, having run out of trash, repacked the driver-side air-bag canister on a Lexus LS-400 with dirt. This particular batch of dirt happened to contain some kind of prolific egg-laying insect, and a week later, while the car's owner was inching home in heavy rush-hour traffic, her steering wheel suddenly popped open and dumped a mass of wriggling larvae into her lap, causing her to leap, screaming, from the car, in the middle of South Dixie Highway.

Fortunately, Kemp had been able to convince the

woman that insect infestation was a common problem in South Florida air bags. He graciously offered to pay her dry-cleaning bill, and he personally made sure that when his shop installed a replacement air-bag canister in her car, it was packed with clean, bug-free newspaper. You had to take care of your customers.

With his air-bag operation running smoothly and cash pouring in, Kemp was looking for another investment opportunity with a steady demand and room to cut corners. He decided on fast food, and opened a restaurant called the Happy Conch. The house specialty was the conch fritter, a South Florida delicacy traditionally made with the ground-up meat of the conch, a large saltwater snail that, when removed from its shell, looks markedly unhappy, even by mollusk standards.

The Happy Conch concept was an instant hit, thanks to amazingly low prices; for $2.49, you could get two dozen fritters, made with Bobby Kemp's special conch-fritter recipe, which was a fiercely guarded secret. The secret was that the fritters contained absolutely no conch. Kemp had figured out that not only did conch cost money, but also that the chewy, funky little pieces of meat were the least-appealing element of the fritter. So he eliminated this element, which meant he was basically selling balls of cheap dough, deep-fried in used fat. It was kind of like fried chicken without the chicken. The public loved it. A tasty seafood meal for the whole family, for only $2.49!

Soon there were more Happy Conch restaurants, now housed in violently pink buildings, which Bobby Kemp designed himself. In front of each was a fifteen-foot-high pink sign depicting a cartoonish conch shell with big goofy eyes, a toothy smile, and a waving hand. This was Conrad Conch, official theme character of the Happy Conch chain. When a new Happy Conch opened, Kemp paid a homeless man twenty dollars to put on a Conrad Conch costume—a big pink foam shell with pink arms and legs—and stand next to the highway all day, waving at motorists. Nobody knew the homeless man's name. Everybody just called him Conrad, which in time is what he called himself.

Using the fast-growing cash flow from his pretend-air-bag and conchless-conch-fritter empires, Kemp moved into what to him seemed the next logical field: medical care. In a matter of months, he was operating a chain of Professional Medical Doctors Discount Laser Eye and Cosmetic Surgery Clinics, based in strip malls. Again, his business strategy was to offer the consumer unbeatably low prices. You could walk into a Professional Medical Doctors Discount Laser Eye and Cosmetic Surgery Clinic, plunk down as little as $150 per eyeball, say, or $1,000 per breast, and walk out with 20-20 vision or vastly enhanced hooters.

Of course, there was a chance you might walk directly into a utility pole. Because the cost-saving secret of the Professional Medical Doctors Discount Laser Eye and Cosmetic Surgery Clinic chain was that it did not employ the highest quality doctors. One of the eyeball men had actually been trained as a veterinarian, although he'd lost his veterinary license because of a tendency to abuse medications intended for horses. He had learned eye surgery from a videotape, and was really not half bad at it, if you caught him early enough in the day.

So there were some lawsuits. But Bobby Kemp was now in the financial position to hire expensive, scruple-free lawyers. Anybody attempting to gain access to his assets faced years of litigation hell. Meanwhile, the money poured in. Kemp got a hairpiece and a red Corvette and a Miami Beach condo facing the ocean. He started getting mentioned in the *Miami Herald* business section. He could walk into Joe's Stone Crab at 9:30 on a Saturday night and get a table right away, walking right past all the loser tourists who'd been waiting three hours, the maitre d' calling him Mr. Kemp, knowing he'd get a fifty later. He began investing in stocks and Miami-Dade County politicians. For the first time in his adult life, he was dating women who had all their teeth.

Just under two years after Kemp opened his first Happy Conch, he held, on the same day, the grand openings of his twentieth restaurant and his tenth clinic. To celebrate the occasion, he treated all of his managers and their spouses to a gambling cruise. He selected the cheapest ship he could find, which happened to be the *Extravaganza of the Seas,* then owned by a Miami hotelier.

They had a little ceremony on the upper deck, with conch-fritter hors d'oeuvres that nobody touched. Kemp gave a little speech, and then Conrad Conch went around and gave each employee a box containing a plastic watch with Bobby Kemp's face on it, a $6.50 value. This was followed by about twenty minutes of awkward socializing, after which the employees drifted downstairs to join the rest of the crowd in the casino.

The dramatic highlight of the evening came two hours later, when Conrad Conch walked up to the roulette table, used his salary for the evening to buy a single $20 chip, put it on zero, and watched as the ball spun around and landed on . . . zero! This meant that Conrad, in one bet, had won $700. He was rich! He clapped his big pink hands.

This did not sit well with the roulette player sitting immediately to Conrad Conch's right, a man named Weldon Mansfield, who had spent the evening drinking far too much rum and diet Coke while losing $870, which was both his rent and his child-support payment. Mansfield had bet, unsuccessfully, on zero eleven times. He was very unhappy to see the little ball finally land there when it did him no good. He was even less happy when he turned to his left and saw who had won.

"You're a *shell*," he said.

Conrad did not respond. He heard very poorly inside his costume, because of the thick padding around his head. Also he was focused on picking up his winning chips.

Mansfield poked Conrad Conch hard.

"Hey, I'm talking to you," he said.

Conrad looked at Mansfield, which required him to turn his whole shell to the right, so he could see out of the black mesh covering his big smiley mouth hole.

"You're a *shell*," Mansfield said. "How the hell do *you* win? You won *my money*, you fucking shell."

Conrad, hearing only muffled, unintelligible sounds, assumed Mansfield was congratulating him. Holding his chips in his left hand, he raised his pink right arm to give Mansfield a high five.

Mansfield responded by throwing a hard right deep into Conrad's soft midsection. Conrad went down like a big pink sack of cement, his chips flying from his hand. Mansfield dove on top of Conrad.

"YOU WON MY MONEY YOU FUCKING SHELL," he shouted, trying to choke Conrad, deeply frustrated by the fact that Conrad had no throat.

Within seconds, two casino employees had pulled Mansfield off and were dragging him away, still shouting for his money. Another employee was pulling Conrad to his feet, when the pit boss, who'd been summoned by the roulette croupier, hurried up.

"What's going on here?" he said.

"They had a fight," said the croupier. "That guy and this . . . shell."

"We don't allow fighting on this ship," the pit boss told Conrad.

Conrad, not hearing this, and concerned about his money, bent over and started frantically looking around the floor for his chips. He saw immediately that many were missing. They had been quietly picked up by alert by-stander gamblers while Conrad was being attacked.

The pit boss, whose name was Manny Arquero, and who did not become pit boss by letting people ignore him, especially not people dressed as giant shells, grabbed Conrad by his pink arm and yanked him up.

"I said we don't allow fighting on this ship," he said.

Conrad, hearing only muffled sounds, and believing that he was once again about to be attacked, decided that the best defense was a good offense. He threw a big, looping, pink punch at Arquero, who easily stepped inside it and drilled Conrad with two very solid body punches. Conrad again went down, this time falling backward onto the roulette table, knocking many thousands of dollars' worth of chips onto the floor. Some of these rolled into the growing crowd of onlookers, where they quickly disappeared.

As casino employees ordered the crowd to move back, Bobby Kemp appeared, drawn by the uproar. With him was his date, a woman named Karli whom Bobby had met as an unhappy client of the Professional Medical Doctors Discount Laser Eye and Cosmetic Surgery Clinic. She had gone in for breast augmentation, and it had gone pretty well, as long as you looked at only one breast at a time. The problem was that when you looked at them together, they were not a matched set, sizewise: The right one was a medium-grade orange, whereas the left one was definitely a member of the grapefruit family.

Karli had complained, and Bobby Kemp, who was a hands-on executive when it came to breast-related matters, had seen to it that not only was Karli's size mismatch corrected, but that she also received, at no charge, an upgrade, so that she was now sporting a pair of serious honeydew melons. Tonight was their first date.

Kemp was holding Karli's hand protectively as he

strode through the crowd around the roulette table. He was not happy when he saw Conrad Conch sprawled on the floor, moaning.

"Who did this?" he asked Arquero.

"You know this asshole?" asked Arquero.

"Who the hell are you?" said Kemp.

"I'm the guy asks the questions on this ship," said Arquero. "And I'm asking you if you know the asshole in the clam suit."

"It's a conch," said Kemp. "And he works for me."

"Whatever he is," said Arquero, "when we get back to Miami, he goes to jail."

Ordinarily, in this situation, Kemp's pragmatic businessman instincts would have prevailed, and he would have papered over the problem with some cash. But with Karli watching, honeydews heaving, Kemp could not back down.

"Listen, my friend," he said to Arquero. "Do you know who I am?"

Arquero sighed. "Yeah, I know who you are," he said. "You're a guy with a hairpiece, looks like Rocky the Flying Squirrel landed on your head, and you want to impress your girlfriend with the big plastic knockers."

"You don't talk to me like that," said Kemp, stepping closer, but only a little. "You hear me? You don't talk to me like that."

"Oh, yes, I do," said Arquero. "That's how I talk to you, unless you own this ship. You own this ship, *my friend*?" He stepped forward, into hitting range.

Kemp stepped back, face burning.

"I didn't think so," said Arquero.

Kemp couldn't stand it. "I don't own it *now,* asshole," he said. "But I will. And when I do, you're gone."

"Oooh," said Arquero. "Look how scared I am."

And that's how Bobby Kemp came to buy the *Extrava-*

ganza of the Seas. The first thing he did, as owner, was go to the ship and personally fire Manny Arquero, from behind two bodyguards. Arquero did not seem troubled at all. He seemed almost *amused,* which made the experience far less satisfying than Kemp had hoped.

Still, it looked as though he'd stumbled into another fine investment. From what he could tell from the books, the casino ship was a marvelous business, with customers handing over money—cash money; *lots* of cash money— in exchange for, basically, nothing. It puzzled Kemp that the previous owner had been willing to sell; in fact, he'd seemed almost eager to get rid of the ship.

It did not take long for Kemp to find out why. Three days after the purchase, he was in his office, on the phone, when his receptionist, Dee Dee Holdscomb, stuck her head in the door, which was how she communicated with him, as she had not learned to operate the intercom. Dee Dee was another client of the Professional Medical Doctors Discount Laser Eye and Cosmetic Surgery Clinics, and Kemp had hired her solely on the basis of having cleavage that a small dog could get lost in.

"There's a guy here wants to see you," she said. Another thing she was not good at was getting names.

"Does he have an appointment?" Kemp asked.

Dee Dee frowned, thinking. "Not as far as I know," she said. "I never seen him before."

"Tell him to make an appointment," said Kemp, turning back to his phone call.

"Mr. Kemp says you . . ." said Dee Dee, but the man had already pushed past her, into Kemp's office. He was a wide, bald man in slacks and a golf shirt. His name was Lou Tarant, and he had, in his career, killed nine people, although none in recent years, since he'd been promoted to management. He walked up to Kemp's desk and put both hands on it. He had very big, very hairy forearms.

"Mr. Kemp," he said. "My name is Lou Tarant."

Kemp looked up from the phone.

"You want to see me," he said, "you make an appointment. I'm on the phone here."

"I just need a few minutes of your time," said Tarant. "I'm with a group of businessmen, we do bus . . ."

"Are you *deaf*?" said Kemp. "I'm on the *phone* here."

"I think you want to hear what I got to say," said Tarant, reaching over and pressing the hang-up button.

"What the fuck do you think you're doing?" said Kemp, standing.

"I'm trying to meet with you," said Tarant. "In a businesslike manner."

"Dee Dee," said Kemp, "call building security."

"Do you know what number that is?" said Dee Dee. "Because sometimes you hafta dial nine, but some other times you . . ."

"Jesus," said Kemp. "Just go downstairs and get a guard, OK?"

"OK," said Dee Dee, hurt, leaving. Tarant turned to inspect her ass as she left, then walked over to the window, which overlooked Biscayne Bay.

"I gotta tell you, Bobby," he said, "this view and that secretary, I wouldn't get nothing done."

Kemp slid open his right-hand desk drawer, where he kept his gun.

"Say you shoot me," said Tarant, still looking out the window. "First, you got to explain it to the cops, why you shot an unarmed guy just wanted to talk to you. Second, you mess up this carpet, which looks to me like wool, has to be, what, fifty bucks a yard?"

"What do you want?" asked Kemp, closing the drawer.

"Like I said, I'm with a group, businessmen, we do business with the *Extravaganza,* which, by the way, congratulations on the purchase."

"What kind of business?"

"This and that. Food and beverage, some personnel, some financial. We had a relationship, very beneficial. Win-win. We want to have the same relationship with you."

"I got my suppliers," said Kemp. "I got my own people. I got a bank."

Tarant turned to face Kemp. "I know that. But I'm telling you, you definitely are better off with us."

Kemp sighed. "Listen, Guido," he said.

"It's Lou," said Tarant. "Lou Tarant."

"I know who you are, Guido," said Kemp. "I seen *The Godfather.*"

"Never heard of it," said Tarant.

"Funny," said Kemp. "Ha-ha. Now you listen to me, Guido. You don't come here, you don't come into *my office* and break my balls. I'm not some little shitball just got into town and opened up a hot-dog stand. I got a very success-ful operation. I know people in this town, people wouldn't let you take out their garbage. I tell a city commissioner I want a blow job, five minutes later he's in here on his knees. And I got friends in your line. Food and beverage, let's call it. I tell my friends you came in here, my office, tried to lean on *me,* they are *not* gonna be happy. And if they're not happy, believe me, *you're* not gonna be happy. *Capeesh,* Guido?"

"Lemme guess," said Tarant. "You're talking about Jimmy Avocado and Sammy Three Nostrils, am I right?"

Kemp said nothing, but those were, in fact, the people he'd been talking about.

"We work with them guys all the time," said Tarant. "We can have a nice smooth transit."

"Get the fuck out of my office," said Kemp.

"Sure," said Tarant. "I got a two P.M. tee time at Doral anyways. You play golf? I can get you on the Blue Mon-ster, name a day."

"Fuck you, Guido."

"OK, then," said Tarant. "How about we get together again tomorrow, hammer out the details? I'll just drop by."

"You know what's good for you, you won't even . . ."

Kemp was interrupted by the entrance of Dee Dee, with a security guard.

"I found one!" she said.

"I want you to escort this man out of the building immediately," Kemp told the guard. "And don't let him back in, *ever*. You understand?"

The guard tore his gaze away from Dee Dee's chest and looked at Kemp, then at Tarant.

"Oh, hi, Mr. T," he said.

"Hi, Vinny," said Tarant.

"Wait a fucking *minute* here," said Kemp. "I'm the goddamn tenant, and I'm telling you to escort this man out."

The guard, speaking to Tarant, said: "Is there a problem, Mr. T?"

"No problem at all, Vinny," said Tarant. "I was just leaving. Thanks for stopping by."

"No problem, Mr. T," said the guard, leaving.

"OK, then, Bobby," said Tarant. "See you tomorrow. You mind if I call you Bobby?"

Kemp said nothing.

"Feel free to call me Lou, Bobby," said Tarant. He left.

Dee Dee said, "The guard told me next time, I could just dial extension one-two-seven."

"Get my lawyer on the phone," said Kemp.

"Which one is that?" said Dee Dee.

"Jesus, never mind," said Kemp, picking up the phone.

"You don't hafta get snippy," said Dee Dee, leaving.

Kemp's lawyer advised him to ignore Tarant.

"He can't *make* you do business with him," said the lawyer, a Harvard Law School graduate who knew his torts. "He's just upset about losing a customer. If he comes back, we'll threaten to file a complaint, and believe me, that's the last you'll ever hear from him."

That reassuring advice, plus five ounces of Belvedere, eased Kemp's worries. He fell asleep that night convinced that he had nothing to worry about, that Tarant was just a big-armed hustler, trying to scare him. Well, fuck *that*. Bobby Kemp didn't scare.

The next morning, every Happy Conch restaurant— every single one—was shut down by county health inspectors. A health department spokeswoman told the news media, which had somehow been alerted, that this was a standard random mass inspection, and that the inspectors had found dozens of violations. These were the very same inspectors who, until then, would not have cared if they had seen human thumbs in the fritter batter, as long as they got their little envelopes of cash.

While a hungover Bobby Kemp was sitting in his office, trying to absorb this news, he got a call from the manager of his largest and busiest Professional Medical Doctors Discount Laser Eye and Cosmetic Surgery Clinic, who informed him that the clinic was being picketed by about a dozen ex-clients, who claimed they were the victims of botched surgical procedures.

"There's a woman out there, she's screaming, she's pulling her goddamn pants down right in front of the TV cameras," said the manager. "Claims we messed up a lipo on her buttocks. I gotta say, between you and me, her ass looks like one of those science-fair projects where some kid lets cottage cheese sit around for two weeks."

Kemp's conversation with the clinic manager was interrupted by another phone call, which turned out to be a supervisor on the *Extravaganza of the Seas*, reporting that there had been a freak accident involving the big supply truck.

"The driver got out," said the supervisor. "He's OK."

"Fuck the driver," said Kemp. "What about the truck?"

"I'm guessing the truck is not in great condition," said the supervisor.

"What do you mean, you're guessing?" said Kemp.

"I mean the truck is on the bottom of the bay."

"Jesus."

"Also, the workers are calling in sick."

"Which workers?"

"Everybody. Dealers, bartenders, waitresses, crew, everybody."

Kemp hung up. He put his face into his hands for a moment, then picked up the phone and punched, from memory, the cell-phone number of a high-ranking elected Miami-Dade County official who had received significant political support from Kemp in the form of paper sacks filled with cash.

"Hello?" said a voice.

"Benny, this is me, Bobby Kemp."

A pause, then: "Benny's not here."

"Benny, goddammit, I know that's you. This is *me*, Bobby Kemp. I got a . . ."

"Whoever this is, I don't hear you. It's a bad reception here."

"Benny, wait, I need to . . . Benny? Hello? Benny?"

Nothing.

"Fuck," said Kemp, slamming down the phone. He thought for a moment, looked up a number, called his lawyer's office.

When the lawyer got on the line, he said, "Listen, you got to get over here right now, because this Tarant asshole is fucking up my entire . . ."

"I, ah, Bobby, I don't think we can do that," said the lawyer.

"What?" said Kemp.

"I just feel . . . that is, *we* feel, here at the firm, that, ah,

in the interest of insuring that you get the best possible legal representation, to which you are absolutely entitled, no
question, it's, ah, our feeling that—and this is, believe me,
strictly for your benefit—to avoid any suggestion of con-
flict, it would be for the best if there was, ah, a *discontinu-
ance,* insofar as . . ."

"They got to you, you little needle-dick weasel," said
Kemp.

"Now, Bobby, there's no call for . . ."

"Three hundred fifty fucking dollars an *hour* I been
paying you to read leases I can already read myself, and
now the one fucking time I need you to actually *do* something, you *bail* on me?"

Dee Dee stuck her head in the door.

"Mr. Kemp? That guy? With the arms? From yesterday?
He's here. You want me to . . ."

"Hey, Bobby," said Tarant, coming around Dee Dee.
"How's things?"

"You know how things are," said Kemp, hanging up on
the lawyer.

"Things look good to me," said Tarant, examining the
front of Dee Dee's dress.

"You want me to get the guard again?" asked Dee Dee.

"No," said Kemp. "Just get out, OK?"

"You don't hafta get snippy," said Dee Dee, leaving.

"Should've come out to Doral with me yesterday," said
Tarant. "Beautiful day, no wind. I'm hitting the ball like
Tiger Friggin' Woods, swear to God. I'll take you out one
of these days."

"What if I go to the feds?" said Kemp. "You ever think
of that, Guido?"

"It's Lou, Bobby. Lou Tarant. Out of curiosity, why
would you want to go to the feds?"

"To tell them I got organized wop greaseballs leaning

on me, my business. I bet they'd love to hear about that."

"Could be, Bobby. Could be. But, sake of argument, say you call them in. First of all, you want to wind up in the Witness Protection Program? You familiar with that? Instead of Bobby Kemp, big-time Miami businessman with a big office, friends with the mayor, has a secretary with a major pair of garbanzos, all of a sudden you're a guy named Hiram Schmutz, living in a trailer in Albuquerque, checking your bedroom slippers for scorpions. And suppose the feds start poking around. You know how they are, always poking around. Maybe they start checking into, I dunno, serial numbers on air bags. Offshore accounts. Immigration violations. Taxes, Christ, just think about the taxes. You know, all that federal shit."

Kemp stared at him.

"Did you know," said Tarant, "you mess with air bags, that's a federal offense? You believe that? Doing time, federal prison, for an *air bag*?"

Dee Dee stuck her head in the door.

"There's some people out here?" she said. "From TV? With cameras? They want to talk to you about some lady, her butt or something."

"Tell them I'm not here," Kemp told Dee Dee.

Dee Dee turned and announced to the reception area: "He says he's not here."

"Jesus," said Kemp. "Just close the fucking door, OK?"

"How come everything around here is always *my* fault?" said Dee Dee, slamming the door.

Kemp sat at his desk, turned the chair, looked out the window.

"OK," he said. "What do you want?"

"Just like I told you yesterday, Bobby," said Tarant. "The group I represent, we want to do business with you. You're gonna find we're very businesslike. You work with us, you got nothing to worry about. For example, looks to me like you got some problems right here today. We can help you with things like that."

Kemp was quiet for almost a minute, then: "OK."

"Good," said Tarant. "Real good." He came around to Kemp's side of the desk, stuck out his hand. Reluctantly, Kemp reached out. Tarant took Kemp's hand and, seemingly without effort, pulled Kemp to his feet. He squeezed Kemp's hand.

"You made the right decision, Bobby." He did not let go of Kemp's hand. His grip tightened. Kemp felt his hand bones grinding.

"Now that we're working together," he said, "couple of minor things." The pain was getting unbearable, but there was no hint of strain in Tarant's voice. "Number one, you never call me Guido again, OK, Bobby? Or greaseball. Or especially wop." When he said *wop,* Kemp felt an agonizing stab of pain in his hand, like something had snapped in there. He whimpered, tried to pull his hand away, but could not move it.

"I said, OK, Bobby?" Tarant said.

"OK," whispered Kemp.

"OK, *Lou,*" said Tarant. "I want you to call me Lou."

"OK, Lou."

"Good, Bobby. Excellent," said Tarant. "I'll be back in touch with you tomorrow, start setting up arrangements." He released Kemp's hand, went to the door, opened it, looked back.

"One more thing, Bobby."

Kemp looked up from massaging his right hand.

"Manny Arquero?" said Tarant. "The guy you fired?"

"What about him?"

"Hire him back," said Tarant, and left.

*   *   *

IN SOME WAYS, BOBBY KEMP'S NEW BUSINESS associates actually did make his life easier. He never had any trouble with labor, with suppliers, with any government bureaucracy. If a problem came up, he'd mention it to Lou, and whatever it was, *poof,* it disappeared.

But that did not make up for the things Kemp hated about the new arrangement. Mainly he hated that he was not really the boss anymore. He was most aware of this when he was on the ship, where Manny Arquero always called him *"Mister* Kemp," acting very respectful, so Kemp knew he didn't mean it. He started to get the same feeling in his other businesses, a vibe from his employees that told him they knew that he wasn't really the man anymore, that he was taking orders from somebody, just like them.

And he was. He still made money; he still was, officially, the CEO. But Lou was the boss. Lou's people were keeping the books now; Lou's people were "helping" Kemp's people manage things. And everybody understood that if Lou's people wanted something done, it was done.

A lot of it clearly involved money laundering. Like, a guy would come on the *Extravaganza* and buy a ridiculous amount of chips—maybe $50,000 worth, way more than anybody ever spent on a sleazeball casino ship. The guy would play some blackjack, some craps, not paying attention, not caring if he was winning or losing, usually losing. At the end of the night, he'd just leave, not cashing in the rest of his chips, leaving a huge profit for the house. Except Bobby Kemp, who was supposed to *be* the house, wouldn't see that money. It'd get spent on something else, some supplier who, as far as Kemp could tell, wasn't supplying anything. Just like that, a big wad of money from God-knows-what became part of legitimate business cash flow.

That part of the operation Kemp understood right away. It took him longer to see the other thing going on. He heard

about it in bits and pieces from his people who spent time
with people who worked on the ship. From what he could
piece together, it happened maybe one or two nights a
month. The tipoff was the presence on the ship of four particular guys—guys who wore crew uniforms, but didn't
perform any crew duties, just kept to themselves. When
they were on board, the *Extravaganza* would, at some
point, break out of its usual pattern of circling just outside
the three-mile limit and move out farther from shore, the
Miami skyline getting small on the horizon. It would turn
north, then slow down, then stop, just drifting with the
Gulf Stream, the captain using just enough throttle to keep
the ship pointed steady.

Then a cabin cruiser, its lights out, would approach
from the east, turn, and back up to the *Extravaganza*'s
stern, where the deck was low to the water. Lines would be
tossed, and when the two ships were tied together, the four
guys would get to work moving heavy canvas sacks. They
went both ways: first, sacks from the cabin cruiser to the
Extravaganza; then, sacks from the *Extravaganza* to the
cabin cruiser. This went on for maybe ten minutes, and
then the ships would untie, the cabin cruiser would head
east, and the *Extravaganza* would go back to circling. The
gamblers never noticed; the stern deck wasn't visible from
the public area, and besides which, they were too busy
yanking slot-machine handles to care what the ship was
doing.

Bobby Kemp spent a lot of time thinking about it, what
was going on out there. He decided it had to be drugs in the
incoming sacks, most likely cocaine. The outgoing sacks
had to be cash, headed for some offshore bank. That had to
be it. These fuckers were bringing in coke, right past the
Coast Guard station on Government Cut, in a ship with
neon lights all over it. And it was *Bobby Kemp's ship*.
That's what really pissed him off. Not that it was illegal,

but that he, Bobby Kemp, who would surely go to jail for this if the shit ever hit the fan, wasn't getting a piece.

This gnawed at him until finally he'd found the balls to ask Tarant to come to his office for a meeting.

"Lou," he'd said. "I realize we got off on the wrong foot, about the *Extravaganza* and all, me saying some things I shouldn't have."

"Forget about it, Bobby," said Tarant. "Water under the dam. The important thing is, we're partners now, everybody's happy."

"Well, that's the thing, Lou."

"What's the thing?"

"What I mean is, I don't feel like, don't take this wrong, I don't feel like a one-hundred-percent full partner here, in some areas."

"What areas, Bobby?"

"Well, OK, this operation on the *Extravaganza,* which, I mean, I'm the *owner,* Chrissakes, so it seems to me . . ."

"What operation you talking about, Bobby? It's a casino ship, makes a nice profit, you get a nice taste of that."

"I don't mean the gambling."

"What *do* you mean?" said Tarant, looking at Kemp hard.

"You know what I mean," said Kemp, making himself look back. "The other shit."

"What other shit, Bobby?"

"Listen, Lou, I got no problem with, I mean, I just think, since I'm taking a certain risk here, it seems to me that . . ."

"Bobby, listen to me." Tarant moved closer. "There's nothing else. Who told you there was something else?"

Kemp didn't answer. It took all his willpower to keep from backing up.

"Because if somebody was to go around saying that," said Tarant, now right in Kemp's face, "I'd want to straighten their ass out. My associates and I can't have people talking like that. You understand, Bobby? I find out somebody is spreading that shit around, believe me, it would not be good for that person. We clear on that, Bobby?"

He put his hands on Kemp's shoulders, squeezed just a little. Kemp felt some pee dribble from his dick.

"I said, are we clear, Bobby?"

"Yeah."

"What?" A little more squeeze pressure. A little more pee.

"Yes, Lou."

"Good," said Tarant, dropping his arms, stepping back. "Was there anything else you wanted to talk to me about?"

"No, Lou."

"OK, then, Bobby. I'll let you go. I know you're a busy man, got important things to do."

As he said this, Tarant glanced down at Kemp's crotch. Kemp looked down, saw the spreading pee stain. He looked up. Tarant was watching him, not moving a muscle on his face, but Kemp could see it, deep in those dark eyes, Tarant laughing at him.

"One more thing, Bobby."

"What?"

"Your secretary out there? With the tits? Who can't work the phone?"

"Yeah?"

"She works for me now."

THAT WAS SIX MONTHS AGO. IT HAD TAKEN Kemp that long to figure out a move he could make, gather the information, work out the plan, get everything lined up. He was very careful. He knew he had one shot at getting himself out of this situation, and that if he screwed it up, he'd be one of those people the Miami-Dade police divers find from time to time inside the trunk of a stolen car on the bottom of a canal, crabs crawling through their eye sockets.

So he couldn't afford to mess up. But things were looking good. The canvas-sack exchange was definitely on for tonight; his source on the *Extravaganza* had assured him of this. In fact, word was that this was a big exchange, which was a piece of unexpected luck. So was this tropical storm, Hector. Weather like this, nobody would see what was going on out there. That was good.

Kemp knew it was going to be tricky. People might get hurt. Probably would, in fact. Too bad. These assholes were going to find out they'd made a big mistake, fucking with Bobby Kemp.

A big mistake.

Three

WALLY FOUND THE PIECE OF PAPER IN HIS WAL-
let, dialed the number.

"Yeah?" said a voice.

"Hi," said Wally. "This is Wally."

"Who?"

"Wally. Hartley. From the band. We're playing on the . . ."

"What do you want?"

"I was just wondering if it's going out tonight. I mean,
I'm *assuming* it's not, what with this—"

"It's going out."

"It is? Because according to the weath—"

"It's going out."

"Well, OK, but, I mean, have you been watching the—"

"It's going out," said the voice, hanging up.

"Shit," said Wally. He dialed bandmate Ted Brailey.

"Hello?" said Ted.

"Hey," said Wally. "It's me."

"Tell me something," said Ted. "How many shooters did I do last night?"

"I would say, conservatively, two hundred fifty," said Wally.

"Feels like more," said Ted. "Feels like dogs humping inside my skull."

"Poetic," said Wally.

"Best I can do," said Ted. "These are *big* dogs."

"You wanna feel worse?" said Wally.

"I don't think I can."

"The boat's going out tonight."

"*What?* Have you looked outside? It's a monsoon out there."

"Technically, it's a tropical storm. Hector."

"Whoever it is, it looks nasty. Maybe we should quit this gig."

"Right. We can quit this gig, and since we have no other gigs lined up, we can live off all the shrewd investments we made over the years. Leather pants, for example."

"Good point," said Ted. "Maybe we need to rethink our careers. Use our skills, get real jobs. No, wait, I forgot. We're musicians. We *have* no skills."

"I'm gonna break the bad news to Jock and Johnny," said Wally. "I'll see you at the boat."

"If I live," said Ted. "These are *really* big dogs."

Wally and Ted's band—which Wally had rejoined after his brief, unhappy foray into the business world—was currently called Johnny and the Contusions. For the past three weeks, they'd been playing nightly on the *Extravaganza of the Seas,* where they replaced a band whose female vocalist suffered from seasickness, as became evident when she released a major stream of projectile vomit while singing "Wind Beneath My Wings."

The band—Wally on guitar, Ted on keyboards, Johnny

Clarke on bass, and Jock Hume on drums—had been together for sixteen years. Wally was much closer to his bandmates than to either of his brothers, both of whom were older and had wives and kids and jobs involving spreadsheets.

For most of the band's existence, they'd called themselves Arrival. This was the pathetically hopeful name they'd come up with when they'd started the band in tenth grade, begging their parents for money so they could buy instruments and amplifiers, figuring out chords, playing way too loud in somebody's family room until somebody's mom made them stop, or some neighbor called the cops. But they kept practicing, because they had a dream, which was to become the first major rock stars ever to emerge from Bougainvillea High School. Or at least get laid.

By their senior year, they were semi-famous in their peer group. They won the talent show and played for a couple of class parties; on occasion, they actually did get laid. Not wanting to see this glamorous lifestyle come to an end, they decided, upon graduating, to stay together in Miami. They enrolled in community college, but only to placate their parents. What they really did was try to make it as a band.

They did not make it far. Despite countless hours of practice, dozens of auditions, many artistic disputes, seven demo CDs, and two radical changes in hairstyle, Arrival never arrived. It wasn't that they were bad; it was just that, as they reluctantly came to understand, they really weren't anything special. They were competent. The problem was, there were competent bands everywhere. Competence wasn't the key to stardom; you needed something else. Whatever it was, Arrival didn't have it.

In time, they accepted their lot and morphed into a generic cover band, taking whatever gigs they could get, mostly bars, sometimes private parties. Eventually, despite having vowed many times that they would never do this, they bought used tuxedos, learned "Wonderful World" and "Hava Nagilah," and began playing weddings and bar mitzvahs.

The worst was this: They'd be in some hotel ballroom on a Saturday afternoon, bone-tired from a Friday-night bar gig, their tuxedos soaked with hangover sweat, trying to feign enthusiasm as they croaked their way through some bogus party-hearty song (*Cel-e-brate good times, come ON! Everybody get out on the floor and help Josh celebrate his special day!*). And then, during a break, a guest would come up and say, "Didn't you guys go to Bougainvillea?" And he'd turn out to be some guy who'd been in their class, some chess-club dork they'd been way too cool to know back then, and now he was giving them that look, the one that said, *I'm a senior partner in an accounting firm; I live in a luxury condo, drive an Audi, and have a big corner office in a high-rise on Brickell Avenue; and you guys are still doing THIS?*

The other bad thing about weddings and bar mitzvahs was song requests. In a bar gig, they could generally slide by these ("Sure, we'll try to get to that in the next set"). But at a private gig, if somebody requested a song, they pretty much had to play it, even if it was a song that, over the years, they had come to loathe, like "Bad, Bad Leroy Brown," or—God forbid—"Feelings."

At one wedding reception, they'd been ordered, by the mother of the bride, to perform "I Will Survive," the angry anthem of dumped women everywhere. The band members played a quick round of Rock, Paper, Scissors to see who had to sing it; the loser was Johnny, who mumbled it in a soft falsetto, staring at his shoes, accompanied by the mother of the bride, who stood in the middle of the dance floor, alone, shrieking the words in the direction of the table where the father of the bride sat with his new trophy wife.

Experiences like that led the band to develop the Retaliation Song. The way it worked was, if they were forced to perform a song they hated, they'd retaliate by playing a song that was even worse. For example, if the band had to play "My Way," it would counterattack with Bobby Goldsboro's sap-oozing piece of dreck, "Honey" (*She wrecked the car and she was sad, and so afraid that I'd be mad, but what the heck!*).

One night, at a wedding reception, an extremely drunk man ordered the band to perform "The Ballad of the Green Berets," and then, a half hour later, demanded that it be played *again*. That night, Arrival struck back with the hydrogen bomb of retaliation songs: "In the Year 2525," the relentlessly ugly Zager and Evans song with the disturbingly weird lyrics (*You won't find a thing to chew! Nobody's gonna look at you!*). Some guests actually fled the room.

In recent years, Arrival's bookings had declined, in part because of the band's growing tendency to become cranky and hostile toward its audience. This trend had culminated in the unfortunate incident that resulted in Arrival's decision to change its name.

It happened a few weeks after Wally returned to the band. Seriously in need of money, he'd booked the band at a west Broward County bar called Boots 'n' Chaps. This was a country-western bar; Arrival was a last-minute replacement for a real country band, whose bus had broken down outside of Jacksonville. The Boots 'n' Chaps owner, with his big Saturday-night crowd only hours away, had been unable to find another country band. In desperation, he called Wally.

"Can you boys play contemporary country?" he asked.

"Sure," said Wally. He, personally, did not know any contemporary country, but he figured somebody in the band would know enough that they could fake it.

As it turned out, nobody in Arrival knew any contemporary country. This was unfortunate, because the Boots 'n' Chaps patrons were very much into that genre, to the extent of wearing actual cowboy-style boots. Arrival tried to please them by opening with the most country-sounding song in their repertoire, "Sweet Home Alabama." The Boots 'n' Chaps patrons tolerated this song as a recognized redneck classic but did not move toward the dance floor. They were waiting for the songs they expected at Boots 'n' Chaps, the songs that enabled them to perform the complex country line dances they learned on Line Dance Lessons Night here at Boots 'n' Chaps, augmented by detailed instructions available on the Internet ("Stomp right foot next to left; kick right foot forward; hook right foot across left ankle; kick right foot forward . . .").

After "Sweet Home Alabama," Arrival moved on to "Honky Tonk Woman," which has the words "honky tonk" in it but is definitely not contemporary country. The crowd's mood darkened, the patrons sucking sullenly on their Budweiser longnecks. As "Honky Tonk Woman" ended, the band members shot one another *What next?* looks. Wally, thinking frantically, came up with Buddy Holly, who at least came from Texas. The band launched haltingly into "That'll Be the Day" in two different keys, which they eventually narrowed down to one. They got through it OK, but the crowd did not move a bone.

When the song ended, a hefty man at the bar, who was wearing not only a pair of cowboy-style boots, but also a cowboy-style hat, a cowboy-style shirt, cowboy-style jeans, and a belt buckle that looked like a hubcap, yelled "'Nuffa that shit! Play some country!" Other patrons hooted cowboy-style, as they had seen done in movies, and banged beer bottles on the tables.

This did not sit well with Johnny, who happened to be a fan of Buddy Holly, and who had fortified himself for this

gig with three tequila shooters. Leaning into his microphone, Johnny said to the hefty man, "So, Buck, how many
head of cattle you got on *your* ranch?"

The room went silent. The hefty man glared at Johnny.

"No, wait, Buck, lemme guess," Johnny continued.
"You don't have a *ranch,* but you drive a pickup, right? To
your job at Wal-Mart? In the housewares department? Am
I right, Buck?"

This left the hefty man—whose name was not Buck, but
Herb Tobin, and who in fact *did* work at Wal-Mart, although in major appliances—with no choice but to defend
his honor. He rushed, boots clomping, across the dance
floor to the low stage and charged into Johnny, who de-
fended himself by thrusting his bass guitar, a 1973 Fender
Precision, into Tobin's face. Tobin grabbed the guitar and
yanked it, along with Johnny, off the stage, and they both
fell to the dance floor, grunting and flailing at each other.

It would probably have been a draw, since neither par-
ticipant was remotely competent at fisticuffs, plus they had
the guitar between them. But the balance was tipped when
a shrieking woman—Tobin's wife and Wal-Mart col-
league, Fran, who worked in the bed-and-bath department—pounced on Johnny from behind and clubbed his
skull with a commemorative Jack Daniel's ashtray that the
police later estimated at two pounds.

That was the finale of the Boots 'n' Chaps gig. Johnny
went off in the ambulance; Herb and Fran went off with the
police. Wally, Ted, and Jock packed up their equipment
quickly under the baleful glares of the Boots 'n' Chaps patrons and left, unpaid. The bar owner told Wally that Arrival would damn sure never play there again. Wally said
that he was sorry to hear that, because they'd really enjoyed meeting the original cast of *Deliverance.* The bar
owner didn't get it.

When Wally, Ted, and Jock got to the hospital emergency room, the nurse behind the desk told them that Johnny was still being examined. They went out to the parking lot to smoke a joint, review the evening, and reflect on their cosmic loserness as a band. Eventually, they got around to the name Arrival, which they agreed had become a marketing liability, not to mention a nagging reminder of their pathetic adolescent fantasies of wealth and fame and incomprehensible amounts of nookie.

By the second joint, they had decided that if they were going to fail as a band, they were at least going to fail with a better name. They were considering various candidates—including "Departure," "The Original Kings of Apathy," "No, We Don't Play Hip-Hop; We're Musicians," and "We May Suck, But We Play Better Than You Dance"—when the emergency-room nurse, whose shift had ended, appeared in the parking lot, headed for her car. She stopped a few feet from the three bandmates and looked at them. Jock, obeying a reflex developed in seventh grade, stuck the joint behind his back.

"You guys want to know about your friend?" the nurse asked.

"Sure," said Wally.

"He's OK," said the nurse. "Scalp wound, fourteen stitches. Some contusions. Nothing serious. He can go soon."

"That's great," said Wally.

"I thought contusions was serious," said Jock.

"You're thinking concussion," said Ted.

"No, I'm not," said Jock, although he had been.

"It's not serious," said the nurse, studying Jock, who was the member of the band women were most likely to study. "It just means bruises."

"Oh," said Jock, studying the nurse in return, and noticing that she was kind of attractive, in a mature-woman, Ann-Margret-ish, potentially-nice-rack-under-that-uniform kind of way.

"That's great," said Wally, again. "Thanks."

The nurse, not leaving, kept her eyes on Jock, who still had his hand behind his back.

"So," she said, "are you gonna offer me a hit of that?"

Twenty minutes later, the nurse, whose name was Sandy, and who was 43, and who had learned that very afternoon that her former husband was going to marry her former Avon representative, drove off with Jock in her Toyota Camry, leaving Wally and Ted to finish the third joint.

Finally, Wally said, "Let's go get Johnny."

"Johnny," said Ted, suddenly remembering Johnny. "And his contusions."

Wally stopped.

"Johnny and the Contusions," he said.

They looked at each other. Then they high-fived, and Arrival was no more.

Three weeks, one wedding, and nine bar gigs later, at 6:30 A.M., Wally was awakened by his cell phone, which he never turned off.

"Hello?" he said.

"You with Arrival?" said a voice.

"What?" said Wally.

"The band," said the voice. "On this business card, where I got this number, it says Arrival, Contemporary Music for All Occasions."

Wally looked at his clock radio.

"It's six-thirty in the morning," he said.

"I know that," said the voice. "I got a watch. What I need is a band."

"Now?" said Wally.

"Tonight," said the voice. "On a casino boat. I need a

band. You show up, do a good job, you get steady work. But you gotta be there tonight. You can do that, Arrival?"

"Actually," said Wally, "that's an old card. Our new name is Johnny and the Contusions."

"What?" said the voice. "The card says Arrival."

"I know," said Wally. "We just changed our name to Johnny and the Contusions."

"Contusions?" said the voice.

"It means bruises," said Wally.

"I know that," said the voice.

"Funny story behind that," said Wally. "Our bass player, Johnny, he got into a . . ." He trailed off, realizing that this was not a good story to tell somebody who was considering hiring the band.

"That's a dumb-ass name," said the voice.

Wally said nothing, because maybe the voice had a point.

"I need to know something about the band," said the voice.

"OK," said Wally, "we do mostly classic-rock covers, but we can do almost any—"

"No," said the voice. "What I need to know, does anybody in the band get seasick?"

"No," said Wally. "I don't think so."

"I don't need a band that pukes on the customers," said the voice.

"No," agreed Wally.

"Two hundred dollars a night," said the voice. "You play five hours."

"I dunno," said Wally. "Usually, for this kind of job, we would charge—"

"Two hundred dollars," said the voice.

"OK," said Wally.

"You know the Chum Bucket?" said the voice. "On the bay?"

"Yeah," said Wally. "In fact we played there a couple of—"

"Boat leaves from there," said the voice. "*Extravaganza of the Seas.* You and the rest of the Concussions be there at five-thirty."

"It's Contusions," said Wally. "Johnny and the Contusions."

"Dumb-ass name," said the voice, and hung up.

ESTELLE WAS ABOUT TO BITE SUMO BOY. FAY could see it in her eyes.

Sumo Boy was the least-pleasant child in Estelle's Tot-a-Rama class, where Fay took Estelle three days a week so she could play with other babies. Except that the Tot-a-Rama instructor did not call it "playing." She called it "interacting." That's how the Tot-a-Rama instructor talked, as a result of taking courses in Child Development. If Estelle was trying to put a ball into a bucket, the Tot-a-Rama instructor would inform Fay that Estelle was working on her spatial relationship skills. Her favorite word was "cognitive."

Fay found this very amusing but had nobody to share the joke with; the other moms seemed to take the Tot-a-Rama instructor seriously. Fay felt out of place in this class, and not just because she was the only mom who drove an eight-year-old Ford Probe as opposed to a new SUV the size of a mobile home. She also believed she was the only single working mom in the group. She was sure she was the only mom who, at night, wore a skimpy costume and served cocktails to groping morons on a casino ship.

So Fay was not crazy about Tot-a-Rama, especially since it cost her money that she didn't always have, and sleep that she desperately needed after long, late nights on the ship. But Estelle loved Tot-a-Rama and got along well with the other babies. Except for Sumo Boy.

Sumo Boy, whose real name was Christopher, was huge for a 19-month-old, weighing in at around 40 pounds, 13 pounds heavier than Estelle. Sumo Boy was very possessive, and right now he was getting on Estelle's nerves, over the beanbags. There were dozens of beanbags, plenty for everybody, but whenever Estelle picked one up, Sumo Boy would yell "MINE!" and grab for it with his chubby hands. Estelle, who was a good sharer, would let go of the bag and pick up another one. Sumo Boy would then drop his current bag, yell "MINE!" again, and grab for the new one.

Fay could see that Estelle was getting tired of sharing and was just about ready to retaliate. Fay kept waiting for Sumo Boy's mother to do something about her son's behavior, but Sumo Mom just smiled, as though this were the cutest thing she'd ever seen.

Fay was not a big fan of Sumo Mom. Once, while the class was developing some cognitive skill or other by playing Marching, Marching Round and Round, Fay had gotten a cell-phone call from her ex-husband, who was pissed off about a letter he got from Fay's lawyer about being behind on his child support. Fay was marching, holding the cell phone to her ear with her right hand, holding Estelle's tiny hand with her left.

"Todd, I can't talk now," she whispered.

"You want another court fight?" Todd said. "Is that what you want?" Todd loved to fight. He spent considerably more on legal fees than it would cost him simply to send Fay the money he owed, but for him the added expense was worth it.

"No, Todd," whispered Fay. "I don't want to fight. I just want you to fulfill your—"

"Well, you're going to *get* another court fight," said Todd, hanging up.

"Shit," said Fay. She said it quietly, but Sumo Mom, who was marching right in front of her, heard it and turned to give her a glare.

"I'm sorry," Fay said.

"There's no need for that kind of language here," said Sumo Mom.

"I know," said Fay. "I'm very sorry."

"Little children have big ears," said Sumo Mom.

Your child also has a big butt, thought Fay, but she said, "Look, I said I'm sorry. The kids didn't hear anything. I'm just having a personal situation that . . ."

But Sumo Mom, having taken the moral high ground, had turned away and was marching righteously onward. Later, Fay saw her talking to the Tot-a-Rama instructor, who pulled Fay aside after class and gave her a little lecture concerning inappropriate contexts for hostile verbalization.

Fay had exchanged no words with Sumo Mom since that day, but she was getting close now, as she watched Estelle, having had enough, yank her beanbag out of Sumo Boy's grasp.

"MINE!" said Sumo Boy, barging into Estelle, hands out. Estelle opened her mouth, clearly intending to chomp down on one of Sumo Boy's plump arms.

"No!" said Fay, grabbing Estelle and swooping her up. "We don't bite, Estelle. We *never* bite."

"MINE!" screamed Sumo Boy, as the beanbag, still in Estelle's grasp, soared out of reach.

Sumo Mom was outraged. "She was going to *bite* him!" she informed Fay. "She was going to bite my son!" Around the room, nine mommy heads swiveled their way.

"MINE!" shouted Sumo Boy.

"I'm sorry," Fay told Sumo Mom. "But your son was taking all her beanbags, and she gets . . ."

"MINE!!" said Sumo Boy, pounding on Fay's leg.

"MINE!!" He hit hard, for a baby; Fay's leg hurt. She was also getting a headache.

"Do you have any idea how dangerous a human bite can be?" said Sumo Mom.

"Yes, but she didn't—"

"MINE!!" (Pound.) "MINE!!" (Pound.) "MINE!!" (Pound.)

"The human bite is very dangerous," said Sumo Mom. "My husband is a doctor."

At that moment, Sumo Boy sunk his sharp little teeth into Fay, penetrating her jeans just above her left knee.

"OW!" said Fay, yanking the leg away. Sumo Boy, suddenly unsupported, fell on his face. After an ominously silent two seconds, he emitted a glass-shattering shriek. It was matched in volume by one from Sumo Mom, who fell to her knees and scooped her wailing child into her arms. He looked unhurt to Fay. She, on the other hand, felt as though she'd been stabbed with an ice pick.

"What happened?" said the Tot-a-Rama instructor, scurrying over.

"She tried to bite my son!" said Sumo Mom, pointing at Estelle.

"We can't have biting behavior in Tot-a-Rama," the instructor told Fay.

"My daughter didn't bite anybody," said Fay. "In fact—"

"She tried to!" said Sumo Mom. "She was going to bite my son."

"We cannot allow aggressive behavior that jeopardizes the physical well-being of our participants," said the instructor.

"But what I'm telling you," said Fay, "is that she didn't—"

"Human bites are very dangerous," said Sumo Mom. "My husband is a doctor."

"Then maybe he could sew your mouth shut," said Fay.

Sumo Mom was stunned speechless. The instructor was very displeased.

"If you and your daughter cannot interact within the parameters of the Tot-a-Rama paradigm," she said, "then I'm afraid you will have to discontinue your participation."

"OK," said Fay. "You bet. We'll discontinue our participation in your paradigm. Although I sincerely doubt that you have a fucking clue what that word actually means."

Around the room, nine mommies emitted simultaneous gasps. Fay, holding Estelle, marched to the door, opened it, and marched out. Then, realizing she was barefoot, she reopened the door and reentered the classroom. The mommies, who had already begun buzzing, fell silent as Fay picked up her shoes and Estelle's tiny sneakers, then left again. She heard the buzzing resume as she closed the door; she knew it would continue for days, maybe weeks.

Still barefoot, Fay carried Estelle briskly through the rain across the parking lot to the Probe. She put Estelle into her car seat, made sure she had her juice cup and her little plastic dolls. Then she put on her shoes and slid behind the wheel. Then she put her face in her hands and cried.

"Mommy crying," said Estelle.

"Mommy's OK, honey," sniffed Fay.

"Mommy OK," said Estelle. "Crying."

"I'm not crying, honey," said Fay, turning to give Estelle a big, fake smile.

"Snow White," said Estelle, holding up a little plastic Snow White doll. It was her favorite toy. She knew, even at age two, the basic story: The girl is beautiful, but sleeping. Then the handsome man comes. He kisses her! She wakes up! She's happy! Forever! Or at least until she encounters a little plastic divorce-lawyer doll.

"Snow White," said Estelle again. "Sleeping. Man kiss."

"That's right, honey," said Fay. "The man kisses her."

She fished a tissue out of her purse, blew her nose, then got her cell phone and called her mother.

"Hello?" said her mother.

"Hi, it's me. Can you come over tonight? I'm sorry, but the ship is going out."

"It's going out? In this hurricane?"

"Yes. I called."

"Well, tell them you can't go."

"Mom, I have to go. It's my job."

"Well, you should get a different job."

Fay sighed. "Mother, just please tell me if you can come over tonight, OK?"

"OK, I'll come over, so later on I can explain to Estelle that her mother was a crazy person who went out and got herself killed in a hurricane."

"Thank you, Mother."

A silence. Fay, from years of experience, knew what her mother would bring up next. And, sure enough:

"I talked to Maggie today."

Maggie was Fay's younger and, in her mother's view, ragingly perfect sister, with a perfect and highly successful husband who enabled her to care full-time for her three perfect children in a perfect modern house with a foyer that could easily swallow Fay's entire apartment.

"Great," said Fay. "How is she?"

"She's fine."

"Great."

"She's doing very well."

Another silence.

"As opposed to me," said Fay.

"I didn't say that," said her mother.

"No, you never *say* it," said Fay.

Another silence. Fay broke it:

"Mom, listen, I'm sorry. I'm just tired. I really appreciate you looking after Estelle. I promise this job will end soon."

"I certainly hope so. That boat is no place to meet a nice man."

"Mother, I am not trying to find a man, OK?"

"That's for sure."

"What is *that* supposed to mean?"

"Nothing. I have to go. *The Young and the Restless* is starting. Good-bye."

Her mother hung up. Fay pressed the OFF button on her phone and told herself that she was *not* going to cry for the nineteen-millionth time over the vast unbridgeable chasm between her life and her mother's expectations.

"Snow White," said Estelle.

"Yes, honey," said Fay. "That's Snow White."

"Man kiss," said Estelle.

"That's right," said Fay. "The man kisses her."

Another silence.

"Mommy crying," said Estelle.

Four

ARNIE AND PHIL WERE IN THE OLD FARTS SENILE
Dying Center recreation room, where no recreation had
ever taken place. Slumped randomly in chairs around them
were a dozen other residents, a few staring into the distance with unfocused eyes, the rest asleep, or—you never
knew here—deceased.

Arnie and Phil were watching the big-screen TV, which
was tuned to NewsPlex Nine, the top-rated local news
show, which specialized in terrorizing its viewers. The
NewsPlex Nine consumer-affairs reporter once did a week-
long series, with dramatic theme music and a flashy logo,
on fatal diseases that could, *theoretically,* be transmitted
via salad bars. The reporter did not find any instance of this
actually happening, but the series did win two awards for
graphics. It was entitled "Death Beneath the Sneeze
Shield."

NewsPlex Nine loved bad weather. At least ten times
per hurricane season, the weather guy—no, make that the

StormCenter Nine meteorologist—would point to some radar blob way the hell out in the Atlantic, next to Africa, and inform the viewers that, while it did not pose any *immediate* threat, he was keeping a close eye on it, because under the right conditions, it could, *theoretically,* strengthen into a monster hellstorm and attack South Florida with winds that could propel a piece of driveway gravel through your walls, into your eyeball, and out the back of your skull.

Needless to say, the members of the NewsPlex Nine team were all over Tropical Storm Hector, which as far as they were concerned was the most exciting thing to happen in South Florida since several weeks earlier, when a German tourist opened his hotel mini-bar refrigerator and discovered what turned out to be the left foot of a missing Norwegian tourist. The meteorologist was already hoarse from speculating about the bad things that Tropical Storm Hector could, *potentially,* do.

"Look at his hair," said Arnie. "Six hours he's talking, he's waving his arms in front of the radar, his hair is perfect. How the hell do you keep hair holding still like that?"

"How the hell do you keep *hair*?" said Phil.

"I hate this channel," said Arnie. "A little rain, they act like it's nuclear war."

"You wanna change the channel, be my guest," said Phil, gesturing toward the remote control.

"You kidding?" said Arnie. "What am I, Einstein?"

The remote control had 48 buttons. No resident of the Old Farts Senile Dying Center knew how to operate it. They were the Greatest Generation, men and women who had survived the Depression, defeated the Nazis, built America into the greatest nation the world had ever seen. But this damned gizmo had beaten them.

Every now and then, a resident would bravely pick up the remote and, with shaking hands, push some buttons in an effort to change the channel. The result was almost always bad. Sometimes the TV would shut off entirely. Sometimes the screen would turn bright blue; sometimes a menu would appear, and nobody could figure out how to get rid of it, and everybody would watch the menu until a staff member wandered by and fixed the problem. So although the center had cable TV and received 98 channels, the residents were limited to whichever one happened to be on when they entered the room. Today it was NewsPlex Nine.

"Look at this," said Phil. "They're showing the super-market morons again."

On the screen, for the third time since Arnie and Phil had started watching, was a reporter in a Publix supermarket. This was a standard element of the NewsPlex Nine storm coverage: the frenzy of food-and-supplies buying by panicked residents, who for the most part were panicked because they'd been watching NewsPlex Nine.

"As we've been seeing all afternoon," the reporter was saying, "the aisles here are jammed with worried shoppers, stocking up for the worst." Behind her, people smiled and waved at the camera.

The reporter turned to a fifty-ish woman in a house-dress, put the microphone into her face.

"What supplies are you buying?" she asked.

"Well," said the woman, looking into her cart, "I got batteries and water, peanut butter, bleach, let's see here . . . soup, cold cuts. Also I got some Vaseline."

"For the storm?" said the reporter.

"No, we're just out of Vaseline," said the woman.

"Back to you in the NewsPlex, Bill and Jill."

"What I wanna know," said Arnie, "is why bleach?"

"What are you talking about?" said Phil.

"Always with the hurricane, people are buying bleach."

"So?"

"So, what do they *do* with the bleach?"

"You need the bleach," said Phil. "In case."

The truth was that Phil had no idea what the bleach was for, even though, like most South Floridians, he firmly believed you needed some. Everybody bought it, because everybody else did. There were hundreds of thousands of gallons of emergency Clorox in cupboards all over South Florida, sitting, ready and waiting, next to the emergency cans of Spam manufactured in 1987.

"In case of *what*?" said Arnie. "A hurricane comes, knocks down your house, you're gonna do a load of laundry?"

Phil looked at Arnie for a moment.

"Does it ever occur to you," he said, "that you think too much?"

"That's exactly what my wife used to say," said Arnie. "She always bought bleach."

"So did my wife," said Phil.

The two old men sat silent for a moment, both thinking about their wives.

On the TV, NewsPlex Nine was now showing a reporter standing on Miami Beach. He was wearing a yellow rain poncho, with the hood off so you could see his hair being blown around.

"The rain has been coming and going all afternoon," he was saying, "and as you can see we're getting some strong gusts."

"Oooh," said Arnie. "Strong gusts."

"We're already seeing some wind damage," the reporter was saying. "Mike, if you could point the camera over here . . ."

The camera swung away, focused for a moment on a large palm branch lying on the beach, fronds fluttering.

"Oh no!" said Arnie. "A branch is down!"

"Call out the National Guard!" said Phil, and now the

two of them were laughing and coughing. This earned them a glare from a man two chairs over, who'd been awakened by the noise. He got up, gave them another glare, and shuffled from the room.

"What's with him?" said Phil.

"My guess," said Arnie, "he's off to take his annual shit."

". . . definitely getting worse out here," the NewsPlex Nine beach reporter was saying. He was squinting, leaning into the wind, as though at any moment he could be blown away. "People are advised to stay away from the beaches, where the surf as you know can be very treacherous."

Two young men appeared behind the reporter, both in bathing suits. They waved happily at the camera, shoved each other in jocular fashion, then plunged into the ocean. A couple jogged past with a Labrador retriever.

"I'll stay out here as long as I can," the reporter was saying. "Back to you, Bill and Jill."

Bill, the male NewsPlex Nine anchor, said, "You take care out there, Justin." He frowned with concern at the female NewsPlex Nine anchor, whom, unbeknownst to either of their spouses, he was porking nightly in his dressing room. "It's looking bad out there, Jill," he said.

"It sure is, Bill," said Jill, turning to the TelePrompTer, so she could read what she was supposed to be alarmed about next. "And things are not any better out on South Florida's rain-slicked highways."

"UH-oh," said Arnie. "Did you hear that, Phil? The highways are *rain-slicked*."

"It's humanity's worst nightmare!" said Phil. "Wet roads!"

"We've already had some fender-benders on I-95," Jill was saying, "and rush hour is shaping up to be a real mess."

"Like it's not a mess every other day," said Arnie.

". . . have a tanker overturned on the Palmetto Express-way," Jill was saying, "spilling some kind of unidentified liquid across all three southbound lanes."

"It's BLEACH!" said Phil.

"WE LOST OUR BLEACH RESERVES!" shouted Arnie, pounding his chair arm. "WE'RE ALL GONNA DIE!"

"Uh-oh," said Phil, looking toward the door. Arnie, fol-lowing Phil's eyes, saw Dexter Harpwell, the assistant day manager, entering the room, trailed by the glaring man who'd left earlier. Harpwell walked tautly over to Arnie and Phil, stopping between them and the TV screen. His right hand was bandaged where the Old Bat had bitten him at lunch.

"Gentlemen," he said, "I've received complaints about your noise level."

"What do you mean, *complaints?*" said Arnie. "You mean Mr. Constipation over there?" He gestured toward the glaring man, who had reseated himself and was now glaring straight ahead.

"Mr. Kremens says you gentlemen are talking so loud he can't watch television," said Harpwell.

"He wasn't watching the television," said Phil. "He was sleeping."

"This is a community," said Harpwell. "You have to re-spect the rights of the other residents."

"No question," said Arnie. "He has a right to sleep. So let him go sleep in his room."

Harpwell heaved a heavy sigh. "Mr. Pullman," he said, "do you recall what I said at lunch today?"

"Yeah," said Arnie. "You said *OOOW.*"

"How's that hand?" asked Phil. "I was you, I'd check the Old Bat for rabies."

"What I said at lunch," said Harpwell, "is that if you gentlemen continued to commit Conduct Violations, I would have to take disciplinary action. I'm afraid you've given me no choice but to do that now."

"How old are you?" said Arnie.

"What does that have to do with anything?" said Harpwell.

"It has to do with, I'm eighty-three, which means I was a grown man supporting a family when you were getting happy-face stickers for making peepee on the potty," said Arnie.

"How old were you then, Dexter?" said Phil. "Fourteen?"

"Very funny," said Harpwell. "But the fact is that . . ."

"The fact is," said Arnie, "we're grown men. We're more grown than you'll probably ever be. Just because we got to live in this cemetery, doesn't mean you can talk to us like we're kids."

"Be that as it may," said Harpwell, "I'm the authority here, and in the interest of protecting the rights of the other residents, I'm going to confine you two to your rooms this evening after dinner."

"What?" said Arnie.

"You're *sending us to our rooms?*" said Phil.

"That's correct," said Harpwell. "This will give you a chance to ponder your responsibilities within the Beaux Arts community."

"And what if we don't go to our rooms?" said Arnie. "You gonna spank us?"

"If you are unable to function within the parameters of the Independent Living Wing," said Harpwell, "I'm afraid I'll have to transfer you to the other building."

"What?" said Arnie. "The loony bin? The International House of Drool?"

The other building was where they kept the truly demented residents, the ones who wore pajamas all day, and wet themselves, and cried out for mommies who'd died forty years ago.

"You can't do that," said Phil.

"It's called the Assisted Living Wing," said Harpwell, "and rest assured, I have full authority, solely at my discretion, to transfer you both there. Unless you prefer to leave Beaux Arts altogether, which is of course your prerogative."

"You little prick," said Arnie.

"You were a hall monitor, right?" said Phil. "In high school? Ratting out the kids who smoked in the boy's room?"

"Just keep it up, gentlemen," said Harpwell, who had in fact been the *head* hall monitor. "Just keep it up. I'm going to have the night security staff check to make sure you're in your rooms tonight. Meanwhile, I think we should change to a channel that Mr. Kremens would find more enjoyable."

He picked up the remote control.

"But he's asleep again," said Phil.

"So he is," said Harpwell, pressing buttons on the remote. "Ah, here we are." The TV was now tuned to a soap opera. In Spanish.

"You little *prick*," said Arnie.

"Have a pleasant evening, gentlemen," said Harpwell, setting down the remote and walking tautly away.

Phil and Arnie looked at each other.

"Can he do this?" said Phil. "Can we call a lawyer or something?"

Arnie shook his head. "First, I don't know about you, but all the lawyers I know are dead. Second, the little prick holds all the cards. This place, believe it or not, there's a waiting list a mile long. My daughter tells me I'm lucky to be here, don't make waves, yadda yadda yadda. They're looking for excuses to get people out of here, so they can bring in new people, charge them more."

"Jesus," said Phil. "So we go to our rooms, like little boys."

"We do," said Arnie.

"So I guess we don't go out on the boat tonight," said Phil, somewhat relieved by this thought.

Arnie thought about that for a moment.

"Not necessarily," he said.

"What do you mean?" said Phil.

"I mean," said Arnie, "I got an idea."

"UH-oh," said Phil.

THE WIND WAS STRONGER NOW, PUSHING THE rain slantwise through the sea-scented Bahamian night. Frank and Juan, wearing ponchos, stood under the yellow dock light next to the cabin cruiser. The boat strained restlessly at its lines even in the shelter of the harbor.

Juan watched the boat shift and heave, and thought about the big waves he could hear crashing out beyond the breakwater. It would be much rougher out there. Juan could not swim. He had never in his life run from anything. He fought anyone who questioned his courage. But now he wanted very much for there to be a reason why he did not have to get on this boat, go out on that dark and violent sea. He would have liked to talk to Frank about this, but he didn't know how.

What he said was: "This asshole, I bet he don't want to take his boat out in this." This was Juan's version of a prayer.

"Oh, he'll take it out," said Frank. "That's why we're here. Make sure he does what he gets paid to do."

"He fucking better," said Juan, because that's what he figured he was supposed to say.

"Time to start the party," said Frank. He cupped his mouth and shouted at the boat: "TARK!"

This time, Tark came right out. In his hand, where his knife had been earlier, was a can of Budweiser, sixteen ounces. He stood easily on the heaving deck, not bracing himself. It pissed Juan off, the way this asshole was un-afraid of the boat, of the roiling water.

Tark exchanged fuck-you stares with Juan for a second, then turned to Frank.

"Nice night, huh?" he said.

"You ready?" said Frank.

"Course I'm ready," said Tark.

"You got the packages?" said Frank.

"I said I'm ready, didn't I?" said Tark. "Question is, are *you* boys ready? 'Cause Pancho here don't look too happy about this. Still on the dock and already looks like he's gonna puke."

"Keep it up, asshole," said Juan.

"OK, *listen,* both of you," said Frank. "Cut this shit right now. I told you before, I don't care what you do when we get back. But I don't want trouble on the boat. On the boat, you work together, like professionals. You under-stand?"

Neither man spoke. Tark pursed his lips, sent a little air kiss at Juan.

"Later, sweetheart," he said. "We got a date."

"That's right, pussy," said Juan. "You better be ready."

They resumed their stare-off. Frank shook his head.

"Christ," he said. "I'm trying to run a business opera-tion, I'm working with the Sharks and the Jets."

Both Juan and Tark looked at Frank.

"*West Side Story,*" said Frank.

Both Juan and Tark frowned.

"Leonard Bernstein?" said Frank.

Both frowns deepened.

"Never mind," said Frank. "Let's get going."

They clambered aboard, Frank first, then Juan, who stumbled as the boat pitched, almost fell, caught himself awkwardly on the gunwale. Tark grinned, opened the cabin door, and went inside. Frank started to follow, then looked back at Juan.

"You coming?" he said.

"No, I stay out here," he said. "Away from that asshole." Truth was, Juan was already feeling queasy. He knew he'd feel worse in the cabin. He hated this goddamn boat.

Frank turned and went into the cabin. It stank of sweat. Tark was crouched by the counter, rooting in the refrigerator. Behind him, sitting in a U-shaped nook around a table littered with an afternoon's worth of beer cans, were three men Frank had never seen before.

"Who's this?" Frank said.

"They're the crew," said Tark, rising from the refrigerator, fresh beer in hand.

"Where's the regular crew?" said Frank. The regular crew was three skinny Bahamians. These were three big white guys.

"I got rid of them," said Tark. "Them spades, all they wanna do is get high. These guys are better. More reliable."

That got a smirk from the man sitting closest to Frank. He wore a black wool cap and a denim shirt with the sleeves cut off, so you could see his big arms, the arms of a dedicated steroid abuser. On his right biceps was a crude tattoo, most likely done in prison, that said "Kaz." The next man was fatter, orange hair in a buzz cut, deep creases in the flesh of his neck. The farthest man, leaner than the other two, had a goatee and wore a bandanna and an earring, like a pirate.

"I don't like this," said Frank.

"You don't like what?" said Tark, showing Frank a big fake-innocent look.

Frank was a big man, and people who didn't know him were always surprised at how quickly he could draw a gun. It was in his hand now, a Glock 31, .357 caliber, 17-shot magazine, serious firepower, popular with law enforcement and professional criminals alike. It was pointed mid-way between Tark and the three guys, who shifted slightly but stayed seated.

"Hey, man," said Tark, "what the fuck is your problem?"

"My problem," said Frank, "is I don't know these guys."

"I know them," said Tark. "I'm vouching for them."

"Somehow that doesn't reassure me," said Frank. "I want to know why you didn't tell me about this."

"I didn't think you'd give a shit."

"You didn't? We use the same crew every time. Suddenly, tonight, we're about to go on a job, a very important job, and there's three guys I don't know from Britney Spears, and you didn't think I'd *give* a shit?"

"I told you, I know these guys. We go back, man. This here is Kaz, this here is Rebar, this here is Holman."

Frank looked at the three of them watching him. The cabin was quiet except for the sounds of the water sloshing against the hull, the lines groaning. Frank reached behind him and opened the cabin door.

"Juan," he said. "Get in here."

Juan came in, saw the situation, the three new guys, the gun in Frank's hand. He reached under his poncho and pulled out his own pistol, also a Glock, the original, smaller, 9-millimeter model 17.

"Who's this?" he said.

"I'm wondering that myself," said Frank. "I'm gonna ask you to keep these gentlemen company while I go outside and call Miami."

"You guys smell beans in here?" said Tark, sniffing the air.

Juan swung his gun barrel toward Tark.

"You want to find out what a bullet smells like, asshole?" he said.

"Easy," said Frank. "Let's not kill anybody just yet, OK? I'll be right back."

He stepped outside, closed the door, pulled out his cell phone and held it up so he could read the display by the dock light. As he'd feared, it said NO SERVICE. He tried to place the call anyway. Nothing.

"Damn," he said. He looked at his watch. Not enough time to go back and use the phone at the inn, which often didn't work anyway.

"Damn," he said again. He rubbed his mouth, thinking, rain dripping down his face. He was in a bind. He needed Tark to run the boat. He needed a crew to transfer the shipments. He needed to get started. With this weather, they were already in danger of being late to the rendezvous.

Frank reopened the cabin door and stepped inside. Nobody had moved.

"OK," he said. "Here's what. My associate is gonna pat you gentlemen down, one at a time." He pointed to Kaz. "Starting with you."

With feigned weariness, Kaz stood, turned, placed his hands against the wall and spread his legs.

"I'm guessing you've done this before," said Frank.

Juan, with practiced efficiency, frisked Kaz, then Rebar, then Holman. Each time, he signaled to Frank: nothing.

"Now you," said Frank, to Tark.

"I don't want that spic touching me," said Tark.

"I don't care what you want," said Frank, aiming the gun barrel a quarter-inch more Tark's way.

Tark sighed, then slowly set down his beer, turned, and leaned against the counter. Juan stepped up and patted him down. As he ran his hand up the inseam of Tark's shorts, Juan considered an uppercut to the crotch, make the man scream, pass out, maybe wind up losing a ball.

"Don't even think about it," said Frank.

Juan finished, finding nothing. He stepped away.

"OK," said Frank. "Here's the plan. You three are gonna stay right at that table until we get where we're going. My associate is going to stay right here keeping you company. You should know that my associate is an extremely good marksman."

"We're supposed to stay here the whole time?" said Kaz.

"That's correct," said Frank.

"What if I gotta take a shit?" said Kaz.

"Then you'll have to shit your pants," said Frank. "So I advise restraint on your part. For my part, I'm going to stay right by our captain's side and assist him with his nautical tasks. I'm confident he'll get us to our destination quickly and efficiently, because he's a team player, because he's a professional, and because if I see even the slightest sign that he's fucking with me, fragments of his skull will come down as far away as Tampa. So is everyone clear on the plan?"

Frank smiled around at everybody. Nobody smiled back.

"Excellent," said Frank. "Anchors aweigh."

Tark, with Frank behind him, went up the small stairway to the bridge, started the engines, checked the gauges.

"I gotta cast off," he said.

"After you," said Frank.

As Tark crossed back through the cabin, he glanced over at the table. He and Kaz locked eyes for a millisecond, traded the tiniest of nods. Everything was going exactly according to plan.

WALLY, TED, JOHNNY, AND JOCK WERE CROSS-ing the causeway, heading from the mainland to Miami Beach in Johnny's 1987 Plymouth Voyager. Johnny was driving; Jock was riding shotgun; Wally and Ted were in the back seat; Muddy Waters was on the tape player. The minivan shuddered as wind gusts hit it, Johnny leaning over the steering wheel to squint into the rainy gloom.

"I can't believe we're going out in this shit," he said. "Are we really *this* desperate for money?"

"I am," said Wally, exhaling, handing the joint to Ted. "I'm very desperate. You want to know how desperate I am?"

"How desperate are you?" said Ted.

"I am so desperate," said Wally, "that today I called the number for that guy who says you can get rich in real estate without putting up any of your own money. You know that guy? On TV? He's in Hawaii, has a major tan, and he has all these people come on and sit with him under the palm trees and give testimonials about how, six months ago, they were living in a refrigerator carton, and now, thanks to this guy's foolproof system, they're making eighty-seven-thousand dollars a month from real estate."

"Why were they living in a refrigerator carton?" said Jock, reaching back to get the joint from Ted.

"I don't mean literally," said Wally. "I just mean, they didn't have shit."

Jock said, "Wouldn't bother me, living in a refrigerator carton, if I lived in Hawaii." He took a hit.

"They don't *live* in Hawaii," said Ted.

"Wally just said it was Hawaii," said Johnny, accepting the joint from Jock.

"I know," said Ted. "But they just fly them out to Hawaii, so everybody thinks, whoa, you do this real-estate deal, you have all this money, you can go to Hawaii."

"If they have so much money," said Jock, "why do they live in a refrigerator carton?"

"Listen," said Wally, reaching forward and getting the joint from Johnny, "just *forget* the refrigerator carton, OK?

There *is* no refrigerator carton. I made the fucking refrigerator carton up."

"But they *are* in Hawaii?" said Jock.

"Yes," said Ted, "but they don't live there."

"How do you know that?" said Johnny. "They might live there."

"He could be right," said Wally, handing the joint to Ted. "Some of them could live in Hawaii. I mean, just randomly."

"Shit," said Ted, "I'm trying to argue for *your* side, and now you're agreeing with *them*."

"I'm not agreeing about the refrigerator carton," said Wally. "I'm just agreeing about living in Hawaii, and I'm only partly agreeing on that."

"Wait a minute," said Jock. "You just said there *was* no refrigerator carton."

"Jesus," said Wally.

"So what happened?" said Ted, handing the joint forward to Jock.

"What happened when?" said Wally.

"What happened when you called the number?" said Ted.

"What number?" said Jock.

"The number on the infomercial," said Ted.

"What infomercial?" said Jock.

"The one we're *talking* about, you moron," said Ted.

"We're talking about an infomercial?" said Jock. He turned to Johnny: "Did you know that?"

"Yeah," said Johnny. "But they're wrong about Hawaii."

"Jesus," said Wally.

"This one's done," said Jock, popping the roach into his mouth.

"So what did happen?" said Ted.

"OK," said Wally. "So I call the number, and this woman wants my credit-card number, so she can charge me fifty-nine ninety-five for the tapes. So I'm like, I don't have any credit left on my credit card. So she's like, well, you can send a check or money order for fifty-nine ninety-five. So I'm like, listen, I don't *have* fifty-nine ninety-five, which is why I need to get into real estate in the first place, so how about you let me have the tapes for no money down, and I pay you the money when I get rich from real estate? And she's like, no, we can't do that. And I'm like, why not? Doesn't the system work? I mean, the infomercial guy says it's foolproof, right? And she's like, well, I wouldn't know anything about that, sir. And I'm like, OK, can I talk to somebody who *does* know something about it? And she's like, well, you can talk to my supervisor. And I'm like, OK, will your supervisor be able to send me the tapes? And she's like, I wouldn't think so, sir, if you don't have the fifty-nine ninety-five. So I'm like, well then, can you explain to me how am I supposed to buy an entire fucking *house* with no money if you won't even let me have some fucking *tapes*? And she's like, sir, there is no call for that kind of language, and she hangs up."

"Sounds like you're on your way to financial independence," said Ted.

"No question," said Wally. "I've taken that critical first step. Do we have another joint?"

"Right here," said Jock, lighting it, taking a hit.

The car was silent, except for Muddy Waters.

Got my mojo workin', but it just won't work on you.

"I bet hardly any customers show up tonight," said Ted, looking out at the rain.

"We still gotta play," said Wally.

"Easy night for the dealers and waitresses, though," said Ted.

"You guys seen that new cocktail waitress?" said Johnny.

"Which one?" said Jock, exhaling.

"Whatshername. With the long hair and the legs," said Johnny.

"Oh yeah," said Jock, handing the joint to Johnny. "What's her name?"

"Fay," said Wally.

"How do you know her name?" said Ted.

"I talked to her," said Wally. He'd tried to strike up a conversation with her, which consisted of him saying hi, I'm Wally, and her saying, I'm Fay, then him saying, I'm in the band, and her saying, huh, not sounding impressed, then an awkward pause, then him saying, so, you work on the ship, and her saying, no I just enjoy wearing this stupid cocktail waitress outfit with the mesh stockings and the uncomfortable shoes, and then him trying to think of a clever comeback but not coming up with anything, just standing there grinning like a moron, and then her saying, I gotta go. He'd hoped to talk to her again, but so far he hadn't seen an opening, because she worked the second deck, and the band played on the third, and when they took a break and he went downstairs, she was always busy, carrying drinks through the smoke and the noise, and besides, he couldn't think of anything non-stupid to say, and besides, a woman who looked like that probably would never be interested in a guy like him, even if he wasn't the world's biggest fucking loser.

Muddy Waters was singing,

Wanna love you so bad till I don't know what to do.

"So what's the deal with her?" said Johnny, handing the joint back to Wally. "She married?"

"I don't know," said Wally. He sure didn't want her to be married.

"She's hot, is what she is," said Jock. Wally didn't like the sound of that, because Jock, even though he had the IQ of a hammer, knew how to make a move on a woman, never seemed to get shot down. If Jock was the competition, you were going to lose, that was Wally's experience.

"What about the roulette woman?" Wally asked Jock. "Tina. I thought you were seeing her." Tina was a croupier, former stripper, blonde, six feet tall, near-cartoon-quality body. She made *serious* tip money. Guys tipped her who weren't even playing roulette. Jock had locked on to her like a Sidewinder missile.

"Oh yes," said Jock. "I've been seeing Tina."

A moment of reverent silence, while all four men thought male thoughts about seeing Tina.

"Are they real?" asked Johnny. "Those things can't be real."

Jock pondered that.

"They're not one hundred percent real," he said, "but they're nice."

"I don't get it, with fake tits." said Ted. "It's the same as squeezing a bag of plastic, right? What's the thrill?"

"Tell you what," said Johnny. "You squeeze a bag of plastic, I'll squeeze Tina's tits, we'll see who gets more thrilled."

"So you're still interested in Tina?" said Wally, handing the joint to Ted.

"Why?" said Jock, turning sideways to look back at Wally. "Are *you* interested in Tina?"

"No, no," said Wally, who was interested in Fay, and thus wanted Jock to remain interested in Tina. "I'm just wondering."

"Tell you the truth," said Jock, taking the joint from Ted, "she's a little weird. She's one of those whaddycallits, they don't eat hardly anything."

"Vegetarian?" said Ted.

"No, worse than that. Like, she won't even eat eggs."

"Eggs aren't vegetables," said Johnny.

"I didn't say they were," said Jock, handing the joint to Johnny.

"What about fish?" said Ted.

"Fish aren't vegetables, either," said Johnny.

"What about fish eggs?" said Ted.

"Shit, *I* wouldn't eat fish eggs," said Jock.

"Sure you would," said Johnny, passing the joint back to Wally. "You eat tapioca, right? That's fish eggs."

"It is?" said Jock.

"Like shit it is," said Ted.

"Well, then, what is it?" said Johnny.

"I don't know," said Ted, accepting the joint from Wally. "But it's not fish eggs."

"How can you say that, if you don't know?" said Johnny.

"Because if it was fish eggs, there would be a fish called the tapioca fish," said Ted, passing the joint to Jock. "You ever see that on a menu? Tapioca fish?"

"I've seen tapioca pudding on a menu," said Johnny.

"But that's pudding," said Ted.

"So?" said Johnny. "It could be made from a fish. Like, tuna fish salad, that's made from tuna fish."

"But there's no such thing as tapioca salad," said Ted.

The car was quiet for a moment, as Johnny tried to think of a good counterattack. Muddy Waters still had the blues.

> *Nothin' I can do to please her*
> *To make this young woman feel satisfied.*

"So Jock," said Wally, "you're saying you're not interested in Tina anymore?"

"What I'm saying," said Jock, "is she farts."

"Everybody farts," said Ted.

"But she farts a *lot*," said Jock. "I think it's from the food she eats. She eats this weird food. Looks like snot."

"Loud farts?" said Johnny.

"Nope," said Jock. "That's the bad part. You don't hear 'em. No warning. Things'll be going great, I'm getting down to it, and then, *whoa,* it smells like a sewer blew up. This one's gone." He popped the roach into his mouth.

"How come you always get the roach?" said Johnny.

"How come he always gets the women?" said Ted.

"When you say you were getting down to it," said Wally, "do you mean you were, like . . ."

"I mean I was right down there," said Jock. "I thought my eyeballs were gonna melt."

The car was silent again as Wally, Ted, and Johnny absorbed this new information about Tina.

"So does that mean you're not interested in her?" said Wally.

"I don't know," said Jock. "I mean, she *looks* good, but I don't want to wear a gas mask to bed, you know?"

"Shit," said Johnny, "I'd wear a gas mask if Tina was in the bed."

"I might take a shot at that waitress with the legs," said Jock. "What's her name? Jane?"

"Fay," said Wally, softly.

"Fay," said Jock, nodding.

"Here we are," said Johnny, pulling the Voyager into the parking lot of the Chum Bucket bar and restaurant. Beyond the building, the *Extravaganza of the Seas* loomed at the dock, lights blazing through the swirling night rain. The four guys sat for a few seconds, nobody wanting to leave the warm, dry car.

Muddy Waters sang:

> *Well don't the heart look lonesome*
> *When your baby find someone else.*

"What I wanna know," said Johnny, "is who the fuck is gonna want to go out and gamble in this?"

"People like us," said Wally. "Desperate losers."

Five

EVENING AT THE OLD FARTS SENILE DYING CEN-
ter. In the common area, the after-dinner entertainment was
Mrs. Bendocker, the killer show-tune woman, who was
shrieking her way through a medley of songs from *South
Pacific*. Her audience consisted mainly of the hearing im-
paired; she did a rendition of "Bali Hai" that could shatter
crystal. Most of the residents, fleeing the din, had shuffled
off to their rooms.

Arnie and Phil had been personally escorted back to the
residential area by Dexter Harpwell, who ordered the security guard to make sure they stayed in their rooms. Phil was
in room 326, at about the midpoint of a long corridor.
Arnie was in room 317, on the other side and closer to the
guard, who sat at a desk at the end of the corridor.

A few minutes after Harpwell left, Arnie stuck his head
out the door. The guard was studying *Juggs* magazine and
working his way through a box of assorted Krispy Kreme
doughnuts, saving his favorite, the blueberry-filled, for

last. He reluctantly tore his eyes from a photo spread entitled "Dairy Queen" and gave Arnie a look. Arnie waved
and retreated into his room. He picked up the phone and
called Phil's room. Phil, who'd been sitting on his bed,
waiting, grabbed the receiver, dropped it on the floor,
picked it up.

"Hello?" he said.

"You ready?" said Arnie.

"I dunno about this, Arnie."

"This'll work. Trust me."

"Why should I trust you?"

"I'm older than you. How many people can say that?"

"True."

"You got your directory?"

"Yup. Right here."

"OK," said Arnie. "I'll take rooms 300 to 325. You take
327 to 350. Remember: There's doughnuts and a free gift.
Make sure you say that. Free gift."

"A free gift," said Phil.

"OK," said Arnie. "Let's do it." He disconnected Phil,
squinted at the directory in his lap, dialed a number, waited
for an answer, and spoke.

"Hello, Mr. Kurtz? This is . . . Hello? Hello? HELLO,
IS THIS MR. KURTZ? THIS IS DEXTER HARPWELL.
DEXTER HARPWELL. MR. KURTZ, WE'RE HAVING
A LITTLE GET-TOGETHER RIGHT NOW AT THE SE-
CURITY DESK, AND WE'RE GIVING EVERYBODY
DOUGHNUTS AND A FREE GIFT. YES, FREE. WITH
DOUGHNUTS. YES. FREE. OK? HURRY, BECAUSE
THERE WON'T BE ANY FREE GIFTS LEFT."

Arnie hung up, dialed another number.

"Hello Mrs. Paris? This is Dexter Harpwell . . . No,
Dexter Harpwell . . . No, Dexter . . . Never mind. I'm calling because we're giving out doughnuts and a free gift at
the . . . that's right, free. Free. But you need to go to the se-

curity desk right now, because it's first come, first served. Yes, free."

Over in room 326, Phil was also getting out the word.

". . . right, a gift. Free. Yes. A free gift, but hurry, because we're running out. And doughnuts. Correct. Tell your friends. Free. Right."

About two minutes later, the security guard, whose name was Albert Fenton, heard a door on the corridor open. A man, wearing a bathrobe and walking with a cane, emerged from a room on the right. Almost immediately, another door opened, and a woman with a walker emerged on the left. They both started moving slowly, but determinedly, his way. A few seconds later, another door opened, then another, then another. Now five people, three of them in bathrobes, were coming at Fenton.

The man with the cane reached him first.

"Where is it?" he said.

"Where's what?" said Fenton.

"What?" said the man.

"WHERE'S WHAT?" said Albert.

"The free gift," said the man. "The doughnuts."

"What are you talking about?" said Fenton.

"What?" said the man.

Behind him, more doors were opening, more bathrobed people coming. And more.

"I SAID WHAT ARE YOU TALKING ABOUT," said Fenton.

"The free gifts," said the man. "The doughnuts."

"I DON'T KNOW WHAT YOU'RE TALKING ABOUT," said Fenton.

"Here's the doughnuts right here," said the man, reaching for one of the Krispy Kremes.

"That's MINE!" said Fenton, snatching up the doughnut with one hand and using the other to swat at the man's hand with *Juggs*.

The man, who was first come and was damn sure not about to be cheated out of being first served, whacked Fenton's arm with the cane.

"OW!" said Fenton, dropping the doughnut, which rolled to the edge of the desk, where it was snatched, with surprising quickness, by the woman with the walker, who had just arrived at the scene of the action. The cane man, protecting what was his, swung the cane at her, but missed. She lifted her walker and brought one of the tips down on his right foot. He yelped, dropped the cane, and grabbed the woman's doughnut hand in both of his, the two of them straining against each other, locked in combat. Fenton started to come around the desk to separate them, then saw two new arrivals grabbing his doughnuts. He turned back and reached for the box, but as he did, he stepped on the cane, which slid sideways, causing him to lose his footing and fall, banging his skull hard on the desk on the way down. He lay dazed for a moment. Somebody stepped on his right hand; something sharp poked his leg. He tried to get up but was too dizzy; he rolled and went fetal, his head throbbing. Through squinted eyes, he saw a forest of ghastly pale skinny legs, with more shuffling his way, and still more. For a fleeting moment, Fenton remembered a movie he'd seen once, called *Night of the Living Dead.* Above him he heard grunting, the sounds of struggle. A stapler bounced on the floor in front of him; they were rummaging through the security desk. A page torn from *Juggs*—"Mammary Lane"—drifted down. He snatched at it, then felt something land on his face, something cold and sticky. He took some in his fingers and licked it: blueberry. *Those bastards.* He reached to his belt, unclipped the walkie-talkie, pulled it to his mouth, pushed the TALK button, and shouted a word that had never been heard before over the Beaux Arts radio system: "Mayday."

Arnie and Phil eased past the mob and walked down the

main corridor toward the common area. A guard came trotting their way, heading for the noise behind them.

"What's going on down there?" he said.

"You got me," said Arnie.

They stopped at the end of the corridor and peered into the common area. Mrs. Bendocker was at the grand piano, still shrieking *South Pacific* to a small audience, most of which was asleep. Straight ahead, through the glass lobby doors, they could see the Beaux Arts van in the driveway. Nestor would be at the wheel, ready to take them to the ship.

"Uh-oh," said Arnie.

"What?" said Phil.

"The little prick," said Arnie, pointing to the right. At the far end of the room, his back to them, was Dexter Harpwell, talking to an underling.

"We gotta move," said Arnie. "Before he turns around."

They started across the common room, going as fast as they could, which was slow. When they'd almost reached the grand piano, halfway to the door, Arnie glanced right. Harpwell appeared to be finishing his conversation.

"Move it," Arnie hissed.

"This is as fast as . . . Oh *no,*" said Phil. He had walked into Mrs. Krugerman, the woman who had the hots for him. She'd been lurking behind the piano and had lunged her walker into Phil's path.

Some enchanted evening, shrieked Mrs. Bendocker, *you may see a stranger . . .*

"Hey, stranger," said Mrs. Krugerman, grabbing Phil's wrist. "Where've *you* been hiding?"

"I have to go," said Phil. He tried to pull his hand loose, but Mrs. Krugerman, who took Tae-Bo for Seniors, was stronger than he was.

"Let me go," said Phil, trying to yank his arm loose.

"You just *got* here!" said Mrs. Krugerman, strengthening her grip. The woman was a python.

"Come *on*," said Arnie. Harpwell was finished with his conversation; he was now looking at some papers in his hand, starting to turn their way.

"She's got me!" said Phil. "You go on without me!"

Arnie looked over at Harpwell. He was still looking down at his papers, but was walking slowly in their direction. Any second now, he'd look up and see them, and that would be it. Arnie glanced back through the lobby doors, at the waiting van. He took a step that way, then looked back into Phil's eyes, his buddy's eyes, the eyes of his only friend left in the world, and he knew what he had to do.

. . . and somehow you'll know . . .

Arnie went to Mrs. Krugerman, stepped up close to her side, his body pressing against her walker, put his arms around her, and said: "I'm the one you want, darling." And he turned her face to his and kissed her on the lips, a real kiss, mouth open, some tongue, the first such kiss he had given a woman who was not his wife since 1946. Mrs. Krugerman, who had never been kissed this way by *any* man, including her late husband of 46 years, went limp, and in her limpness released Phil's wrist. Arnie pulled his lips from Mrs. Krugerman's, put his arms on her shoulders, looked her in the eyes, and said, "I must go now, my darling. Wait for me." He released her and stepped back, and only her walker kept her from collapsing in a rapturous swoon.

Arnie looked over at Harpwell, still looking down at his papers, but only yards away now.

. . . once you have found her, never let her go . . .

"Go go *go*," Arnie hissed, shoving Phil toward the lobby doors, which sighed open automatically to let them through. As they sighed closed again, Harpwell looked up from his papers. His eyes registered the two departing shapes, and there was something about them that tickled something somewhere in his brain, something that he almost started to retrieve. But before he could get to it, all thoughts were blown from his brain as Mrs. Bendocker took her shrieking to a new level, aiming gamely for, but missing, those big final notes . . .

. . . ne . . . ver . . . let . . . her . . . GOOOOOOOOO.

Outside, in the driver's seat of the van, Nestor said, "What the hell is *that?*"

"Mrs. Bendocker," said Arnie, climbing into the back.

"Sounds like some kind of human sacrifice," said Nestor.

"I don't think she's human," said Arnie.

Phil got in next to Arnie.

"Jesus, that was close," he said. "Listen, Arnie, what you did back there, that was, Jesus, I mean, thank you."

"Forget it," said Arnie.

"What'd he do?" said Nestor.

"I said, *forget* it," said Arnie. He still had the taste of Mrs. Krugerman in his mouth. It was not an unpleasant taste. It was the taste of Fixodent. Arnie would not admit this to Phil—he could barely admit it to himself—but he kind of liked it, tasting Mrs. Krugerman. Maybe he would look her up some time, see if she played pinochle.

"OK, then," said Nestor, putting the van in gear, easing out of the covered driveway. "I still think you boys are crazy, going out on a boat in this weather."

"Yeah," said Phil, watching huge drops splatter on the windshield. "It's gonna be ugly out there."

"Hey," said Arnie, "after what we've been through already, how bad can it be?"

* * *

"THIS IS GONNA BE BAD," SAID EDDIE SMITH, on the bridge of the *Extravaganza of the Seas,* looking out at the bay.

Eddie Smith was captain of the *Extravaganza.* He was a good seaman, a natural boathandler, always had been. He once had a very promising nautical career. He hadn't expected it to lead to this, driving this butt-ugly neon-smeared tub around in circles, going nowhere.

In the '80s, he'd been a hotshot mate in the cruise industry, rising fast through the ranks on the big ships that sailed from the Port of Miami, loaded to the gunwales with chunky Midwesterners wearing active leisurewear and blindingly white sneakers, ready to spend a fun-filled week at sea, getting chunkier.

In those days, Eddie had cut a fine figure. He looked good in his white officer's uniform, reminding people of Kevin Costner. He was tall and lean, hair going just a little gray, indicating seriousness, offset by an easy smile, indicating a desire to get laid.

Which he did, a lot. Single women went to great lengths to be in Eddie's vicinity. So did married women. That was Eddie's problem: the married women. The truth was, he liked it *better* when they were married. He liked the excitement, making plans to meet them on deck, looking around to make sure nobody saw, climbing into the lifeboat where he kept a blanket stashed. Or sometimes, when their husbands were in the casino, Eddie would even go to their cabins—into their damn *cabins*—and the sex was even better, because of the danger of getting caught.

So for a while there, Eddie was one happy ship's officer. But like most men whose brains are in their dicks, he was not really thinking things through.

Imagine you're a guy who drives a snack-food van.

You're out there every freaking day, rain or shine, hot or cold, fighting traffic, busting your hump to refill vending machines with Doritos, Snickers, all that crap that office workers eat. You're constantly being hassled by cubicle dwellers who claim the machine ate their dollar, acting like you're supposed to reach into your pocket and just hand them a dollar, these people who make more than you do for sitting on their Snickers-padded asses all day. You don't like this job, but you've been doing it for twelve years, and you're probably going to keep doing it for twenty-five more because you have a wife and two kids and no college degree and this is what you do.

Now imagine that your wife talks you into taking a cruise, which you really can't afford, but, hey, you haven't had a real vacation, just the two of you, since you went on your honeymoon, which was in Atlantic City, and it rained both days. So you figure, OK, what's another two grand on the Visa, you're never gonna pay the goddamn thing off anyway.

And so you go on the cruise, the two of you, and it really is nice—Jesus, the *food* they give you—and you're having a good time, even winning a little at the slots. And then on the third night, this officer sits at your table, tall guy, big smiler, white teeth, you can tell he thinks he looks like hot shit in his uniform. The women, your wife included—your wife *especially*—are looking at him like he's a movie star. You even hear your wife tell somebody else's wife this guy looks exactly like Kevin Costner, whom your wife loves. The guy is talking about what it takes to handle a big ship like this, how *complicated* it is, and your wife is eating this up, and you're thinking you'd like to see this pretty boy handle a truck in the traffic you deal with every day, without 97 crewmen to help, but you don't say anything, you just order another beer.

After dinner, you want to hit the casino again, maybe

try blackjack tonight, and your wife says she's tired, she's just going to take a walk on the upper deck and maybe turn in early, and you say suit yourself, because to be honest you're a little pissed off at her anyway. When you get back to the cabin, she's acting like she's asleep, but you can tell she's really not. You get in bed, and after a while you hear her crying. You ask her what's wrong and she says nothing. You say, OK, then why are you crying? She gets out of bed and goes into the bathroom and closes the door and stays in there doing God knows what, and you fall asleep.

For the rest of the cruise, she acts weird, like she's off in space. A couple more times, you hear her crying in bed, but she still won't tell you why. You figure she probably got her period.

But when you get home, even after a week, she's still acting weird. And then one night, after the kids are asleep, you come into the bedroom and she's sitting on the floor, back against the wall, sobbing like a baby, and when you ask her why, all she says is I'm sorry, over and over, I'm sorry I'm sorry I'm sorry I'm sorry I'm sorry, and you sit down next to her and put your arm around her and hug her, and that makes her sob even harder, and finally she turns to you, and she tells you about that night on the ship, how he took advantage of her, he gave her something to drink, she didn't know what was happening, it was all hazy in her mind, she was too scared to say anything afterward. Somewhere in your mind is the suspicion that this might not be exactly what happened, but you believe her, because you need to believe her.

That's how Eddie Smith's cruise-ship career ended. Cruise lines depend heavily on repeat business, and have a near-pathological obsession with customer satisfaction. The last thing you want, if you're a cruise executive, is to pick up the phone and hear a customer screaming that he's calling the police, calling a lawyer, calling the TV stations, that he didn't pay your company two thousand fucking dollars to have one of your employees jump his wife.

Eddie's ship was at sea when this call came. The cruise line sent a helicopter to pick him up. That's how badly they wanted to get him off the ship, bring him back to Miami, and fire him.

In the end, the D.A. didn't press charges, because it was pretty obvious to everybody but the husband what had really happened. But the cruise line had to pay $50,000 to make the couple shut up, and there was no way it was going to hire Eddie back. None of the major lines would even talk to him. He was cancer. He had traded his career for a sexual experience that had lasted maybe eight minutes. And it hadn't even been particularly *good* sex.

Eddie quickly ran out of money and started working as a mate on day-charter fishing boats out of Bayside, playing caddie to guys who, on their own, couldn't catch a fish if it jumped into their shorts. He baited their hooks, rigged their lines, told them when they had a fish on, told them how to play it, half the time pretty much hauled the damn thing in himself. On the way home, he opened their beers, lit their cigars, listened to their bullshit, pretended to laugh at their moron jokes, hustling for tips.

He was drinking a lot now, getting those veins on his nose. He lost some hair, didn't take care of his teeth, no longer reminded people of Kevin Costner. He discovered cocaine, which was not difficult in Miami in the '80s, when it was everywhere, it was falling out of the damn sky. He used it a little at first, and then more, and then more, and pretty soon he didn't have enough money to support his habit. This is when the guy who supplied it asked him if he was interested in getting into the supply side of the business.

And so Eddie embarked on a new kind of nautical career, living in the Bahamas, piloting a 38-foot go-fast boat, twin turbocharged 500-horsepower engines, screaming across the Gulf Stream in the dead of night at sixty, seventy, sometimes eighty miles an hour, lights out, rafting up with a transfer boat off the U.S. coast, offloading the cargo, then getting the hell out of there.

The money was very, very good, enough to retire on soon if Eddie had saved it instead of putting it up his nose and leaving thousand-dollar tips for barmaids, just to get their attention. He'd go to Freeport, to one of the big casinos, with $15,000 cash in his pocket and wake up three days later with nothing, not even a memory of where it all went, and he didn't care because there was always more coming. He figured there would be time to settle down, one of these months, but time ran out one night at Fowey Rocks, about ten miles out from Miami. Eddie had just rafted up and was about to transfer 1,400 pounds of cocaine and 600 pounds of pot when *oh shit* there's a Coast Guard helicopter screaming over the horizon, searchlight blazing, making it look like daylight out there at 3:30 A.M.

Eddie cast off instantly, left his crewman there on the transfer boat, yelling hey what the fuck, but Eddie was gone, gunning the engines, starting east but turning around when he saw two Coast Guard boats coming from that way—they'd set a trap for him—leaving him no choice but to run for the Florida coast.

He was faster than the Coast Guard boats, but not that goddamn chopper, that thing was on him the whole way, trying to blind him, but he kept running, his plan being to get to Miami, get ashore somehow, lose himself in the city.

He came screaming through the flats at Stiltsville faster than anybody sane would try, turning toward the big condos in Coconut Grove, blasting into the channel to the Dinner Key Marina, zigzagging out of the helicopter spotlight for a second, yanking back on the throttles to slow the boat enough so he could jump without killing himself, then shoving them forward again just as he dove, the water feeling like concrete when he hit it doing thirty miles an hour.

He surfaced, took a quick look around, saw a sailboat moored about twenty yards away, inhaled, and kicked back under water. He came up for breath, heard a crash, loud, dove back under, kept swimming, reaching the sailboat in a couple more breaths. He grabbed the mooring line and hung on, gasping, and looked over toward the marina, where he saw a ball of fire, just like in the movies, where his boat had smashed into the dock on the far right end. He started swimming toward the left and *oh shit* the chopper was on him again, the searchlight putting him in the middle of a brilliant white circle, following him as he paddled to shore, where he was greeted by what appeared to be everybody involved in local, state, and federal law enforcement.

That was the end of the '80s for Eddie. He spent most of the '90s in prison. He could have got out sooner, maybe; the feds promised him that he would do less time if he told them whom he was moving drugs for. They also promised that they could protect him. Eddie was considering this offer when he received a message, which was that if he cooperated with the feds, he would soon be exceedingly dead, and the feds could not protect him. Eddie took this message seriously, because the person who delivered it was a prison guard.

And so he did his time, and when he got out he went back to being a mate on a fishing charter, because charter captains don't care what your background is if you know your way around a boat. Eddie stayed clean and sober and found a small room in a run-down apartment building in Hialeah.

One night there was a knock on his door. It was a slight, dark-eyed woman holding a little boy; he'd seen them around the building. She offered, in a combination of

Spanish and English, to do his laundry for two dollars. He told her he hardly had any clothes to wash, except what he was wearing. She looked at his faded cutoffs and fish-gut-stained T-shirt, smiled, and said he was even worse off than she was, and she'd wash his clothes for free. He said if she'd do that, he'd buy her dinner, anything she wanted, as long as they sold it at Burger King. She laughed and said it was a deal.

Her name was Luz. She'd come up from Nicaragua and lived common-law for a couple of years with an El Salvadoran man, who left her when she got pregnant. She was supporting herself and her boy by washing clothes and, when she could, cleaning rich people's houses in Coral Gables, if they didn't mind a cleaning lady who brought a kid along.

The boy was three. His name was Alejandro. He was very small and sick a lot, but always smiling. For whatever three-year-old reason, he thought Eddie was the coolest thing ever. Eddie called him "Magnet," because of the way he stuck with Eddie whenever Eddie was around. Sometimes, when Luz had work and Eddie didn't, he'd watch the boy, take him on the bus out to the new mall by the turnpike, the two of them walking around, looking at the stores, the fountains, enjoying the air-conditioning. Eddie would swing Alejandro up on his shoulders—man, the kid weighed nothing—and carry him, holding him by his skinny legs, Alejandro thrilling to the view.

When they got back to Luz's room, they'd share a pizza and Alejandro would tell Luz about his day, babbling bilingually. Then he'd fall asleep, and Luz would put him in his little mattress on the floor. Then she and Eddie would make love, silently yet spectacularly.

Pretty soon, Alejandro was calling Eddie *papi*. Pretty soon, the three of them were living together in Eddie's little room. It was the happiest Eddie had ever been.

The happiness lasted three months. Then Alejandro started getting sicker. The doctors said that he had a problem with his heart, that he needed surgery. Neither Luz nor Eddie had insurance. They descended into the part of hell reserved for poor people who need medical care, a world of waiting and worrying and paperwork and more waiting and worrying. Luz spent her days fighting hospital bureaucracies, her nights stroking her boy's head, weeping. Eddie spent his nights in a fever of helpless self-loathing, thinking about the money he'd pissed away, what it could have done for this little boy.

Days, Eddie kept working the charters, struggling to keep his eyes open out on the water. One evening when the boat got back to Bayside, a man was waiting on the dock, a big guy in a golf shirt. He gave Eddie a big smile, stuck out a hand. Eddie did not take the man's hand. He'd spent enough time in prison to know immediately when a guy was dangerous, as opposed to just big.

The guy said, "Hey, Eddie."

Eddie said, "Do I know you?"

"My name is Lou Tarant."

Eddie definitely knew that name.

"I gotta go," he said.

"Whoa whoa *whoa*," said Tarant, holding up his hands, palms out. "I just want to talk, Eddie."

"We got nothing to talk about," said Eddie. "I did my time, I'm out, I'm clean. I never said anything. I don't plan to say anything. So leave me alone, OK?"

"Eddie," said Tarant, "I'm here to help."

"I don't need your help," said Eddie, turning away.

"Maybe you don't," said Tarant. "But Alejandro does."

Eddie stopped, turned back around.

"How do you know about him?"

"We know all about you, Eddie. We got an interest in you. We know you could use some help. When you're drowning, somebody throws you a life preserver, you don't swim away, you grab it. I'm your life preserver, Eddie."

Eddie thought about it, about Luz and Alejandro, about the bills piling up, about how much money he had in his shorts, forty-two dollars and change, which was also how much money he had in the world.

"OK," he said, finally. "I'm listening."

"We want you to run a boat," said Tarant.

"No way," said Eddie, starting to turn away again. Tarant gripped his arm.

"Not like that, Eddie," said Tarant. "This is a legit job, on a big boat."

"What boat?" said Eddie.

"Casino boat," said Tarant. "The *Extravaganza of the Seas*. You know it?"

"I know it," said Eddie. "You want me on the crew?"

"No," said Tarant. "We want you to be the captain."

"Real fucking funny," said Eddie.

"I mean it," said Tarant.

He had to say it five more times before Eddie's mind could even start to accept it. *Captain*. Jesus. When he finally believed it was for real, he said, why me, and Tarant said, because you did your time like a man, and we don't forget our friends. Tarant did not say, *Also we own you and want to keep you where we can see you*. But Eddie understood it.

Eddie said there was no way, with his record, he'd be allowed to work as a ship's captain; he'd never get the papers, never get his parole officer to approve. Tarant laughed out loud at that. Eddie said what's so funny, and Tarant said this is Miami, for Chrissakes. Look who they got running the damn *government*. You think anybody's gonna care who's running a boat?

And he was right. The rules got bent; the obstacles magically dissolved; the paperwork zipped right through, no

questions asked. Eddie did his training, took command of
the ship, was bringing home a nice paycheck. Alejandro
got his operation and was doing better, though he still
needed a lot of care, which thank God was mostly covered
by Eddie's insurance. Luz quit cleaning houses. They
moved into a nicer apartment, with actual bedrooms. They
talked about having another kid. Life was good for Eddie
Smith, family man, ship captain, solid citizen.

He tried not to think about the other side of it, which
was, when you got right down to it, that he was still running dope. And maybe more. He didn't know, because nobody told him what was going on back at the stern when
the *Extravaganza* rafted up with the cabin cruiser out in the
Gulf Stream. They just told him when and where.

But he knew that, whatever it was, it sure as hell wasn't
legal, and if they ever got caught, nobody would believe
that he didn't know what was going on, not with his record.
He'd be in just as deep as everybody else, maybe deeper,
because it was allegedly his ship. Which of course is exactly why they gave him this job: He had the most to lose if
anything went wrong.

So he took the money and steered the ship, and he tried
not to think about the rest of it. He never talked to Luz
about it. She thought it was just a miracle that had happened in this great and wonderful country, America,
where, just like that, you could go from being a guy with
no money and no prospects to being captain of a great big
ship. He didn't tell her why, on certain days, he became
edgy.

He was very edgy this day. When he'd called Tarant that
morning about the weather, he was sure that the rendezvous would be called off, and was appalled when
Tarant told him it was on. He knew that if he were a real
ship's captain, if he had any balls at all, he'd have told

Tarant forget it, absolutely no way was he going out in this weather with civilians on board.

But of course he wasn't a real ship's captain, and he didn't have the balls to defy Tarant, because he knew what Tarant could do to him, and because he couldn't go home and tell Luz that their happy new miracle life was over, that they were poor again. Luz was now six months pregnant. If it was a boy, they were going to name him Eddie Jr.

So he was going out, out in this mess. And as he'd feared, there would be customers on the ship. He could see them now, scurrying through the rain, buying their tickets at the booth on the dock, scurrying to the gangway. Coming out on a night like this just to lose money. Morons.

"This is gonna be bad," he repeated.

"I heard you the first time," said Hank Wilde. In theory, Wilde was the *Extravaganza*'s first officer. In fact, he was Lou Tarant's main guy on the ship, which meant he was the real authority. He knew almost nothing about ships and deferred to Eddie on purely nautical matters. But, bottom line, Eddie answered to him.

"I'm sorry, but I don't like this," said Eddie.

"You made that point," said Wilde. "Time to move on."

"I'm asking you one last time, just call them, tell them it'll be a lot safer to do this another night," said Eddie. "A little delay is all I'm talking about."

"And I'm telling you, one last time, they told us to do it tonight, and we do what they tell us," said Wilde.

"Yeah, but they're not going out in this," said Eddie. "We are."

"That's right," said Wilde. "We are. So shut up and do your job. OK, *Captain?* Me, I'm gonna go get a drink. You want one?"

Eddie didn't answer.

"Oh yeah, I forgot," said Wilde. "You gotta drive."

Laughing, he left the bridge, leaving Eddie to stare out at the storm.

JUAN HAD NEVER IN HIS LIFE FELT THIS NAU-seous, this stomach-churningly, cold-sweatingly, room-spinningly sick. The goddamn boat would *not* stop moving—rolling, then rising, then making a gut-heaving plunge, then rolling, rising and plunging again, over and over and over. It felt like this had been going on for hours, but when Juan checked his watch, he saw it had been only forty minutes.

The cabin was hot and stank of b.o. and beer. Juan was standing with his back braced against the galley counter, his legs aching from the strain of fighting the boat's inces-sant motion. He wanted desperately to go out on deck, get some air, stick his head over the side. Or, better yet, die. But he had to stay there, had to keep watching the three men at the table. They were watching him back, giving him hard-ass looks, but he could tell they weren't doing so great either, especially the fat guy in the middle. He looked like he was about to puke.

Up on the bridge, Frank wasn't feeling much better, watching the heaving sea, the waves sometimes breaking over the bow. Tark, braced against the captain's chair, looked his way every now and then, giving him a big smile, clearly enjoying his discomfort. Frank suspected that Tark was deliberately steering the boat in such a way as to make the motion even worse, but there was no way he could tell. Frank had decided that he didn't care who this scumbag knew in the organization, this was definitely the last time Frank was going to make this run on this boat.

As he'd been doing every ten minutes since they left the marina, Frank went down the ladder to the cabin to check on Juan, stopping at the bottom, where he could still see Tark on the bridge.

"You OK?" he asked Juan. Juan nodded that he was, but Frank could tell he wasn't.

"Hang in there," he said, heading back up.

"How's bean boy doin'?" asked Tark. "He puke yet?"

"He's fine," said Frank.

"I bet he is," said Tark, smiling big. "Maybe I should go down there and make him a nice big plate of corn beef hash. You think he'd like that? How about you? You want a nice big old plate of greasy hash? That sound good?" He yanked the wheel half a turn, and the boat lurched sickeningly.

Frank grabbed a railing, hung on, fought down the nausea. When he recovered, he said, "You know, I almost hope you do have something planned for tonight, because it would be a real pleasure to blow out your tiny brain."

"Hey, I'm just messin' with you," said Tark. "You know I'm a company man all the way. 'Sides which, you ain't gonna shoot me, not out here, not tonight." Now Tark's smile was gone. "You and bean boy'd never get back alive."

The bitch of it was, Frank knew he was right.

Six

FAY STOOD BY THE BAR WITH MARA PURVIS, ONE
of the other cocktail waitresses and the closest thing she
had to a friend on the ship. They were watching the passengers, a steady stream of them, wet from the rain, coming into the big casino room on the first deck.

"Am I imagining this," Fay said, "or are there actually
more of them than usual tonight?"

"Definitely," said Mara. "We're the only boat stupid
enough to go out, so they're all coming here. You know
Bobbi? In the ticket office? She told me she was getting
calls all day, 'Are you going out? Are you going out?'
These people are crazy to gamble."

"I was hoping for an easy night," said Fay. "Estelle
woke up this morning at six."

"You want easy nights," said Mara, "you picked the
wrong career."

"I'm not planning to do this forever," said Fay.

"That's what I said, fourteen years ago," said Mara. "I

thought I was gonna be an accountant, you believe that? Debits and credits. Whatever debits are. I even enrolled for night courses at Miami-Dade. And then I met a basketball player at a bar, and went to Cancun the day I was supposed to start classes. And now here I still am, two husbands later, bringing drinks to guys who think if they tip me a buck it means they can grab my ass."

Mara was in her mid-thirties, dark hair, dark eyes, her face getting a little hard around the edges, but still pretty, friendly smile, good eye contact, the kind of look that always made men, especially men who were drinking, think she was more interested than she actually was. She would never admit it, but she was proud that she still averaged two marriage proposals per month from semi–complete strangers, and she would be depressed when the number declined.

"Hey," she said, "did I tell you what this guy said to me last night?"

"No," said Fay.

"Get this," said Mara. "This guy, he's playing black-jack, and he asks me for a gin and tonic, and I bring it to him, and we're talking a little, back and forth, and he seems like a nice guy, cute, possibly even human, and then, after maybe three sentences, he says, 'Don't take this wrong, but you got a great pair of tits.' Can you believe that?"

Fay shook her head.

"Don't take it *wrong*?" said Mara. "This guy I just *met* is talking about my boobs like I'm his 4-H Club cow, and he doesn't want me to take it *wrong*? Jesus. If they ever invent a vibrator that also takes out the garbage, I'm quitting men altogether. Here come the *abuelas*."

A clot of a half dozen elderly Cuban women waddled through the doorway, all talking loudly in Spanish. They would spend the evening shoving quarters into slot machines, yanking the handles, and complaining to each other that they were getting nothing back, nothing.

"Ni agua," they would say, over and over. *"Ni agua."* This meant *Not even water.*

The *abuelas,* remaining in clot formation and all continuing to talk simultaneously, waddled over to their usual corner of the room, claiming the spaces in front of their favorite slot machines, so they'd be ready to start losing money as soon as the ship reached the three-mile limit.

"Great tippers, those ladies," said Mara.

"Really?" said Fay.

"Oh yes," said Mara. "Sometimes they'll give you an entire quarter like it was *nothing.* I think they buy their *cars* with quarters. Here comes the Grateful Dead."

Johnny and the Contusions appeared in the doorway, trying to look alert. Jock, who had extremely sensitive Woman Radar, spotted Mara and Fay instantly and swerved their way, trailed by Johnny and Ted, Wally bringing up the rear, carrying his guitar case.

"Ladies," said Jock. "How're you ladies doing tonight?" Jock's approach to women was: move in close, keep talking, allow the women to be overcome by his studliness. This didn't always work, but it worked often enough that Jock had no reason to try another approach.

"We ladies are doing great," said Mara. "We're gonna spend four hours schlepping drinks in a hurricane. What could be better than that?"

"Huh?" said Jock, who, even when not stoned, often failed to recognize sarcasm. He went to his smoothest move: "You ladies are looking fine tonight."

"And you gentlemen are smelling like a giant reefer," said Mara.

Ted and Johnny giggled. Wally reddened. Jock bored straight ahead.

"How about," he said, "when we get back tonight, you

ladies go with us over to the Road? We can party over there. You ladies be up for that?"

"Will Tina be joining us?" said Mara.

"Tina?" said Jock.

"Tina, the playmate of the month, who you're dating," said Mara.

"Oh, Tina," said Jock, thinking as fast as he could, which was not fast. "No, she's not . . . we're not . . . I was just thinking you ladies would wanna party with us, over at the Road."

"Gosh," said Mara, "I'd love to, but I have a two A.M. dental appointment."

"Huh," said Jock. "How about you, Jane?"

"Fay," said Fay.

"How about you, Fay?" said Jock. "You wanna party with the band?"

"Are you kidding?" said Fay.

"Kidding about what?" said Jock.

"Seriously," said Mara, "would you say she has a great pair of tits?"

Fay snorted into her hand.

"What?" said Jock.

"Never mind," said Mara.

Jock frowned, his overloaded brain seizing up, then rebooting. He said: "You ladies are looking fine tonight."

Mara rolled her eyes. Fay snorted again. Johnny and Ted, laughing, grabbed Jock by the arm and pulled him toward the stairs. Wally stepped forward.

"Don't mind him," he said. "He's just . . . he's . . ."

"We ladies know what he is," said Mara.

"Yeah, well," said Wally. "Anyway." He aimed his eyes at the floor, then at Fay. Big breath. "Hi," he said.

"Hi," said Fay.

This is where Wally very much wanted to say something that would get Fay's attention, something articulate yet winning, something smart yet modest, something that would clearly distinguish him from Jock, from men in general, so that Fay would see that he was intelligent and sensitive but also funny; and that he was very much attracted to her, but not just in a physical way, although he *was* attracted to her physically—very attracted—but not in a *cheap* physical way; and that even though there was no way he could ever compete with a guy like Jock in the looks department, he was somebody that she could talk to, and laugh with, and get to know on a deep and passionate yet meaningful and spiritually satisfying level. That's what Wally wanted to get across here.

What he said was: "So."

"So?" said Fay.

"We're going out," said Wally.

"We're going out?" said Fay.

"I mean the boat," said Wally. "The boat is going out."

"Yes," agreed Fay.

"Yup," said Wally. He stood there for ten agonizing seconds, desperately hoping his brain would come up with something, anything, that was not as lame as what he had just said. *The boat is going out. THE BOAT IS GOING OUT. You MORON.* But his brain was not there. His brain was a spooked groundhog that had scuttled deep into its burrow and wasn't coming out anytime soon.

"Yup," he said again. "Well, OK, then, good luck."

Good luck? GOOD FUCKING LUCK??

"Thanks," said Fay.

Wally, afraid of what idiot statement his mouth would emit next, turned to follow his bandmates, a defeated man.

Watching him go, Mara said, "He has it *bad* for you."

"Lucky me," said Fay.

"He's kinda cute, in a cuddly way," said Mara. "He's not a bad guitar player."

"Just what I need in my life," said Fay. "A cuddly guitar player."

"The drummer, now *he's* cute," said Mara.

"The stupid one? The one dating Tina, who thinks he's God's gift? 'You ladies are looking fine'? Are you *serious*?"

"He's actually a good drummer," said Mara. "And he's nice to look at. Put duct tape over his mouth and you got something."

"Him, you can definitely have," said Fay.

"I just might, one of these nights," said Mara. "And speaking of studs, here comes my boyfriend." She waved at Arnie and Phil, coming into the room. Arnie saw her and headed over, Phil trailing.

"Hey there, gorgeous," Arnie said. "You ready to run off with me for endless nights of wild, passionate sex?"

"I dunno, Arnie," said Mara. "You make all these promises, but you always go home with Phil." Behind Arnie, Phil snorted.

"I know, I know," said Arnie. "He's like my senile old uncle, who I gotta take care of. So howzabout this: You run off with me for nights of wild, passionate sex, and we'll fix up Phil here with your friend, this lovely lady here, I don't believe we been introduced."

"Fay," said Fay.

"A pleasure, Fay," said Arnie. "I'd make an indecent proposal to you if I didn't have this thing going with Mara here."

"I appreciate the thought," said Fay.

"You're new on the ship," said Arnie.

"A few weeks," said Fay. "I work upstairs."

"I don't get up there much," said Arnie.

"His age," said Phil, "he *can't* get up."

"Don't listen to my senile uncle," said Arnie. "It's a

whole new world, with this Viagra. So howzabout it, ladies? Whaddya think?"

Mara said: "Arnie, I think what I always think, which is I wish you were forty years younger."

"Me, too," said Arnie.

"Especially when he tries to pee," said Phil.

"What is *that*?" said Fay. The other three turned to follow her eyes, which were looking at the doorway, through which was coming, in all his pinkness, Conrad Conch. He was walking unsteadily, arms out, feeling his way along, not seeing all that well through his mouth hole. Next to him, looking concerned, was one of the *Extravaganza*'s dockside security guys.

"That's the conch from the Happy Conch, whatshisname, Conrad," said Mara. "Who says we don't get glamorous celebrities on this ship?"

"He's a regular?" said Fay.

"He was here once before," said Mara. "He got into a fight."

"Who would fight a giant pink shell?" said Arnie.

"Who would *wear* a giant pink shell?" said Phil.

"Who'd he fight with?" said Fay.

"Several people," said Mara. "Manny, for one."

"Manny fought a *shell*?" said Fay.

"Looks like he wants to again," said Mara.

Manny Arquero, the pit boss, was striding across the casino floor, looking angry. He stopped in front of Conrad and put his face up to the mouth hole.

"What the hell are you doing here?" he said.

"Mmmmwmf," said Conrad.

"What?" said Arquero.

"Mmmmwmf," repeated Conrad, adding, "Mmmmwmf."

"What's he doing on the ship?" said Arquero, to the security guy.

"Mr. Kemp sent him over," said the security guy.

"What do you mean?" said Arquero.

"I mean, Mr. Kemp called the ticket office, and he said the conch is going out on the boat tonight," said the security guy. "Some kind of promotion thing. He came in a limo."

"Kemp did?" said Arquero.

"No, the conch."

Arquero thought about that.

"OK," he said, speaking into Conrad's mouth hole. "But there better not be no trouble, you hear me?"

"Mmmmwmf," said Conrad.

"And you two," Arquero said, turning to Fay and Mara. "You're supposed to be waiting on customers."

"Yes, sir," said Mara.

"We're customers," said Arnie.

"I don't see no drink in your hand, Pop," said Arquero.

"I ain't your pop," said Arnie.

"Easy, Arnie," said Mara, putting her hand on Arnie's arm. "Mr. Arquero here's right, OK? We gotta get to work."

"That's right," said Arquero, turning, striding away.

"Asshole," said Arnie.

"True, but he's the boss asshole," said Mara.

"Why do you got to get into it with *everybody*?" said Phil.

"Not everybody," said Arnie. "Just the assholes."

"Right," said Phil, "but to you, practically *everybody* is an asshole."

"True," said Arnie.

"Nice to meet you gentlemen," said Fay. "I gotta go upstairs."

"Our pleasure," said Arnie. "I'm only sorry Mara here claimed my heart first."

"We came this close, Arnie," said Fay, holding her fingers an inch apart. "I'll always treasure what we had." She turned and went upstairs.

"Classy lady," said Arnie.

"I know," said Mara. "I can't figure out what she's doing here."

"Hey," said Arnie, "you got class, and you're here."

"Thanks, Arnie, I appreciate the thought, but I know what I am, which is a high-school dropout. This is all I ever did, hustle drinks. But Fay is . . . I dunno. She doesn't belong here."

Fay was thinking pretty much the same thing when she got to the second deck and surveyed the crowd waiting to gamble. Most of the males were gathered around Tina, the tall and abundant roulette croupier. She was putting on a demonstration of how roulette was played. Almost all the males watching her knew exactly how roulette was played—it is not a complex game—but they were watching Tina intensely, the way a dog watches a hamburger being carried across a patio, in case maybe, somehow, you never know, the dog is going to get some.

Fay's job was to go up to these people and ask them if they wanted anything from the bar. It was her experience that, on average, two out of every three of them would respond to this simple question by making basically the same joke, which was: *Yeah* (looking down at some specific part of Fay's body), *I want something all right, heh heh.* And that was the subtle version. Sometimes they'd point at what they wanted; sometimes they'd try to touch it.

The first time this happened, Fay was unprepared. She asked a guy—middle-aged, clean-cut, not obviously drunk—if he wanted anything, and with no hesitation he put his right hand on her left breast and said, "This'd be nice." She whacked his hand with her drink tray. He grabbed his hand and yelled what do you think you're doing you bitch. Manny Arquero, always on patrol, was there instantly asking what happened, and Fay said this guy grabbed me, and the guy said I was just kidding around and this psycho bitch tries to take my hand off, and Arquero said to the guy, look, she's new, no harm done, next drink's on the house, and the guy said yeah well that's fine but you oughtta fire that psycho bitch. Then Arquero took Fay aside and said what's wrong with you, and she said what's wrong with *me*? This slimeball gropes me and you want to know what's wrong with *me*? And Arquero said that guy is a customer, happens to be a very *good* customer, and you don't hit a customer again, ever, if you want to keep your job, you understand? And Fay said nothing, because she needed to keep this job.

So now, whenever she approached a male customer she didn't know, she held the drink tray between them, her body tense, ready to step away quickly. She'd also learned, when men said things to her, how to put on exactly the right smile—just enough to let the customer know she got that he was making a joke, ha ha, but not so much that he'd think it was OK with her for him to take it any further, or make a grab. Fay had to make these calculations, recalibrate her expression and posture, hundreds of times a night, which was one reason she almost always went home with a headache.

She felt one starting already as she picked up her drink tray from behind the bar and headed over to the crowd of dedicated roulette aficionados surrounding Tina. She circled the perimeter, searching for somebody relatively noncarnivorous-looking to ease her into the evening. She settled on a seventy-ish, gray-haired, grandfatherly man wearing neatly pressed chinos, loafers, and a button-down shirt, his reading glasses hanging from his neck.

Fay approached, put on her fake perky cocktail-waitress smile, and said, "Would you like anything from the bar, sir?"

He gave her a grandfatherly smile and said, "I'd like a cranberry juice on the rocks, please."

"You got it," she said, her fake smile melting into a genuine one.

"And a blow job," he said.

SOMEWHERE ON THE DARK SEA BETWEEN THE Bahamas and Florida, Frank peered out at the alarmingly large waves. He was now seriously seasick, his clothes soaking with cold sweat, his gut churning from the boat's relentless rolling and lurching, his head pounding from the *thrum-thrum-thrum* of the engines.

Frank had been making a conscious effort not to think about how lousy he felt. Unfortunately, this got him to thinking about how much water there was out there, all around him, beneath him. It was a *lot* of water, he was thinking. A *shitload* of water. It was starting to bother Frank that the only thing between him and all that water was this boat, which to Frank now seemed small and frail, especially compared to these waves. It occurred to him that he didn't really know how boats worked. It didn't make sense, the more he thought about it, that if he dropped, for example, his car keys into the ocean, they'd sink immediately, even though they weighed far less than this boat. Frank wondered—he couldn't help himself—*What was keeping the boat up?* And what if it suddenly stopped working, out here? Wherever the hell *here* was.

Frank looked over at Tark, at the helm. Tark, who always seemed to sense when Frank was looking at him, looked back and grinned, clearly loving how much Frank was clearly hating this.

"Are we on time?" said Frank, trying to sound businesslike, in control, unafraid.

"We're good," said Tark. "Timewise, anyway. You don't look so good, though."

"Don't worry about me," said Frank.

"Who said I was worried?" said Tark.

"I appreciate your concern," said Frank.

"Some people just can't get used to it, the rough water," said Tark. "Me, I love it. Rougher the better, far as I'm concerned."

Frank said nothing.

"Probably gonna get a lot rougher," said Tark. "Storms like this, I've seen 'em capsize bigger boats'n this."

"Shut up," said Frank.

"You're the one started this conversation," said Tark.

Frank looked at his watch, saw it was time to check on Juan. Bracing himself against the motion of the boat, he moved toward the ladderway. Just before he reached it, the boat lurched violently. Frank almost fell, caught a railing with his non-gun hand, hung on. He looked back at Tark, who was spinning the wheel, grinning.

"Better watch yourself," Tark said. "You could get hurt."

"Next time that happens," Frank said, "I shoot you in the knee, you got that? Hurts like a bitch, and you'll never walk right again. But you can still drive the boat, unless you want me to shoot the other knee."

"Hey," said Tark, "you can't blame me for what the ocean does."

Frank aimed his Glock at Tark's left eye, so Tark could see right down the barrel, which Frank had always found to be a strong attention-getter. He said, "You can't blame me for what my gun does."

Tark tried to keep his grin up, but it faded just a hair, enough to make Frank feel momentarily better as he turned and headed down the ladder. He immediately felt worse when he got into the cabin, which stank of large, unhygienic bodies radiating their odors into stale, humid air. Tark's three friends—Kaz, Rebar, Holman—were still sitting at the table, staring at Juan, who was still facing them, his back to the counter, gun in hand. He didn't look good. His eyes were glazed, his face slick with sweat.

"You OK?" Frank said.

Juan responded by handing Frank his gun—Juan *never* let go of his gun—then whirling to the sink and vomiting copiously. Frank jumped back, trying to avoid the splatter. At the table, Kaz, the one on the left, with the big arms, said "Oh *shit*" and started to rise.

"Don't move," said Frank.

"Come *on*, man," said Kaz, sitting back down. "You can't keep us in here with *that*."

"I said *don't move*."

The acrid stench of puke was hitting Frank now, and he knew his stomach was close to open revolt. Juan, between heaves, looked up from the sink and said, "Ag sagg manng"—Frank took this to mean *I'm sorry, man*—then went back to retching. Frank fought to regain control of the snakes writhing in his gut so he could figure out how to play this.

Rebar, the fat guy next to Kaz, said, "I'm gonna puke."

Kaz said, "Oh man, no DON'T . . ." but this is not one of those areas where people take directions, and even as Kaz spoke, Rebar blurted onto the table what had at one time been an abundant seafood lunch, now transformed by Rebar's digestive system into a rancid sloshing horror. At that instant, the boat hit a wave trough and pitched violently forward, dumping Rebar's spewage into the lap of Holman, who responded milliseconds later by launching his own lunch in a gush that shot across the table and splashed onto the floor. Kaz was now scrambling sideways, away from his two puking cohorts, trying to stand up but getting only partway to his feet before the chain reaction reached him and *BLARRRGGHH,* he, too, released a mighty river of ralph.

Frank was now in a small enclosed space with four men who were actively regurgitating, their stomach contents mingling on the pitching, heaving floor, forming a reeking gumbo from hell. The stench was unbearable, and at that moment, Frank, normally the ultimate professional, did not care about making the rendezvous or keeping an eye on Tark or anything else except getting out of there *right now.* He lunged toward the cabin door, but as he did, the boat lurched again, and he stepped on some unspeakable, slippery thing and lost his footing. With a gun in each hand, he was unable to grab for support, and so he went down, backward, cracking his head against the counter, landing on his butt, which continued to slide out from under him until he was lying on his back, momentarily blacked out, regaining consciousness to feel wetness on his back and . . . *Oh no . . . Oh God no, it's in my hair . . .*

And then Frank lost it, too, joining the chunk-blowing chorus, the barf brigade, five men in a tossing boat who might have reasons to kill each other, but who, for the moment, could think about nothing except when the next retch would come, and what it would bring up.

"IS EVERYBODY HAVING A GOOD TIME?" SAID Wally. "Is everybody ready to *party*?"

Wally surveyed the dance floor on the third deck of the *Extravaganza of the Seas.* This did not take him long, as there was nobody actually on the dance floor. There were a dozen or so passengers on the deck, but most of them were at the far end of the room, buying drinks at the bar or picking warily through the buffet.

The buffet was included in the *Extravaganza's* $8.95

admission price ($5.95 for seniors). It was advertised as the Sumptuous All You Can Eat Gourmet Buffet, but nobody ever ate much of it. Experienced *Extravaganza* passengers did not even approach it.

The Sumptuous All You Can Eat Gourmet Buffet consisted of a row of dented industrial chafing dishes, each containing an unidentifiable entrée, generally random lumps of something that could have, at one time, been part of a living thing, but not a healthy thing—medallions of weasel, perhaps—soaking in semi-coagulated gravylike liquid, generally a yellowish-brown in color, sometimes with a tinge of gray or green.

The buffet was tended by a hatchet-faced, hostile-looking man wearing a chef's uniform with large permanent stains. This man never spoke. The band called him "Emeril." Emeril did not appear to actually cook anything. At the start of the night, he produced the chafing dishes and lit the burners. During the cruise, he sat behind the counter on a stool, arms folded, glaring into the distance, refusing to answer customers' questions (the most common question being, "What *is* this?"). At the end of the night, he removed the chafing dishes.

It was Ted who had proposed the theory that Emeril was setting out the same food, night after night.

"Why not?" Ted said. "Hardly anybody eats it. It could last for months."

"I think some of it is actually getting larger," said Johnny. "On its own."

Ted had decided to test his theory that Emeril was recycling the food. He'd gone through the buffet, pretending to be selecting his dinner, and slipped a baseball card—Cliff Floyd, long-ball-hitting outfielder formerly of the Florida Marlins—under one of the weasel medallions. The next night, plate in hand, he'd searched the buffet, dish by dish, poking through the mystery lumps. He thrust his fork triumphantly into the air when, in the fourth dish, he uncovered the gravy-soaked but still-smiling face of the Marlins slugger.

This discovery led to the creation of a betting pool among the band members, five bucks a man to see who could predict how long Emeril could keep the Cliff Floyd dish alive in the Sumptuous All You Can Eat Gourmet Buffet. Each night, Ted had gone through the buffet; each night, sooner or later, he'd turned up the baseball card.

Tonight was critical. It was exactly seven days from the initial card placement, and the only two bandmates still in the pool were Johnny, who'd bet on six days, and Ted, who'd put his money on an even week. Thus there was considerable tension in the room, or at least in the band, when Ted, his bandmates watching closely, went down the row of chafing dishes. There were eight of them, and as of the seventh one, Ted had found nothing. Painstakingly, he began poking through the eighth, and . . .

"YES!" he shouted, reaching into the chafing dish, pulling out the dripping card, holding it aloft.

"Shit," said Johnny.

"Emeril," said Ted, "you da MAN!"

Emeril, from his stool, continued glaring into the distance.

"What do you think," Ted asked the band, "you want to start another pool?"

"I don't know, man," said Wally. "Maybe we should warn somebody about this. I mean, what if somebody *eats* this? They could *die*."

"The way I see it," said Johnny, "anybody who eats this *wants* to die."

"That's a point," said Wally.

So Ted slid the Cliff Floyd card back into whatever it

was in the chafing dish, and the band started a new pool, with Jock taking two more days, Wally three, Johnny six, and Ted betting on another full week.

"I have faith in Emeril," he said. "The man is *loyal* to this food."

With that settled, they set up their equipment and tuned up. A few minutes before departure time, they went up on the deserted top deck and huddled out of the wind and rain against a stack of rubber lifeboats for one last pre-gig joint. Then they went down and got some beers. Thus prepared for the grim evening ahead, they returned to their instruments and launched into their traditional first number of the evening, a blues instrumental in the key of whoever started playing first.

This was a little game the band played. Jock, a purely self-taught idiot savant of rhythm, would start off on the drums with a hypersyncopated introduction whose structure was deeply obscure, sometimes even to Jock. Wally and Ted would listen hard, competing to see who could discern the tempo first; the winner would jump in, playing in the key of his choice. If Wally started, he'd usually go with A or E, easy guitar-player keys, where you can mess around with open strings. If Ted jumped in first, he'd pick something more convenient for a keyboardist, but worse for a guitarist, like F. If, as sometimes happened, Wally and Ted started simultaneously, they'd play musical chicken, each trying to force the other to yield. Johnny would usually end the Battle of the Keys by coming in with his bass on one side or the other, unless he felt like playing in a *third* key, in which case the band would usually be laughing too hard to keep going.

Tonight, Ted had cleanly won the faceoff, picking B-flat, and they'd jammed for ten minutes, getting into it, taking their solos, trading fours for a while, not caring that nobody was listening to them, because they were listening to one another. This was Wally's favorite thing about being in the band—the time when they'd just started playing, had just soared free, for the moment, from the swamp of failure and rejection they were usually mired in, and they were tuned up good and had a little buzz on, and they were doing the one thing they really knew how to do, and damned if it didn't sound all right. That's what always struck Wally when they started a gig: *We sound pretty good.* Not great, but pretty damned good. Wally figured they were as good at making music as most businessmen were at whatever business thing they did. The difference, of course, was that even semicompetent businessmen could make money, whereas even very good musicians could go their entire lives without owning a decent car. But still, this part was fun, just the playing.

It usually became a lot less fun when they had to stop making music and start trying to entertain. Wally, as he had been since the days at Bougainvillea High, was the front man. Reluctantly, he turned from his bandmates, toward the microphone.

"We'd like to welcome you all to the party deck of the fabulous *Extravaganza of the Seas,*" he said. "You look like a great crowd out there!"

At the moment, the crowd consisted of those few people poking through the buffet and buying drinks at the bar, and three dudes, each holding a Bud Light and wearing a ball cap turned around backward, standing at the edge of the dance floor, watching the band with expressions that said: Don't even *think* about entertaining us.

"We're Johnny and the Contusions, and we'll be playing for you all night long," said Wally. "We want you to have a good time, so if you have any requests, let us know, OK?"

"Play quieter!" shouted one of the Bud Light dudes, and the other two cracked up.

"Ha ha, good one!" said Wally. "We never heard that one before." He looked around at the band. "Have we?"

"Never," said Ted.

The shouter dude frowned, not sure how to take this.

"Anyway," said Wally, "we want to remind everybody that the world-famous *Extravaganza of the Seas* all-you-can-eat buffet is open, with some unforgettable classic dishes prepared by our award-winning chef; ladies and gentlemen, give it up for the culinary genius we call . . . Emeril!"

Jock hit a rim shot. There was no other reaction in the room.

"Thank you," said Wally. "Ladies and gentlemen, you are a beautiful crowd, and we'd like to kick things off for you with a party song, because it's a party ship, and a party kind of night, and . . . the tiki bar is OPEN!"

Wally went straight from there into chopping out the minor chords for the John Hiatt song "Tiki Bar." The other guys smiled, because this was a song they *never* did; this was pure self-indulgence on the part of Wally. But they jumped right in, Johnny walking the bass line, Jock pounding on the two and the four, Ted doubling Jock on the keyboard. Wally growled the lyrics, Hiatt-style, and all three bandmates joined him to shout out the chorus:

> *Thank God the tiki bar is open*
> *Thank God the tiki torch still shines . . .*

They had one dancer for this song: a tall, cadaverously skinny man who bore a startling resemblance to Strom Thurmond and who, to judge by the way he weaved over from the bar, had been drinking nonstop since roughly 1967. He stood in the middle of the dance floor and, looking down at his feet, concentrating hard, did a slow but determined version of the Funky Chicken.

Wally sang two verses of "Tiki Bar" and then took a solo, keeping it short but getting some nice riffs in there, grabbing a beer bottle and playing slide guitar for the last two bars. The band finished the song with a perfectly synchronized stop, then a nice little reprise ending, strong and tight, as if they'd practiced it for years. They were rewarded with: nothing. Strom Thurmond kept dancing, apparently unaware that the band had stopped playing. Across the room, a few bold buffet pioneers continued their search for edible food. The Bud Light dude who'd told them to play quieter stuck out his fist and, when he caught Wally's eye, made a thumbs-down gesture. This cracked the other two dudes up.

"Thank you!" said Wally. "Thank you very much."

Strom Thurmond, just now realizing the music had stopped, weaved over to Wally.

"Hey," he said, emitting a cloud of whiskey fumes that made Wally's head jerk back. "Play that song."

"Which song would that be?" said Wally.

"You know that song," said the man. "About the thing. With the car."

Wally looked over at Ted.

"Ted," he said. "Do you know that song about the thing? With the car?"

"Sure," said Ted. "We'll get to that in the next set."

"OK," said Strom Thurmond, who made the OK sign with his hand, then fell down. This was not totally his fault; the ship had moved discernibly. Usually it was very steady, but tonight, in the storm, it had a definite rolling feeling. Slowly, with great concentration, Strom Thurmond struggled back up on his feet. Once he was fully erect, he made the OK sign again, almost losing his balance a second time, but making a nice save.

Wally leaned into the microphone. "Ladies and gentlemen," he said, "right now for your continued enjoyment, we're gonna let Mr. Ted Brailey on the keyboards here do a little Van Morrison for you."

Johnny counted "two, three, four" and they were into "Moondance," that staple of a zillion bar mitzvahs and wedding receptions, a song that the Contusions, like most bands, could play in a coma. Strom Thurmond resumed the Funky Chicken. A few more people were in the room now, passengers wandering around the ship, waiting for it to get to the three-mile limit. The veterans went straight to the bar; the newcomers headed for the buffet, from which they recoiled in various stages of horror.

The band, having had its musical fun, was now on auto-pilot. From "Moondance," it would go into a set of similarly mellow, easy-listening, low-stress tunes, to which, on most nights, hardly anybody would listen—the band members themselves would basically tune out—and nobody would dance. Once the casino opened below, there would rarely be any passengers in the room at all. This is the way it was every night on the *Extravaganza of the Seas*.

But tonight something different happened. Midway through "Moondance," a group of giggling women emerged from the stairway and flowed onto the dance floor, eight of them, young and attractive, especially for *Extravaganza* passengers. Wally guessed that they were a bachelorette party; they'd obviously been partying hard for a while. They began dancing directly in front of the band, which responded by finishing "Moondance" early and going straight into the Commodores' "Brick House," a song that, in the band's experience, was a lot of fun to watch women wearing tight, low-cut tops dance to. They responded nicely and, when the song ended, applauded.

"So," said Wally, into his microphone. "Is somebody celebrating a special occasion tonight?"

"Yes!" said several, pointing to a petite woman with short blonde hair. "Connie!"

"And is the lovely Connie getting married?" asked Wally.

"Nope," said Connie. "Divorced!"

"Congratulations!" said Wally. "Who's the lucky guy?"

"An asshole," said Connie. This set off a round of whoops and high-fives among the women. One of them high-fived Strom Thurmond, who went back down like a sack of grain. As some women helped him back up, Wally asked Connie: "Is there anything special you'd like the band to play?"

"Yes," said Connie.

"What?" said Wally.

Connie pointed at Jock and said, "I'd like him to play doctor with me."

The women whooped; Johnny spat out his beer in mid-swig; Wally and Ted exchanged laughs. They were used to women hitting on Jock, but this was an indoor record.

"How about it, Dr. Jock?" said Wally. "You want to play doctor with Connie here? Help her through this difficult time in her life?"

Jock pointed a drumstick at Connie and said, "You are looking *fine* tonight." More whoops from the women. Connie did a little bump and grind, inadvertently knocking into Strom Thurmond, who went down again.

"I feel a lot of love in this room," said Wally. "This calls for a very special song, a very romantic song, a very tender song for this very special lady, Connie, on her very special night."

Then he stomped on his distortion pedal, cranked up his volume knob and slashed out the opening riff to "I Want Your Sex Pootie," by the Seminal Fluids. Jock caught it instantly and came in right behind him, and in a heartbeat everybody on the floor, including Strom Thurmond, was bouncing up and down, chanting with Wally:

I want your sex pootie
I want your sex pootie
I want your sex pootie
I want your sex pootie

There were more people coming up the stairs now, drawn by the noise. Some of them watched; some of them joined the dancers, a couple dozen out there now. This was, by far, the best response the band had gotten on the *Extravaganza*: an actual audience, including actual babes, actually dancing. As the band reached the end of "Sex Pootie," Wally shot a glance back at Jock to let him know that he was going to keep it moving and blasted into the high-energy opening chords, E-A-D-A, of the Romantics' "What I Like About You." The crowd responded as it always did to that song, a song so danceable that even middle-aged white men can sometimes locate the beat.

Still more people were coming up the stairs. Even the Bud Light dudes drifted onto the floor, assuming the pseudo-soulful facial expression of men dancing and insinuating themselves into the clot of gyrating divorce-party women. Somebody bumped into Strom Thurmond and he went down again, but this time he wisely elected to stay on the floor and dance in a prone position.

As "What I Like About You" ended, the band followed Wally right into AC-DC's "You Shook Me All Night Long," which begins with a tender couplet of almost Shakespearean eloquence:

She was a fast machine
She kept her motor clean

Midway through the song, Connie, the grieving divorcée, pulled up her top and flashed her breasts at Jock, although the rest of the band was in a position to benefit visually. The dance floor was actually crowded now; Wally saw all ages and types out there, old people and young people, and . . . Jesus, was that a *shell*?

Sure enough, out there in the middle of the mob, clearly disoriented, flailing his pink arms around, was Conrad Conch. He'd come up the stairs and started feeling his way toward the buffet when somebody had grabbed him and pulled him onto the dance floor, where he was being bounced from dancer to dancer like a giant pink beach ball. He got shoved toward the band, where the divorce-party women surrounded him and began feigning lewd acts of human-mollusk sex, one of them dropping onto her knees and applying her mouth vigorously to what would be the penile area of the shell, if conchs had penises. The crowd was going insane, stomping its feet and cheering the women on. At the microphone, Wally was laughing so hard that he had to stop singing.

This was precisely the moment when Manny Arquero appeared. He didn't even have to tell the band to stop playing; the fury of look he gave them made it almost physically impossible to continue. The sound drained from the room; the crowd quieted down, interested in this new drama. Arquero stepped around the microphone, got his face right into Wally's. He was exactly Wally's height, but somehow he gave Wally the impression of being three or four times Wally's size.

"What the *fuck* are you doing?" he said, quietly but violently.

"We're just—"

"Shut the fuck up," said Arquero.

"Yes," said Wally.

"Now you listen," said Arquero. "From now—"

"Hey!" said Strom Thurmond.

Arquero turned around, noticed the old man on the floor. "What the hell happened to you?" he said.

"Tell 'em to play that song," said Strom Thurmond. "About the thing. With the car."

Arquero turned back to Wally.

"Hey!" said Strom Thurmond, again.

Arquero whirled back around, pissed off, and said, *"What?"*

"I think I shit myself."

This got a big laugh from the crowd, which pissed Arquero off even more. He turned back and grabbed Wally by the arm. He had a painful grip.

"Listen," he said. "You don't play that kinda music on this boat, you understand?"

"What kind of—"

"Shut the fuck up."

"Yes."

"You don't play the kind of music that's loud and sounds like somebody's up here killing a bag of cats with a shovel and makes the customers crazy, that's what you don't play."

"But the crowd was—"

"Shut the fuck up."

"Yes."

"You play the kind of music you been playing since you got this job, which is quiet music people can maybe listen to a little bit and then go back downstairs, you got that?"

Wally said nothing, because he figured Arquero would just tell him to shut the fuck up.

"I said you *got* that?"

"Yes."

"Good. Because the way we make money on this boat is, people gamble downstairs. We don't make money if we got all our customers up here listening to you killing cats and watching some bimbo give a fucking blow job to a fucking shell."

"But we didn't—"

"Shut the fuck up."

"Yes."

Reminded of the conch, Arquero turned around, grabbed Conrad by one of his pink arms, yanked him over, stuck his face into the mouth hole.

"I told you I didn't want no trouble," he said.

"Mmmmwmf," said Conrad.

"Shut the fuck up."

Conrad nodded.

"I got half a mind to throw you off this ship," said Arquero. "You, too," he said to Wally. He now was gripping each of them, the guitarist and the shell, by the upper arm. "Anymore trouble from either of you, you are gonna be very fucking sorry, you got that?" He gave each of them an extremely painful biceps squeeze.

"Ow!" said Wally.

"Mmmmwmf!" said Conrad.

"Good," said Arquero. "Remember that." He let go of their arms, turned to Wally. "Now you and your so-called band play some nice quiet music, doesn't cause any problems with our customers."

"Yes, sir," said Wally, to Arquero's retreating back.

Wally turned to the band and said, "Thanks for the backup, guys."

"Hey," said Ted, "looked to me like you had him right where you wanted him."

"I was this close to beating the shit out of him," said Johnny.

Wally shook his head, smiled. "OK," he said. "Bar mitzvah time. Count it off, Jocko."

". . . two, three, four," said Jock, and the band, once again, launched into "Moondance." Drifting up from the stairway came the electronic *boop-boop-boop* that the slot machines made incessantly, and the clank of quarters landing in the tray, signifying that somebody had won something. The crowd, including the divorce party, headed toward the stairs, leaving Johnny and the Contusions playing for an audience of two: Conrad Conch, who resumed making his gingerly way toward the buffet; and Strom Thurmond, who got back onto his feet and resumed dancing the Funky Chicken, more aromatically now.

Seven

ON THE BRIDGE OF THE *EXTRAVAGANZA OF THE Seas*, Hank Wilde, looking snappy in his first-officer whites, sipped Jack Daniel's from a foam cup. At the helm, Captain Eddie Smith studied the navigation and radar displays. Eddie usually stayed at the helm for the entire trip. He never let Wilde run the ship, not for a second, even if Wilde hadn't been drinking.

Wilde didn't care. He had no interest in the operation of the ship. All he cared about was making sure Eddie did what he was told, and occasionally cell-phoning reports to Tarant. The rest of the time, Wilde drank and looked for ways to amuse himself. One of these ways was to hang around the bridge, trying to goad Eddie into having a conversation, which he could usually do, because it was pretty boring on the bridge.

"Hey, Captain," said Wilde.

"What," said Eddie, still watching the displays.

"You know that roulette croupier?"

"Which one?"

"Like you don't know," said Wilde. "Like when I say 'roulette croupier,' what comes to your mind is the fifty-year-old bald guy with the potbelly. Like you're not immediately thinking about the six-foot blonde with the bazooms that're a hazard to navigation."

"Oh, her," said Eddie.

"Yeah, oh her."

"She is hard to miss," said Eddie.

"She makes me hard, tell you that," said Wilde. "But here's the thing. You ever spend any time around her?"

"No," said Eddie. "I'm up here, running the ship. Maybe you noticed."

"Well, as first officer, I feel like I got to check out the ship from time to time, make sure it's shipshape, you know?"

"It's a load off my mind," said Eddie.

"So anyway, one of the shapes I like to check is Tina's, which is not easy because there's always like fifty guys around her table, waiting for her to bend over. And here's the thing. I think she's a farter."

"A what?"

"A farter. I think she farts."

"Everybody farts. I fart."

"Right. I fart also. But she farts a lot."

"How do you know it's her? It's probably one of the customers."

"That's what I thought, the first few times. I'd be over there by the roulette wheel, and I'd be like, whoa, somebody cut a major chunk of cheese here, and I'm looking around at all these guys, because you figure it's a guy. You don't figure a woman for a farter."

"No," agreed Eddie. He was in his twenties before he was even sure women *could* fart.

"You can live with a woman for years and never hear

her let one rip," said Wilde. "You live with a woman, right?"

"A year now," said Eddie.

"You ever hear her fart?"

Eddie said nothing, not sure he wanted to be having this conversation.

"Come on," said Wilde. "I'm not asking you to say she farts. I'm asking you to confirm you never heard her fart, which I bet you didn't. She'd be happy to know you were sticking up for her."

"OK," said Eddie. "I never heard her fart."

"Exactly. She's whooshing on you."

"She's what?"

"Whooshing. Women have some kind of technique where they do something with their butt muscles, and they just whoosh 'em out."

"Whooshing?"

"That's what they call it."

"How do you know that?"

"This woman I lived with once, up in Jersey, she told me about it. She said they all do it."

"How do they know how?"

"That she didn't say. Could be instinct. Could be it was on *Oprah*. All's I know is, that's the secret. Whooshing."

"Huh," said Eddie.

"So anyway," said Wilde, "I'm smelling this smell, and I'm figuring it has to be one of the customers, right? Some guy ate a bad burrito or whatever. But next time I'm there, whoa, there it is again. Next time, same thing. Different nights, different guys, same smell. And finally I realize it has to be Tina. The woman is like permanently surrounded by a green cloud."

"But she still draws a crowd?"

"Oh, hell, yes. A woman looks like that, she's gonna have guys around no matter what she smells like. She could be dead, worms coming out her nose, and there'd still be guys asking her what is she doing later. Plus which, the customers all probably think it's some other customer doing it."

"True," said Eddie. Then: "Why're you telling me this?"

"Just in case," said Wilde. "I mean, one of these days, somebody's gonna light a match around that woman, and the whole goddamn ship could blow up, like that blimp, whaddyacallit, the *Hindenburn*. I figure you should know, being the captain."

"I appreciate the information," said Eddie.

"Just doing my job as first officer," said Wilde, taking another sip of Jack Daniel's.

The ship lurched, just a little, but a little is a lot on a ship the size of the *Extravaganza*.

"What was that?" said Wilde.

"Wave," said Eddie. "Big one. Case you didn't notice, this is a storm, which we shouldn't be out in."

"We already talked about that," said Wilde. "That's a closed subject."

They were quiet for a minute.

"The boat we're meeting," said Eddie. "It's the same one as usual?"

"Yeah, same boat, same guys, same everything. Why?"

"Because I wouldn't want to be them," said Eddie, looking at his radar. "Can't be comfortable, a boat like that, out in this."

"They're fine," said Wilde. "They're professionals."

IN THE MAIN CABIN OF THE SHIP OF PUKE, Frank, gagging, struggled to a sitting position, his back against the counter. He looked around for Juan's gun, which he'd dropped when he fell, but he didn't immediately see it. He still had his own Glock in his right hand.

Directly in front of him, Kaz was on his hands and knees in the repulsive spew, moaning. Rebar and Holman were still at the table, both retching loudly. Juan was slumped over the sink, not moving.

Frank reached his left hand up, grabbed the edge of the counter, pulled himself upright. His plan was to get back up to the bridge, away from this reeking hell. He saw Juan's Glock now, on the floor next to Kaz, covered in vomit. He couldn't leave it there. He still hadn't made up his mind about the three new guys, and he wasn't going to let them have a gun. With great reluctance, moving slowly to keep his balance in the pitching boat, he stepped forward and leaned down to pick up the Glock.

That's when Kaz came up under him, very fast, pushing off the floor with his hands and driving his left shoulder into Frank's chin, snapping Frank's head back, Frank feeling his teeth biting deep into his tongue, going black for an instant, dropping his gun. He staggered backward, catching himself on the counter. His brain cleared a little, and he saw Kaz leaning over to pick up Juan's gun. Frank kicked him, aiming for his face but slipping a little on the wet floor and catching just the top of his forehead, the kick causing both men to fall again. Kaz recovered fast and scrambled toward Juan's gun, but Frank lunged forward and met him, the two of them grappling on the floor now, each unable to grip the other firmly because they were both hideously slick with digestive juices. Kaz tried to put a knee into Frank's balls, but Frank got his leg in the way. Kaz drew back his right fist to try to throw a punch, which gave Frank, who was usually quicker than guys his own size, an opening to sink a left deep into Kaz's gut, then a hard right into his face, sending him back and down, not moving after his head hit the floor.

Frank spat blood from his mouth, and felt more leaking from his lacerated tongue. He found Juan's gun by the counter, reluctantly picked it up, stuck it into his pocket, retrieved his own gun, and looked around the cabin. Kaz looked to be out. Rebar and Holman looked too sick to be a problem. Juan was still sagged motionless over the sink. Frank thought about trying to get Juan out of there but decided that it was more urgent to get back to Tark.

He staggered to the ladderway and started up, holding the railing with his left hand, keeping his gun in his right. As he neared the top, his shoulders level with the bridge floor, he saw that Tark wasn't at the wheel, and he yanked his head back, which is why the two-foot metal bar, coming from his left, missed him. It clanged into the ladder, and before Tark could pull it up again, Frank got his hand around Tark's wrist and yanked hard, the two of them falling down the ladderway, Tark on top, Frank losing his gun again on the way down. As they hit the bottom, Frank felt Tark struggling to pull something from his belt. Frank rolled sideways and shoved himself back just as the knife came up, intended for his gut, just missing. Frank slapped Tark's knife hand sideways and drove his forearm into Tark's windpipe. From the feel of it, he knew Tark would have trouble catching his breath for a while. If he ever did.

As Tark writhed on the floor, clutching at his neck, making a sound like *uck uck uck,* Frank rolled to his hands and knees, spat out another mouthful of tongue blood, and started struggling upright, trying to clear his head, to figure out how he was going to get the boat to the rendezvous, or anywhere, without Tark to drive it.

He was halfway to his feet when his peripheral vision registered that Kaz was no longer lying on the floor. He started to move, but as quick as he was, he was too late to get out of the way of the eight-pound marine fire extinguisher coming down on the back of his head.

* * *

FAY STOOD AT THE WAITRESS STATION OF THE
bar, waiting for Joe Sarmino to finish her drink orders. Joe
was a 67-year-old Cuban who, before he became a bartender, raised a family and put four kids through college by
cleaning pools in the expensive homes of Coral Gables and
Pinecrest, going house to house in his pickup with jugs of
chemicals in the back, dawn to dusk, six days a week, 34
years.

"I think sometimes I pee chlorine," is how he described
it to Fay.

Once, when the bar was slow, he told her about things
he'd found in his clients' pools. Alligators, for example;
he'd encountered at least a dozen. Also the occasional
snake. Hundreds of frogs. These were to be expected in
South Florida, which as far as the native wildlife was concerned was still a swamp, no matter how many houses got
built on it. But Joe had also found numerous non-wildlife
things in pools, the most memorable being a naked human
corpse; natural causes, the coroner said. Joe had also found
a bowling ball, a trombone, a wide variety of cellular tele-
phones, dozens of car keys, and a riding lawnmower,
whose owner had decided at 5 A.M., after a night of alcohol
and cocaine consumption, that it would be a good idea to
spruce up his backyard. Joe had found a rifle, at least ten
brassieres, a laptop computer, and three television sets, all
of which had been deep-sixed following fourth-quarter-
collapse losses by the Miami Dolphins. ("That prevent defense," Joe said. "It don't prevent nothing.")

Joe had also once serviced a pool containing the business wardrobe of a prominent, and well-dressed, Miami attorney. When Joe arrived, the attorney was in the deep end,
wearing a dive mask and flippers, going down to the bottom and coming back up with a silk tie, a suit jacket, a

wingtipped shoe, a dress shirt. He'd fling it onto the pool deck, take a breath, then go down for a new article of clothing.

"You need help with that, Mr. B?" Joe asked.

"No, thanks, Joe," the attorney said. "I'm fine."

The patio door opened, and a hand-stitched Italian loafer came sailing out, just missing the attorney's head, splashing into the water.

"VERY MATURE," said the attorney. "THAT'S VERY MATURE."

"DON'T TELL ME ABOUT MATURE, YOU BASTARD," said a woman's voice from inside the house. "YOU DON'T KNOW WHAT THE WORD MATURE MEANS." The other loafer came sailing out.

"Maybe I come back another time," said Joe.

"No, no," said the attorney. "Do what you have to do." He dove back under, came back up with a belt, holding it up like he'd caught an eel. Joe started around the pool, cleaning the basket filters. Something came flying out the patio door, splashing into the shallow end. As it settled on the bottom, Joe saw that it was a golf club. He didn't play, but sometimes on Sundays, on the sofa, he'd nap while watching the PGA on TV. This looked to him like a five iron.

"OH, THAT'S INTELLIGENT," said the attorney. "THAT'S GOING TO ACCOMPLISH A LOT."

"INTELLIGENT?" said the voice from the house. Another club came sailing out. Driver. "YOU WANT TO TALK ABOUT INTELLIGENT? HOW INTELLIGENT IS IT TO COME HOME WITH YOUR GIRLFRIEND'S PANTIES IN YOUR FUCKING GLOVE COMPARTMENT? Oh, hello, Joe."

"Hi, Mrs. B," said Joe. "I think maybe I come back later."

"No, no," she said. "You go right ahead." Another club

splashed into the water, a putter, with one of those offset shafts. The attorney, treading water, watched it sink to the bottom.

"YOU WONDER WHY WE HAVE INTIMACY IS-SUES," he said. "YOU SHOULD LISTEN TO THE TONE OF YOUR VOICE."

Joe told this story to Fay deadpan, polishing the bar. Fay shook her head.

"Intimacy issues," she said.

"Next week I go back there," he said, "they on the patio together, drinking coffee, reading the newspaper, like nothing happen."

"Just like that," said Fay.

"But I bet he have to buy some new shoes," said Joe.

Tonight on the *Extravaganza,* there wasn't time for long conversation, just a few minutes here and there while Fay waited for Joe to fill her drink orders. Mounted over the bar was a TV set, usually tuned to ESPN, but tonight tuned to NewsPlex Nine. On the screen a reporter was in a supermarket, interviewing panicked shoppers lined up with their overflowing carts, then showing bare shelves, the reporter explaining that the store was running out of certain emergency supplies—water, batteries, bleach.

"Let me ask you something," said Fay. "What's the deal with the bleach?"

"The bleach?" said Joe.

"Yeah," said Fay. "In a hurricane, people always buy bleach, but I don't get what they do with it."

Joe paused for a moment from pouring margarita mix, pondering. Then he said: "I don't know, but they tell you to buy it, the bleach."

On the screen, the supermarket reporter had been re-placed with a blob of red that whirled around in the center of the screen, counterclockwise, like a hurricane, and then turned into the words NEWSPLEX NINE BREAKING STORM

NEWS BULLETIN. These words then whirled around and got smaller and went to the upper right corner of the screen, which now showed the NewsPlex Nine NewsCenter, where the male and female anchors/lovers were looking even more frowny than usual, indicating that something bad, and therefore exciting, had happened.

"I'm afraid we have had a tragic development in connection with Tropical Storm Hector," said the female, who then looked to the man to continue the story, because NewsPlex Nine anchors generally did not say more than a sentence at a time.

"We have had an apparent electrocution caused by a power line down in some flooding in the Westchester area," said the male anchor.

"Westchester, I used to live there," said Joe Sarmino. "They getting flooding every time a dog take a leak."

The female anchor was saying, ". . . to NewsPlex Nine Storm Specialist Todd Ford, on the scene of this tragic development."

On the screen was a blond young man in a yellow NewsPlex Nine rain poncho, standing at the middle of a flooded residential street, the water coming up to his mid-shins.

"Bill and Jill," he said, "police are telling us the tragedy occurred about forty-five minutes ago, when a young boy was electrocuted while playing with some friends in the street about two blocks behind me. As you can see, there's about a foot and a half of water here, and there are power lines down, so police and fire rescue are warning the public that they must not, I repeat not, go into this flood water, because it is extremely dangerous."

"Why is HE in the water?" said Fay.

"That's what I'm wondering," said Joe.

Now NewsPlex Nine was doing a picture-in-picture effect, with the reporter in the main picture and the anchors frowning in a smaller picture on the upper left. The upper right still said NEWSPLEX NINE BREAKING STORM NEWS BULLETIN.

"Todd," said the male anchor, "do we have any identification yet on the victim?"

"As of now," said the reporter, "police are saying only that—"

The larger picture went dark. In the smaller picture, the two anchors continued frowning for a second. The male said: "Todd?"

Nothing.

The female said: "Apparently, we're having some technical difficulties from that location."

Joe Sarmino said to Fay, "Maybe we safer out here."

AT A THREE-DOLLAR BLACKJACK TABLE ON THE

first deck, Arnie was staring at his cards, a six and a three. He tapped the table for another card; the dealer flipped him a two. He tapped again; another six. Seventeen.

"I should stand on this," he announced to the other players—two Latin guys—and the dealer. "That's the smart strategy, stand on seventeen. But I'm not gonna stand, and you know why?"

Nobody said anything.

"Because I been following the smart strategy all night, and you know what I won?"

Nobody said anything.

"I won bupkis," said Arnie. He looked at the Latin guys. "You familiar with bupkis? They got bupkis in Cuba?"

"Not Cuba," said one of the Latin guys. "El Salvador."

"You got bupkis down there?" said Arnie.

"What is it?" said the guy.

"It's nothing," said Arnie. *"Nada."*

"Oh yeah," said the guy. "We got a lot of that."

"You want a card?" the dealer asked Arnie.

"Isn't that what I'm saying?" said Arnie.

"I got no idea what you're saying," said the dealer.

"I'm saying hit me," said Arnie.

"Then tap the table," said the dealer. "So *they* know what you're saying." He pointed up at the surveillance camera.

Arnie waved to the camera, then tapped the table. The dealer flipped over another card. The queen of clubs.

"NOW the smart strategy works," said Arnie, as the dealer took his chips.

"How you doing?" said Phil, coming up to the table.

"If the object of blackjack was to get twenty-two or more," said Arnie, "I would own this boat. You?"

"Tell you the truth, I did pretty good at the roulette," said Phil. "Playing my grandchildren's birthdays. I hit three times, you believe that?"

"I can't remember my grandchildren's birthdays," said Arnie.

"Neither can I," said Phil. "But from now on, they're on the twelfth, sixteenth, and twenty-seventh."

"Are you in?" the dealer said to Arnie.

"Of course," said Arnie, putting three one-dollar chips in the circle. "Lady Luck is gonna change her mind. I feel it."

The dealer dealt one card, two cards. The first El Salvadoran had blackjack. The second took a card, stood on eighteen.

"So how come you left, if you were winning?" Arnie said to Phil.

"There was a smell," said Phil.

"A smell?" said Arnie.

"Like somebody took a dump."

The El Salvadorans laughed. Phil turned to them.

"What?" he said.

"You playing roulette upstairs?" the closer one said. "With the lady?" He made the international hand gesture for large bosoms.

"Yes," said Phil. "Why?"

The El Salvadorans laughed again. The dealer snick-ered.

"What?" said Phil.

"You want a card?" the dealer asked Arnie. Arnie had a king and a three. He tapped the table.

"Come on, Lady Luck," he said.

The dealer flipped him a nine.

"Bupkis," said the El Salvadorans.

"Lady Luck is a bitch, you know that?" said Arnie.

"THAT'S GOOD," SAID LOU TARANT. "RIGHT there."

Tarant was sitting, naked, on a leather sofa in the living room of his 4,200-square-foot North Miami Beach pent-house condominium with ocean view, in front of his $8,000 42-inch, flat-screen plasma-monitor TV. In his right hand, he held the remote control. His left hand was on the neck of Dee Dee Holdscomb, Bobby Kemp's former secre-tary, who was kneeling between Tarant's thick hairy thighs.

"That's real good," Tarant said.

"Mmmmwmf," said Dee Dee.

"What?" said Tarant.

Dee Dee lifted her head. "Don't squeeze my neck so hard," she said. "I tole you that a hunnert times."

"Sorry," said Tarant. "You're doing real good, baby."

"Mmmmwmf," said Dee Dee, back at work.

Tarant clicked over to ESPN, now showing video of John Daly hitting a tee shot. Christ, that guy could rip it. That thing had to go half a mile. Tarant had a titanium driver, took lessons, worked on his stance, practiced his swing every chance he got, went to the driving range every week, and he couldn't come within a hundred yards of this guy's tee shots, this fat slob who wouldn't last five seconds against Tarant in a fight. It pissed Tarant off, the way this guy could hit the ball.

"*Dammit* Lou," said Dee Dee, lifting her head again, yanking his hand away from her neck. "I just *tole* you, don't *do* that."

"Sorry, baby," he said, putting his hand back, pushing her head back down. "It just feels so good, what you're doing there, is all."

"Mmmmwmf," said Dee Dee, her tone a little hurt.

Tarant clicked through some more channels, stopping on one with a big whirling red blob on the screen, which turned into NEWSPLEX NINE BREAKING STORM NEWS BULLETIN, which whirled again and went to the upper-right corner of the screen, which was now showing a man and a woman, the man older, gray around the temples, the woman younger, blond, lots of lipstick. Tarant wondered if he was banging her. They were both looking sad, the man saying something, the woman shaking her head. Tarant had the mute on, but he could read the headline crawling across the bottom of the screen: NEWSPLEX NINE TRAGEDY: REPORTER, CAMERAMAN ELECTROCUTED.

"Morons," said Tarant.

"Mmmmwmf?" said Dee Dee.

"Nothing, baby," said Tarant, patting her neck. "Keep doing that."

The phone rang, the business line, which meant it was a call he should take, as opposed to a call from his wife, off shopping in Spain or Sweden, some fucking place in Europe.

"Shit," said Tarant. It was getting so a man couldn't get

a simple blow job in his own home from his secretary anymore. He picked up the phone.

"What," he said.

"Lou, I hate to bother you," said a voice, which Tarant
recognized as belonging to Gene Shroder, the guy he had
handling the books for Bobby Kemp's businesses. Shroder
would not call without a reason.

"What," said Tarant.

"Our boy, he's been making some moves I think you
should know about. I should have found out about this earlier, but I was home from work the last two days, my wife
is having that chemo."

"Yeah, sorry about that," said Tarant. "What kind of
moves?"

"OK, one thing, today he went around to most of the
restaurants and collected the cash receipts."

"He ever do that before?"

"No, and that's not the way it's supposed to work, but if
the owner of the restaurant chain walks in and says he
wants his money, the managers aren't gonna say no."

"What else?"

"When I heard about that, I called our bank guy, and
turns out our boy also cleaned out his personal bank accounts, plus his money market. He didn't touch the Bobby
Kemp Enterprises checking account, but there's not much
in there, and he'd know I'd hear about that right away."

"Anything else?"

"I called his broker, who didn't want to talk about it,
said it was confidential, so I had the Wookie go see him."

Tarant had an image flash into his mind here, of an incident a few years ago involving the Wookie. This was the
name they called a very large individual they sometimes
sent out to talk to people who needed to grasp the urgency
of a situation. In this one incident, the Wookie had gone to

see a member of the Miami-Dade County School Board, who had been paid, fair and square, to vote in favor of the district buying a certain tract of land to build a school on, but who now was making noises about opposing the deal because some fuckknuckle newspaper reporter had found out that the land was, half the year, more what you would classify as a lake.

So the Wookie goes out to see this guy and finds him on his patio, grilling some steaks on his Weber gas grill. The guy, figuring out right away what the situation is, says he's not going to keep the money, he's going to give the money back, all of it, every dime. And the Wookie nods, not saying anything, meaning either the refund concept is OK with him, or just that he hears what the guy is saying, the guy doesn't know which. So the guy keeps talking talking talking, waving his long-handled barbecue spatula around, telling the Wookie that he's not about to charge for a service he can't deliver, but he can definitely be counted on in the future, and in fact he will probably be even more valuable in the future, because this vote will establish that he has integrity, so it's really *better* this way, for all parties concerned, blah blah blah. All this time the Wookie is nodding, nodding, and finally the guy figures, OK, this is gonna work out, and he thanks the Wookie for his understanding and steps forward to shake the Wookie's hand. Which is when the Wookie picks him up by his arms and puts his ass down on the grill, holds him there for maybe five seconds, which is a long time under these particular circumstances.

Two weeks later, the guy voted in favor of the land deal. He stood up throughout the school board meeting, because of what he said was a medical problem. People assumed it was hemorrhoids.

"And?" said Tarant.

"And," said Shroder, "the broker said he cashed out, everything, stocks, bonds, mutual funds."

"Where is he right now?" said Tarant.

"That's the thing. I been calling his numbers, leaving messages, nothing. I had people check his house, other places he could be, but nobody's seen him."

"*Fuck,*" said Tarant.

"*Mmmmwmf,*" said Dee Dee, shoving his hand away from her neck.

"Sorry," said Tarant.

"What?" said Shroder.

"Nothing," said Tarant. "Listen, I want you to find him, OK? Get some guys on this. And stay by the phone, OK?"

"OK," said Shroder. "Listen, I feel bad about this. I should've found out sooner, but I was home when it started and I didn't check in until this afternoon because, I don't mean this as an excuse, but my wife is having a pretty rough time of it right now."

"OK," said Tarant. "You tell Laurie I'm thinking about her."

"OK," said Shroder, whose wife's name was Linda.

"And find that little prick," said Tarant.

Eight

ON THE THIRD DECK, JOHNNY AND THE CONTU-
sions were on cruise control, drifting through a mellow set,
EZ-listening music. Strom Thurmond was still on the floor,
dancing whether the band was playing or not, his eyes focused intently on his feet, as though they were performing
brain surgery down there. The only other customers were
two elderly women, ship regulars, who were waiting for
the song to stop so they could request, as was their usual
practice, an old standard song that the band either did not
know or hated. Lately, they had been pushing for "My
Funny Valentine."

At the moment, the band was doing "Desperado," the
sad and soulful Eagles song. Ted was singing lead, doing a
nice job, sounding as though it was coming straight from
his heart . . .

You better let somebody love you

. . . although in fact Ted was thinking about his 1989 Mazda, whether he should try to get the a/c fixed again or just accept that it would never work right and he was doomed to drive around hot, his pants soaked with sweat and permanently wedged into his butt crack. Maybe he should sell the car, but what would he get for it? Nothing. Maybe he should just push the goddamn thing into a canal. That's what he wanted to do, push it into the canal and collect the insurance. Except that he had not had insurance on the car since 1994.

Johnny, on bass, was thinking about a show he'd heard about on TV where people ate sheep eyeballs to make money. *Eyeballs.* Man. He was wondering how much money it would have to be before he would eat a sheep eyeball. It would have to be a LOT of money, like $5,000. No, make that $7,500, because there would be taxes. Although Johnny was not 100 percent sure about that, because he had never filed a tax return. He was wondering which he would want to eat less: a sheep eyeball, or the *Extravaganza of the Sea*'s Sumptuous All You Can Eat Gourmet Buffet. Tough call.

Jock was thinking about sex, which was what Jock usually thought about, but at the moment he had an unusually compelling reason. A few minutes earlier, while the band had been playing "Tupelo Honey," Connie, the grieving divorcée, had walked into the room, strode up to Jock, and dropped a condom on his tom-tom. The other three guys exchanged looks, their faces saying, "Man, she put a condom on his *tom-tom.*" It sat there a few seconds, the little pale-blue foil packet vibrating on the drumhead, Jock and Connie staring at each other. Then Jock flipped the packet up with a stick, caught it in midair, stuck it into his shirt pocket—it almost looked like he practiced this—and said, "We'll be taking a break pretty soon." Connie turned and left, her hips traveling about a yard in each direction. So now Jock was thinking about logistics, where they could go on the ship that word wouldn't get back to Tina.

Wally was thinking about Fay. His plan, when they took their break, was to go down to the second deck and spontaneously bump into her, maybe say, "Oh, hey, how're you doing?" But he would need a good spontaneous thing to say next, something he could memorize and not screw up, something that could lead to a meaningful conversation. All he'd come up with so far was, "This weather sucks, huh?" He knew he had to do better than that. Maybe go the other way, something like, "Nice weather, huh?" Sarcasm. She was smart and would get sarcasm. That seemed like a better approach, a little more intellectual. Maybe, "Lovely evening, isn't it?" She'd probably say, yeah, maybe crack a smile. But then what? Talk a little more about the weather? No, she wasn't going to stand around talking about the weather. Maybe he could make a ship joke, like . . . OK, how about a *Titanic* joke? Something like: "Hey, I don't want to make you nervous, but I think I saw Leonardo DiCaprio over at the craps table." But would she get the reference? Had it been too long since that movie was out? No, everybody knew that movie. OK, so that was the plan: "Lovely evening," would be his spontaneous opener, and then Leonardo DiCaprio, and then maybe she would see he wasn't just some moron hitting on her; he was a witty conversationalist, probably with some depth.

As Wally was thinking this, he and Johnny, who was still thinking about sheep eyeballs, were singing the high harmony on the last verse of "Desperado":

Let somebody love you

And then Ted, who was at that moment deciding he was going to try one more time to get the goddamn a/c fixed, but this time using a different mechanic, sang the last line a capella:

Before it's too late.

When the song ended, the two elderly ladies started walking toward Wally. They were both widows and both lived in Surf Breeze Villas, a widow-infested retirement condominium located in Hallandale a good two miles from the Atlantic Ocean. They had become friends when they discovered that they were both from New York and both named (what are the odds?) Rose. They went out on the *Extravaganza* twice a week to play the quarter slots, although they made a point of listening to the band—even though they did not like the music the band played, they figured they had paid for it. (They also had paid for the buffet, but they drew the line at that.) They were approaching Wally now, Rose I and Rose II, taking a circular route around Strom Thurmond, who was still on the floor cutting an imaginary rug.

"I'd like to request a song," said Rose I.

"'My Funny Valentine,'" said Wally.

"That's right," said Rose I, a little surprised.

"We'll get to that in the next set," said Wally.

"You said that last time," said Rose II. "But you never played it."

"Is that right?" said Wally.

"So maybe you could play it now," said Rose I. "'My Funny Valentine.'"

"Absolutely," said Wally. "Johnny here does a great version of that song. Right, Johnny?"

"What?" said Johnny, who had been thinking about sheep eyeballs and had just mentally raised his minimum price to $8,000.

"'My Funny Valentine,'" said Wally, playing the mournful opening chords.

"What about it?" said Johnny.

"I was just telling this lovely lady how you do a great version of it."

"I don't know the words," said Johnny.

"Sure you do," said Wally. "It's your signature tune. Take it!"

Johnny shook his head, then leaned into the mike and crooned:

"My funny valentine. *(pause)* You sure are lookin' fine. *(longer pause)* You make me toe the line. . . ."

"Those aren't the words," said Rose I.

"It's a special arrangement," said Wally.

"Don't shave your hair for me," Johnny crooned. "Wear underwear for me . . ."

"What is he singing?" said Rose II.

"These are the original lyrics," said Wally. "A lot of the other artists who did this song took liberties with it."

"Don't shoot a bear for me," crooned Johnny, getting into it now, "Blow Fred Astaire for me . . ."

"C'mon, Rose," said Rose I, pulling Rose II toward the doorway. "I don't think they know this song."

"Fall down the stair for me," crooned Johnny. Wally stepped up to his mike and said, to the departing Roses and Strom Thurmond, "Ladies and gentlemen, we're going to be taking just a short break right now, but don't go away, because we'll be coming back with much more music for your enjoyment here on the beautiful *Extravaganza of the Seas.*"

As the two Roses disappeared through the doorway, the band ended "My Funny Valentine." Strom Thurmond held his arms out horizontally, did a slow, stately, 360-degree spin, and fell down.

"Thank you very much," said Wally. "We're Johnny and the Contusions."

"Unfortunately," said Ted.

* * *

THE RAIN BROUGHT FRANK BACK TO CONSCIOUS-ness, cold drops hitting his face. He was choking, his throat clogged, his mouth full of warm liquid. He rolled onto his side and spat it out, a big gush of blood. He spat again, then again, but each time he immediately felt more blood seeping from the wound in his tongue. His tongue felt huge.

Frank tried to feel inside his mouth, but he couldn't move his arms. His wrists were bound behind his back. It felt like plastic, maybe those disposable handcuffs the cops used in riots. He tried to rise and felt that his feet were also bound tight.

He was lying against the gunwale at the back of the boat. The sound of the sea was loud out here, the big waves lifting the boat, dropping it, lifting it. He felt a surge of panic, thinking about what it would feel like if they threw him over the side like this, arms and legs bound; how long it would be before he lost consciousness, how many seconds, maybe minutes, before he couldn't hold his breath anymore, before he started swallowing water, before it was over. He fought to calm himself, to think about what he would say to Tark, what he had to negotiate with that would keep him alive. Nothing came to mind. He didn't even understand why he was alive now: Tark was smart enough to know that, no matter what Frank promised him out here, if Frank ever got back to land alive, Tark was dead. Tark was almost certainly dead anyway, for daring to freelance on this deal; there would be a very serious effort to track him down and kill him in a very unpleasant manner, as a warning to anybody else who might be thinking about freelancing. Tark had to know that, had to know he had no reason at all to keep Frank alive. But Frank had to come up with one right now.

He heard shouting, arguing, coming from inside the cabin. Mostly Tark's voice, but also the big guy, Kaz. And then a scream, Juan's voice. So Juan was also still alive. Although to judge from the sound, maybe he didn't want to be.

Frank rolled so he could see the cabin door, which was open. Somebody was coming out, backward; it was one of the big guys, Holman, carrying somebody by the feet. Juan. Kaz came out next, holding Juan's shoulders and arguing with Tark, behind him.

Juan wasn't moving. His hands and feet were bound, and his face was covered with blood. Something else was wrong with his face, but there wasn't much light and Frank couldn't see exactly what. Kaz and Holman dumped him on the deck.

". . . get it over with," Kaz was saying. "We don't got time for this shit."

"We'll be there in time," said Tark, his voice raspy from the hit he'd taken to his throat. "Rebar can run the boat. I want to take care of this."

He crouched next to Frank, peered into his face. He had his knife in his hand.

"Well, well," he said. "Looks like the big boss is awake. You want to give me some orders now, big boss?" Casually, he tapped his knife blade against Frank's face. Frank started to talk, but his mouth was full again. He turned his face sideways and spat out more blood.

"That's a nasty cut you got in there," said Tark. "You oughtta have that looked at."

Frank tried to say "You're making a mistake," but his tongue had swollen, and his words were unintelligible.

"What's that, boss?" said Tark, cupping his hand to his ear. "I'm not following you."

Frank turned sideways and spat out more blood. He tried to speak again but was stopped by the feel of Tark's knifepoint against his throat.

"You know what, boss?" said Tark. "I'm not in the mood to listen to you right now, after the way you and the spic here puked all over my boat. It's a mess in there, you know that? It stinks bad. Makes me want to hold my nose. But I can't, you know why?"

Frank stared at him. Tark prodded his neck with the knife.

"I said you know why I can't hold my nose?" Tark said. Frank shook his head.

"I can't hold my nose 'cause"—Tark smiled a big, happy smile—"I'm holding the *spic's* nose."

Then he thrust it at Frank, a bloody lump of flesh. Frank jerked his head away, banging it against the gunwale. Tark pushed the grotesque thing into his face. Frank could feel it pressing against his own nose.

"Get it?" Tark said. "I'm holding his nose!"

"Come on, man," said Kaz. "Let's finish this, OK?"

"Relax," said Tark, over his shoulder. "Problem with you is, you're always in a damn hurry. You got to learn to stop and smell the fucking roses." To Frank, he said, "I got to hand it to your boy, he put up a pretty good fight, for a sick little spic, one against four. That boy did *not* want the plastic surgery."

Frank tried to talk again but could only spit blood.

"That's a bad cut, all right," said Tark. "I'll take care of that for you in a minute. But first Dr. Tark needs to go tend to your boy. You hang on to this for me, OK?"

Tark tucked Juan's nose into Frank's breast pocket, then moved over to where Juan was lying. Juan was regaining consciousness, moaning. Tark grabbed his shoulders and shook him.

"Hey, spic," he said. "How you doing?" He examined the gaping wound in the middle of Juan's face. "You're *looking* a lot better, tell you that."

Juan's eyes opened, focused, looked at Tark with a mixture of agony and hate. He spat into Tark's face, a gob of bloody saliva.

Jesus, he's brave, thought Frank. *But stupid.*

Tark wiped off the spit with the back of his hand, taking his time, showing how calm he was, in control.

"I gotta hand it to you, spic," he said. "You got some balls." He looked at Frank. "Don't he got some balls, boss?"

Frank shook his head. He suspected where this was going, though he hoped he was wrong.

"Let's take a look," Tark said. "Let's see those spic balls a' yours."

He slid his knife blade under Juan's belt, sliced through it easily. It was a very sharp knife. Now Juan was realizing what was happening. He shook his mutilated head, spraying drops of blood from the place where his nose had been. He jerked his body sideways, pulling his hips away from the blade.

"Hold him down," said Tark, to Kaz.

"Man, can't we just . . ."

"I said hold him down," said Tark. "Holman, hold his legs."

"Jeez, Tark, I . . ."

"Hold his fucking legs."

They held him down, Juan struggling but weak from shock and blood loss, no match for the big men. Tark crouched over him, letting him see the knife. Frank tried to yell, but it came out as a gargling sound. Tark glanced over.

"I'll take care of you in just a minute, boss," he rasped, rubbing his neck. "I ain't forgot about you." He turned back and began slicing through Juan's pants, then his underpants, those ridiculous black mesh briefs Juan wore, which Frank made fun of, but which Juan said his wife thought were sexy, and so did both his girlfriends. Juan was writhing desperately now, shouting something in

Spanish, the only word Frank understood being *madre*. Frank turned away and tried not to hear, but there was no way not to hear, as the shouts turned into a scream, and then the scream turned into something much, much worse.

AT THE MIAMI COAST GUARD STATION, THE commander and the lieutenant commander, who also happened to be fishing buddies, were in the officers' break room, getting coffee.

"So far," the commander was saying, "it's amazingly quiet, knock on Formica. Biggest excitement was this afternoon, when we had a couple of hardy mariners who thought this would be a good time to try to go over to Bimini in a twenty-three-foot Donzi."

"You're kidding," said the lieutenant commander.

"It gets better. They had no radio, no navigational equipment, and no life preservers. They did, however, have the foresight to take along two cases of Miller Lite."

"You can't be too careful. So what happened?"

"Using their seamanship skills, they got approximately five-hundred yards off Government Cut, at which point they experienced serious maritime distress and shot off every flare they had, in the process setting fire to their boat. We rescued them, but the Donzi sank."

"I bet we get sued," said the lieutenant commander.

"I have no doubt," said the first. "I mean, they did lose their beer. But other than that, it's actually been pretty quiet."

"What about that casino ship?"

"The *Extravaganza*."

"Yeah. I'm surprised he went out. Did we think about ordering him in?"

"We've been in contact. He says he's fine."

"Do we believe him? I mean, some of those guys,

they'd stay out in a hurricane if they were making money."

"Well, I'm not one-hundred-percent sure we believe him, but we do have reason to believe the ship is OK."

"What do you mean by that?"

"I mean that ship happens to have a CGIS agent on it." CGIS meant Coast Guard Investigative Service.

"Really."

"Yup. Civilian, undercover."

"And that's in connection with?"

"Officially, I have no idea."

"Our little friends at the Chum Bucket?"

"Like I say, I have no idea. It's pure coincidence that I'm nodding my head in an affirmative manner."

"And this agent is in contact with us?"

"Only if there's a problem."

"And so far?"

"Nothing."

They sipped their coffee for a moment, watching the TV on the end of the break-room counter. On the screen, an older male anchor and a younger female anchor were looking grim. Above their heads, to the right, were pictures of two men, bordered in black, with red letters below the border spelling out NEWSPLEX NINE TRAGEDY.

". . . had only been with NewsPlex Nine for six weeks," the male anchor was saying, "yet Todd Ford had already established himself as a reporter to watch." He turned toward the female anchor.

"Bill," she said, "Todd Ford was the kind of newsman who was not about to let personal risk stand in the way of getting the story for our NewsPlex Nine viewers." She turned toward the male anchor.

"Already," he said, "tributes are starting to pour into the NewsPlex Nine Newscenter as the South Florida community remembers these two courageous journalists."

"What are they talking about?" said the commander.

"You didn't hear?" said the lieutenant commander. "These two TV guys, they're doing a story about somebody getting electrocuted by a power line down in floodwater. So they go out and stand in the water, warning everybody not to stand in the water. And guess what?"

"Tell me you're joking."

"Nope."

"When'd this happen?"

"Maybe a half hour ago."

"And they already have a *graphic* for it?"

The TV screen was now showing a whirling red blob that turned into NEWSPLEX NINE BREAKING STORM NEWS BULLETIN. The male anchor was saying, ". . . just received word that the NewsPlex Nine NewsChopper is now en route to the scene."

"They're sending a *helicopter* up?" said the commander. "In *this*?"

"Got to keep the public informed," said the lieutenant commander.

"If I was the public," said the commander, "I'd be nervous."

"HOW LONG NOW?" SAID FIRST OFFICER HANK Wilde.

"About fifteen minutes," said Captain Eddie Smith.

"OK, then," said Wilde, taking a sip of Jack Daniel's. "Time to mobilize the crew."

"Let's try and do this as fast as possible, OK?" said Eddie.

"Relax," said Wilde. "It's gonna be fine. It's always fine."

"We never did it in this kind of weather before."

"That's not gonna be a problem."

"How in the hell can you say that?"

"Because," said Wilde, holding up his foam cup, "I have been drinking."

"TWO BUD LIGHTS, ONE HEINEKEN, ONE BOURBON rocks, one Stoli diet Coke," said Fay.

"Stoli and diet Coke?" said Joe Sarmino.

"That's what the lady said," said Fay.

"OK," said Joe, picking up the Stolichnaya bottle. It did not actually contain Stolichnaya vodka; it contained a vodka called Wolf Dog, which was made in Dayton, Ohio, and which the *Extravaganza* purchased in ten-gallon plastic jugs. All the other vodka bottles displayed on the bar— Finlandia, Absolut, Smirnoff, etc.—were also filled with Wolf Dog. It had been the experience of the *Extravaganza* management that, although the customers often specified premium brands, most of them could not tell the difference, especially in mixed drinks, between Stolichnaya and Vick's VapoRub.

On the TV screen, a man was broadcasting from a helicopter. Above him and to the right were big red letters that said NEWSPLEX NINE NEWSCHOPPER HELICAM. He was gesturing out of an open hatchway, pointing toward a scene below him, a residential neighborhood flooded with dark water, a half-dozen police and fire-rescue vehicles down there with their lights flashing. The image was bouncing around.

"What's going on?" said Fay, pointing to the TV.

"I think maybe somebody got hurt," said Joe, putting drinks on her tray. "I wasn't watching too close."

The reporter in the helicopter was saying, ". . . can see, these gusting winds are making it very difficult."

"I'm surprised a helicopter can even fly in this," said Fay.

"Must be a big story," said Joe.

Now there was a little window on the lower left of the screen, showing the male and female anchors.

"Clark," the male anchor said, "can you see from there exactly where the downed lines are?"

"Bill, I . . . hold it," said the reporter. The helicopter appeared to be gyrating wildly now, the hatchway behind the man showing sky, then ground, then sky. The reporter appeared to be grabbing for something, then he disappeared from sight. A muffled voice said *shit*.

"Did somebody just say 'shit'?" said Fay.

"Sound like," said Joe.

"Clark?" said the male anchor.

On the screen, there was more gyrating, then, suddenly, blackness.

The female anchor said, "We seem to be having some technical problems with that live feed."

The male anchor said, "We'll be right back."

"They're busy tonight," said Fay.

"Lotta news happening," said Joe, putting the drinks on Fay's tray. "Here you go. Stoli and diet Coke, man."

"Thanks, Joe," said Fay. "Listen, after I deliver these, I'm gonna duck outside and call my mother, so if Manny asks where I am, tell him I went to the ladies' room, OK?"

"OK, but I don't think we see Manny for a while."

"Why not?"

"You feel that?" said Joe, pointing toward the floor. "We slowing down."

Fay listened for a moment, then said, "Why?"

"I don't know, but sometimes the boat slows down out here, and when that happens, Manny goes to down there in the back with some guys, and you don't see him again for a while."

"Why? What's going on?"

"I don't know," said Joe. "I don't want to know. On this boat, the less you know, the better."

* * *

ON THE FIRST DECK, THE *ABUELAS* WERE IN THEIR usual corner, punching the PLAY buttons on their usual quarter slot machines, complaining in Spanish about their usual bad luck.

Ni agua, they were saying, mantralike. *Not even water.* But their poor return on investment did not keep them from shoving more quarters into the slots. They did not notice that the boat was slowing, and they barely glanced up as Conrad Conch passed by, a mass of shuffling pinkness, heading toward the stern.

Nine

THE INSTANT THAT JOHNNY AND THE CONTUSIONS stopped playing, Connie, the grieving divorcée, reappeared, and before the other band members had put their amps on STANDBY, she and Jock were in a full-body clamp, mouths locked, with major tongue penetration.

"Hey, Jock," said Ted, to Jock's back. "Your wife asked me to remind you to pick up some Pampers on the way home."

"For the baby," said Wally.

"He means the babies," corrected Ted. "The three little babies you have at home, with your wife."

"Who you're married to," said Wally.

Jock unlocked his mouth from Connie's and said to her, "They're just messing with you. I don't have kids."

"I don't give a shit," said Connie, locking back on.

"So," Ted said to Wally, "Johnny and me were gonna go out on deck and try to identify constellations in the subtropical sky."

"I'll catch up with you," said Wally. "I'm going downstairs for a little while."

"Really?" said Ted. "What's downstairs?"

"Nobody," said Wally.

"With the legs," said Ted. "Good luck with *that*. How much time you figure we have?"

Wally looked at his watch. The band was supposed to take a fifteen-minute break. "You think we can get away with a half hour?" he said.

"Fine by me," said Ted. "Question is, can Jock *survive* a half hour?"

Jock unlocked. "I'll be fine," he said.

"You'll be fine more than once," said Connie.

"We'll be in the kitchen," said Jock, heading toward the buffet area, his right hand on Connie's butt, her left hand on his.

"They make a nice couple," said Ted.

"A lot in common," said Wally.

"He's gonna do her in Emeril's *kitchen*?" said Johnny.

"That's Jock," said Wally. "Always with the romantic gesture."

"Nothing says true love," said Wally, "like getting nailed on a stainless-steel counter."

"Twice," said Ted. "In a half hour."

"I bet there's roaches in there the size of raccoons," said Johnny.

"They'll just have to wait their turn," said Wally. "Jock is only human."

"Sometimes I wonder," said Ted. "Anyway, we'll catch you later."

"Don't get blown off the ship," said Wally. "Or, if you do, leave the car keys."

"Seems to me," said Ted, "you're the one who's gonna get blown off."

* * *

ON THE FIRST DECK, MARA PURVIS WAS AT-tempting to explain a point of etiquette to the three dudes wearing ball caps backward.

"What you need to understand," she was saying, "is that just because you buy a Bud Light from a person, that doesn't mean you can grab that person's ass. Even when you give the person four dollars and say keep the change, which is a tip of a whole fifty cents, that is not the same thing as an agreement between you and me that you have purchased the right to touch any portion of my body, OK?"

"We were just having some fun," said the first dude.

"But it's not fun for *me*," said Mara. "Don't you get that?"

"Get what?" said the dude.

Mara sighed. "Let me ask you something," she said. "Do you have a sister?"

"Yeah," said the dude.

"Would you want one of these guys grabbing *her* ass?" said Mara.

"I grab his sister's ass all the time," said the second dude, who then dodged a punch from the first dude.

"His sister is a ho," said the third dude, dodging a second punch.

"But seriously," said Mara. "You get my point, right?"

"Yeah," said the first dude.

"Then tell me what it is," said Mara.

"If I want to touch your ass," said the first dude, "I need to give you a bigger tip." All three dudes cracked up.

"Jesus," said Mara, shaking her head.

Arnie walked up, trailed by Phil. "Hey there, gorgeous," he said. "These ruffians giving you any trouble?"

"Not really," said Mara. "They're just young and stupid.

Some day they'll be older. Although probably just as stupid."

"If we're so stupid, and you're so smart," said the third dude, "how come we're college students, and you're a cocktail waitress?"

"College students," said Arnie. "Now THAT'S an achievement. They only let in, what, seventy-eight million people a year?"

"What's this got to do with you, Pops?" said the first dude.

"I ain't your pop," said Arnie. To Phil, he said, "How come everybody thinks I'm their pop?"

"You got a paternal way about you," said Phil.

"We'll catch you later, sweets," said the first dude, to Mara. "When we need more beer." He faked a grab at Mara's butt, and she flinched.

The dudes drifted off, laughing. Mara watched them for a moment, shook her head, said, "What am I *doing* here?"

"Hey," said Arnie, touching her shoulder, "you're not taking those idiots seriously, are you?"

"No," said Mara. "I'm just, I think maybe I'm getting too old for this, you know? Night after night."

"Hey," said Arnie, "you're not old."

"Trust us," said Phil. "We know from old."

"You got your whole life ahead of you," said Arnie.

"I know," said Mara. "That's the problem. I mean, I look ahead at my whole life, and all I see is more nights like this, and more idiots like that." She patted Arnie's hand. "Anyway, thanks for the rescue, but I got to get back to work. You guys need anything?"

"No, thanks. We're heading outside, get some air. Getting smoky in here."

"It's blowing pretty hard out there," said Mara.

"We're going out the back of the boat," said Arnie. "Out of the wind."

"That's supposed to be crew only back there," said Mara. "They don't even let us go back there. Manny's real strict about that."

"So if he sees us, he'll tell us to leave," said Arnie. "That's the beauty of being an old fart. We go wherever we want, but nobody ever gets mad. They just figure we're senile."

"Which we are," said Phil.

"Speak for yourself," said Arnie. "I have all my faculties."

"You *have* them," said Phil, "but you don't always bring them *with* you."

"Anyway," said Mara, "be careful out there."

She headed back into the crowd for more drink orders. Arnie and Phil headed toward the stern. They paused by the first-deck bar to look up at the TV set, which showed a male announcer and a female announcer, both looking grim. In the upper right-hand corner of the screen were large red letters spelling out the words KILLER STORM DEATH TOLL MOUNTS, and under that, NEWSCHOPPER NINE CRASHES WITH 3 ABOARD.

". . . apparent death toll raised to six in this killer storm," the male was saying, "as, incredibly, the lives of three more members of the NewsPlex Nine news family apparently were claimed just minutes ago in a tragic helicopter crash in Westchester." He looked at the female anchor.

"We have dispatched the NewsPlex Nine Satellite NewsVan to the scene," she said, "and we hope to have a live report from there shortly." She looked at the male anchor.

"Already," he said, "tributes have begun flowing in to the NewsPlex Nine NewsCenter in memory of these three courageous . . ."

"Are they saying six people are *dead*?" said Phil.

"Sounded like that," said Arnie.

"Six people dead in this storm," said Phil, "and I let you get me out on a boat."

"Don't be an old lady," said Arnie. "This is a big boat here, run by professionals. They wouldn't leave the dock if it wasn't safe. You see anybody dying out here?"

"Not yet," said Phil.

FRANK LAY ON HIS SIDE WITH HIS FACE TOWARD the gunwale, keeping his mouth open so the blood could flow out. It felt like the bleeding was worse now. He wondered how much longer he could keep losing blood at this rate. Although currently that was not his biggest concern. His biggest concern was what Tark was going to do to him. He understood now that Tark wasn't keeping him alive for any rational purpose, something that might give Frank a tactical chance, a bargaining lever. No, Tark was keeping him alive because Tark was a psycho dirtbag who enjoyed hurting people. He had taken his time doing whatever he did to Juan, Kaz telling him hurry up, man, get it *over* with, Tark answering relax, we got plenty of time, then resuming his knife work, humming along to Juan's agony, sometimes whistling.

Whistling.

Juan had still been alive when they heaved him over the side. Even in the noise of the storm, Frank could hear him moaning. Then the splash. Frank hoped for his friend's sake that he would die quickly.

That had been a few minutes ago. Frank thought he'd heard somebody go back into the cabin, but he wasn't sure; he couldn't tell if Tark was still out here, behind him. And he didn't want to roll over and look. He hated to admit it, but he was *afraid* to look. He felt like a child, pretending that if he held still and closed his eyes, the monster wouldn't see him.

More minutes went by. Frank still heard nobody behind him. He began to feel a tiny tickling of hope. It had to be time for the rendezvous. That would keep Tark busy. Obviously, Tark was planning some kind of ambush, but maybe somebody on the ship would notice something wrong. Maybe somebody would see Frank lying here. Maybe they'd be ready for whatever Tark was planning to do. Maybe they'd rescue Frank. Maybe . . .

"Hey there, Chief," said Tark's rasping voice, right in his ear. "Bet you thought I forgot about you, huh?"

FAY UNLOADED HER DRINKS, COLLECTED HER money, pretended not to see a couple of customers waving her over, looked around for Manny, and started for the port door to the outside second deck. She was almost there when she was intercepted by Wally, who was pretending that he just happened to spontaneously be in the area.

"Oh, hey there," he said, in an unnaturally perky voice.

"Hi," said Fay. "I'm just on my way out to . . ."

"Lovely weather, huh?" he said. He sounded to Fay as though he were reading a script.

She said, "Yeah, well, I don't mean to be rude, but . . ."

"I thought I saw Leonardo da Vinci," said Wally.

"What?" said Fay.

"*DiCaprio,* I mean," said Wally. "Leonardo *DiCaprio.*" Sweat beads were popping out on his upper lip.

"Leonardo DiCaprio?" said Fay.

"From the *Titanic,*" said Wally. "Leonardo DiCaprio. So I don't want to make you nervous. Ha ha!" He wiped his lip with his sleeve.

"Listen," said Fay. "I'm going to walk away now, and you're going to stay right here, OK?"

"OK," said Wally. "I just meant, the weather . . ."

"I have to go now," said Fay, going.

Wally watched her until she was through the door, then he turned and began slowly and methodically banging his forehead against the front of a slot machine. A large woman, a veteran slots player holding a plastic cup of quarters, paused on her way to the ladies' room and watched Wally for a moment. Then she put her hand on his shoulder and said, "Honey, I know *exactly* how you feel."

AT THE STERN OF THE *EXTRAVAGANZA*, MANNY Arquero, Hank Wilde, and four other men stood on the deck above a platform that jutted out from the ship, just above the water, illuminated by two bluish lights mounted flush on the ship's hull. Arquero was holding an AK-47 set on full automatic. Wilde was holding a cell phone. Stacked behind them were twenty-two extra-large black polyester duffel bags, each one jammed with cash.

"There he is," said Arquero.

Wilde peered through the rain and saw the pale shape of the fishing boat, its lights out, moving slowly toward the ship. He speed-dialed a number on his cell phone.

Lou Tarant answered immediately.

"What," he said.

"We're bringing home Chinese food tonight," said Wilde.

"OK, good," said Tarant. "Before you hang up, you seen the guy that owns the restaurant?"

"The guy that *owns* it?"

"Yeah. Is he there? At the restaurant?"

"Nope. Least not as far as I know."

"Well, keep an eye out, and let me know if you see him, OK? Because I want to talk to him right away. I don't want him to go nowhere 'til I talk to him, understand?"

"OK," said Wilde, but Tarant had hung up. Wilde turned to Arquero.

"You seen Bobby Kemp tonight?" he said.

"No," said Arquero. "He don't come on the ship much. Why?"

"Lou is looking for him. Says he wants to talk to him right away. Says don't let him go nowhere."

"That don't sound too good for Bobby," said Arquero, smiling.

The fishing boat was close now, coming into the shelter of the massive bulk of the *Extravaganza,* which was pointing straight into the wind, not moving on its own power, just drifting with the Gulf Stream. The fishing boat began to turn, getting ready to back in and raft up with its stern against the ship. Arquero unclipped a two-way radio from his belt and held it to his lips.

"Captain," he said.

"Right here," said the voice of Eddie Smith.

"It's time," said Arquero. "Hold it steady."

"OK, lemme know when you're done."

"This won't take long," said Arquero.

Ten

ON THE TOP DECK, JOHNNY AND TED HUDDLED
behind a stack of rubber lifeboats, Johnny holding in a
lungful of smoke, Ted examining the minuscule roach to
see if there was any hope for it.

"OK," said Johnny, exhaling, "here's my point."

"What?" said Ted. He popped the roach into his mouth.

"They're in Hawaii, right?" said Johnny.

Ted swallowed, then said, "Who is?"

"The infomercial people," said Johnny. "Who don't live
in the refrigerator cartons."

"You're still thinking about *that*?"

"I just want to explain my point, which is, some of them
might be there already."

"Be where?"

"In Hawaii."

"Of course they're in Hawaii. Nobody said they weren't
in Hawaii. The whole *point* is, if you sell real estate, you
can go to Hawaii and party with the infomercial guy."

"But my point is, they might be there *already.*"

"Who?"

"The Hawaiians."

"What about them?"

"They're already there. In Hawaii."

"So your point is, there's Hawaiians in Hawaii? That's your point?"

Johnny sighed, fished in his jacket pocket, pulled out another joint, lit it, took a deep hit, passed it to Ted, exhaled.

"OK, listen," he said. "Try to follow me here, and don't interrupt all the time, OK? What I'm saying, there *could* be—I'm not saying I *know,* I'm just saying *could* be—some Hawaiians who were already in Hawaii when the infomercial guy got there, and so the infomercial guy has them come on the infomercial, and he saves on his hotel bill."

"Why would he save on his hotel bill?"

"Not the infomercial guy's hotel bill. The *Hawaiians'* hotel bill."

"Why would the Hawaiians have a hotel bill?"

"They *wouldn't* have a hotel bill. That's my *point.*"

"Why not?"

"Because they *live* there."

"They live in the hotel?"

"No, they live in Hawaii. That's why they're *Hawaiians,* for Chrissakes."

"I *know* that. We *established* that. Hawaiians live in Hawaii. You keep saying that like it's E equals M-I-T fucking squared. We *agree* on that, OK? Hawaiians live in Hawaii. No duh. What's your *point*?"

Johnny took the joint back, took a hit, looked at Ted for a few moments.

"OK," he said, finally. "What I'm saying is, when the infomercial guy decides to go to Hawaii, it's *possible,* I'm not saying I know for sure, but it's *possible* there were some Hawaiians who were already *in* Hawaii, and the . . ."

"Hold it," said Ted, holding up a hand. "Let's finish this in the back of the boat, OK? I'm getting wet here."

"You're not supposed to go back there," said Johnny. "That's crew only. Manny saw me and Wally coming outta there one night and he got really pissed."

"Yeah, well, Manny's not gonna be out here tonight," said Ted. "You coming?"

"OK," said Johnny. "But you need to listen to the point I'm making, and not interrupt all the time, OK?"

"We might need another joint," said Ted.

BREATHE THROUGH YOUR NOSE, FRANK TOLD himself. *Breathe through your nose.* He felt panic again seeping into his brain, as he felt blood again seeping into his mouth. *Swallow,* he told himself. *Swallow it. Now breathe through your nose. . . .*

Frank had expected Tark to cut him. He had felt Tark crouching over him, had waited for the feel of the blade, wondering where it would come, eyes closed, body clenched, waiting . . .

"You think I'm gonna cut you, Chief?" Tark had said. "Like I cut your friend?" Frank had felt the tip of the knife touch his left eyelid, just touching it. *Not my eyes Jesus not my eyes nononono . . .*

A bit more pressure now, the blade point digging into the thin eyelid skin just a little . . .

Nonononono . . .

And then a raspy laugh, and the knife point had pulled away, and Tark had said, "Don't worry, Chief, I ain't gonna cut you. In fact, I'm gonna stop that bleeding."

Frank had heard the sound then, a familiar, mundane sound: duct tape being ripped off a roll. Then he'd felt the tape across his mouth, Tark wrapping it around his head, then around again, then again, making a tight seal. Immediately, Frank had felt the blood backing up in his mouth. He'd begun to choke, to thrash, but he couldn't spit out the blood, couldn't reach the tape, couldn't do anything.

He'd heard Tark's voice again, rasping in his ear: "Best thing for you to do, Chief? Swallow that blood. That'll work for a while, anyways. How long you think a man can swallow his own blood, Chief? How about we find out?"

And that's what Frank was doing, forcing himself to swallow his blood, to breathe, to swallow again, keeping alive another minute, then another.

He felt the fishing boat slowing now. He rolled onto his back, looked up and saw, through the rainy gloom, the gaudy neon lights of the upper deck of the *Extravaganza*. He felt a momentary surge of hope. Then he felt himself choking again.

Swallow.

ON THE STARBOARD SIDE OF THE *EXTRAVAGANZA*, on the second deck, outside, Fay was on the cell phone, talking to her mother.

"She won't go to sleep, and I don't know what she wants," her mother was saying. Estelle was crying in the background. "She's saying something over and over, but I don't know what it is."

"Can I talk to her?" said Fay.

"Do you want to talk to your mommy, Estelle?" Fay's mom said.

"No!" shouted Estelle. "Namenowhy! Namenowhy!"

"She just keeps shouting that and crying," said Fay's mother. "She's giving me a headache."

"She's saying her name is Snow White," said Fay. "She wants you to call her Snow White."

"Why?"

"She's pretending. Sometimes she pretends she's Snow White, and you have to call her that, or she gets upset."

"Well, it's driving me crazy. And she wouldn't eat anything tonight."

"Did you give her that kiddy alphabet soup, in the microwave?"

"I looked at that, and it's all chemicals in there. I don't think she should be eating that. I tried to give her some nice fish, but she won't eat it. You want some nice fish, Estelle?"

"Namenowhy! Namenowhy!"

"Mom, just call her Snow White, OK?"

"OK, Snow White, you want some nice fish?"

"No!"

"She doesn't want any."

"Mom, she hates fish."

"Fish is good for her."

"Yes, but she won't *eat* it."

"You don't want a nice piece of fish, Estelle?"

"Namenowhy!"

"She's giving me a headache."

"Mom, just please for Godsakes *call her Snow White, OK?*"

"You don't have to take that tone with me."

"I'm sorry, Mom. You're right. It's just that . . ."

"By this hour, your sister's children are asleep."

"Mom, I really don't see what good it does for . . ."

"Just a minute. Don't put that in your mouth, Estelle."

"NAMENOWHY!"

"Fay, you're going to have to call back, because now she's . . .

"NAMENOWHY!NAMENOWHY!NAMENOWHY!"

"Mom, please, just . . ."

But her mom had hung up. Fay started to press REDIAL,

then decided to first walk around to the stern of the ship, out of the wind. She found her path by a low, locked gate, with a sign on it reading CREW ONLY NO ADMITTANCE AT ANY TIME. She looked around, and seeing nobody—Who would be outside in this weather?—she stepped over the gate.

THIS WAS HOW IT WAS SUPPOSED TO HAPPEN:

The fishing boat would raft up to the *Extravaganza,* stern to stern. The men on the fishing boat would form a chain and haul heavy black polyester bags containing product out of the specially made storage compartment in the hull. They would heave these over the transom, onto the platform on the back of the *Extravaganza,* where they were grabbed by the ship's crew. The ship's crew would then heave the bags of cash over the transom onto the fishing boat. Arquero would oversee the operation, holding his AK-47 with the safety off. His policy, understood by everyone involved, was that if he saw any person do anything that he considered suspicious, that person was hamburger. When the transfer was complete, the fishing boat would cast off and get the hell out of there, and Hank Wilde would call Lou Tarant to tell him the Chinese food had been delivered. In good weather, the whole process took about twenty minutes, during which, depending on market conditions, somewhere between $50 million and $100 million worth of money and narcotics changed hands.

That was how it was supposed to happen.

Of course, tonight the weather was bad. That was one difference. Another one was that usually Frank and Juan were standing at the back of the fishing boat with the three Bahamian guys. Tonight, as the boat backed toward the *Extravaganza,* Arquero and Wilde both noted that there was only one man standing in the back of the boat, and it was Tark, the guy who usually drove the boat. He was at the stern on the starboard side, holding a big coil of rope in his right hand.

When the boat was about ten yards off, Arquero shouted, "WHERE'S FRANK?"

"INSIDE, PUKIN'," Tark shouted back. His voice was strained, raspy. "HE'S NOT DOIN' TOO GOOD."

That sounded plausible to Wilde, who didn't feel so great himself. It almost sounded plausible to Arquero, for a second or two. But then it struck him: If *he* were puking sick, he wouldn't be inside the pitching boat. He'd be outside, hanging over the rail. So why wasn't Frank? And where were the Bahamians?

The fishing boat was now just a few yards away. Tark drew back the coil of rope, getting ready to toss it. One of the *Extravaganza* crew guys moved forward, getting ready to catch it.

Arquero raised the barrel of the AK-47 and shouted, "Hold it!"

"Hey, man," said Tark, holding up his left hand, "what's your problem?"

"Stop the boat NOW," said Arquero.

Tark turned and shouted "Hold up!" toward the bridge of the fishing boat, but to Arquero's eye there was something wrong with the way Tark was standing, the way he'd raised only his left hand, the way he was holding the coil of rope in his right. To Manny Arquero, these things, combined with the fact that he had never liked this scrawny redneck prick anyway, were enough to justify conviction and execution. He put the AK-47 to his shoulder and in that instant knew he'd made the right decision, because now Tark had dropped the rope coil, and Arquero saw that it had been concealing a gun. Arquero also knew that he was going to win this one, because Tark had to bring the barrel up, which meant Arquero had time to aim and squeeze the trigger nice and easy, the way they teach you, which is what he was just about to do, when the first bullet made a small hole in his back and exited, much less neatly, through the front of his chest. The second and third bullets weren't really necessary, as Arquero was already going down, and there was no way for him to get any deader than he was about to be anyway.

The four members of the ship crew had absolutely no chance. Before Arquero landed facedown on the platform, Tark opened fire with his gun, a TEC-9 semiautomatic with a 50-shot magazine, an effective weapon used in countless drug-related slayings. Tark started with the two crewmen to his left, the ones farthest away, taking them with two shots apiece, *pop-pop, pop-pop,* easy targets, as neither had time to move. As Tark shot the second crewman, he heard, to his right, a *pop-pop-pop-pop-pop-pop,* which told him that Kaz, who'd been crouched behind the transom on the port side, was up and firing at the other two crewmen, both turning to escape the platform, neither getting more than a step.

This left only Hank Wilde, whose alcohol-fogged mind had reacted less quickly to the eruption of carnage, still only a few seconds old. As the two bullets, one from Tark's gun, one from Kaz's, struck Wilde virtually simultaneously, he was still staring in bafflement at the back of the platform, at the shooter who'd appeared from the ship and gunned down Manny Arquero from behind, and who was still standing there, still clasping a pistol in both of his hands.

His very big, very pink, hands.

Eleven

"THIS IS BAD, MAN," WHISPERED JOHNNY. "THIS is *bad*."

"Oh man," whispered Ted. "Oh *man*."

They were crouched on a dark catwalk at the stern of the *Extravaganza,* starboard side, second-deck level, over-looking the stern platform. They had just lit a joint when they saw the fishing boat backing toward the ship. They had seen Manny Arquero holding a gun and heard him shouting something to the man in the back of the boat. They had heard the man shouting something back. They had seen Manny aiming his gun, and then they'd seen the shell—the *shell*—appear and *pop-pop-pop* shoot Arquero in the back. Then suddenly there'd been two guys in the boat shooting, and in a few seconds there were six bodies down.

Now the fishing boat was tying up, and the shooters were climbing onto the *Extravaganza* platform. For the first time in his entire life, Johnny dropped a perfectly good joint.

"Jesus," he said, "they're coming on the *ship*. What are we gonna *do*?"

"Oh man," whispered Ted. "Oh man."

"Ted," whispered Johnny, "we have to *do* something."

"OK," whispered Ted, fighting to clear the pot fumes from his brain. "OK, listen. We have to tell somebody."

"Who? We can't tell Manny. Manny is *dead,* man."

"I *see* that. You think I don't see that? Lemme think."

"We should tell the captain."

"Shut up and let me think, OK?"

"OK," whispered Johnny.

Ted thought for a moment.

"OK," he whispered. "Here's what we need to do."

"What?" whispered Johnny.

"We need to tell the captain," whispered Ted.

"I just *said* that," whispered Johnny.

"When?"

"Just *now.* I said, 'We should tell the captain.'"

"All right, Jesus, whatever, let's just *go*," whispered Ted.

"All right," whispered Johnny. "But you got to learn how to listen."

FAY SAW IT, TOO. SHE WAS ON THE SAME CAT-walk as Johnny and Ted, but on the port side. She had just come around the corner, out of the wind, and was about to call her mother again when she'd seen the fishing boat, seen Manny Arquero, seen Conrad Conch, seen the shootings. Before the guns had stopped firing, she was pressing buttons on her cell phone, holding it to her ear.

Beepbeepbeepbeepbeep.

"Shit," Fay whispered.

She backed around the corner, out of sight of the platform, held the phone up to catch the light from a porthole. The phone screen said NO SERVICE.

"*Shit.*"

Fay peeked around the corner. The fishing boat was tying up to the *Extravaganza,* the gunmen getting ready to board. Fay turned and ran, heading for the bow, for the stairway to the bridge.

ARNIE AND PHIL SAW IT, TOO, OR MOST OF IT. They'd gone down a stairway at the stern, past a sign that said CREW ONLY KEEP OUT. At the bottom, they'd followed a corridor to the left, which took them to another stairway. They followed that down, went out a doorway, and found themselves on a small recessed deck, mostly filled with a large inflatable dinghy, suspended from davits, with an outboard motor. Just below this recessed deck was the starboard end of the stern platform. Arnie and Phil could hear men talking out there, so they stayed back, behind the dinghy. There was a stack of life vests there; Arnie had seated himself on it.

"Perfect," he'd said. "You got comfortable seating, fresh air, a view of the ocean; what else could a man want?"

"He could want to be on land," said Phil. "With the sane people."

"Stop your bellyaching," said Arnie. "Tomorrow you'll say to me, 'Arnie, that was another great idea you had, going out.' "

"If we see tomorrow," said Phil. "I'm looking at those waves out there, and . . . What the hell is that?"

"What the hell is what?"

"We got another boat coming up here. Backward."

"What the hell are you talking about?" said Arnie, getting up off the life vests and joining Phil, peering out from behind the lifeboat. "Christ, look, there's that shell that we . . . Christ, what is he . . ."

That was when they saw Conrad Conch open fire. As soon as they heard more gunshots, they were on their way out of there, moving stiffly but at a higher velocity than either man had achieved since the Reagan administration.

THE INSTANT THE FISHING BOAT TOUCHED THE bumpers hanging from the *Extravaganza* stern, Tark, TEC-9 in hand, was over the transom and catching a line tossed by Kaz. Tark cleated the line down, then quickly caught and cleated another.

Conrad Conch was waddling toward him, gesturing with the pistol in his big pink right hand and shouting something unintelligible through his mouth hole. Tark gave him a hold-it gesture, then pointed to Kaz, who was pointing his TEC-9 right at Conrad.

"Put down the gun gently," said Tark.

Conrad Conch set the gun down on the platform, stood up, started to shout and gesture again.

Tark pointed his gun at Conrad and said, "Shut up."

Conrad shut up. Tark quickly went to each of the six bodies on the platform, checking for signs of life. Satisfied that there were none, he turned back toward the fishing boat and shouted, "OK."

Holman emerged from the cabin. In one hand, he carried a gym bag. In the other, he carried a gray metal case, rectangular, about the size of a desktop computer, with a carrying handle and an antenna on the top. He handed these to Tark, then climbed over the transom, onto the *Extravaganza*. Kaz followed him, also holding a gym bag, into which he was stuffing his TEC-9.

Tark pointed to the metal case. "Is it on?" he asked Holman.

"It's been on," said Holman, pointing to a small green light.

"Is it working?"

"Yup. I just checked it."

"And you made the call to Miami?"

"Yup."

"You got through?"

"Yup."

"OK, get going," said Tark. "Then get back here soon's you can and help move the shit."

Holman picked up the metal case and the gym bag. He and Kaz crossed the platform, climbed the port-side ladderway, and disappeared through the doorway into the ship.

Tark turned back to the fishing boat. Rebar had come down from the bridge and was standing at the stern.

"OK," Tark said to him, "you start moving them bags. I'll give you a hand soon's I finish with the shell." Rebar went over to the pile of duffel bags filled with cash, grabbed one off the top, dragged it to the edge of the platform, then went back for another bag.

Still holding his TEC-9, Tark walked over to Conrad Conch, who started shouting again through his mouth hole, obviously very pissed off.

"MMMWMF!" he said.

"I got no idea what you're saying," said Tark. "Take off the damn head."

Conrad reached his big pink hands up and stuck them into the area where his shoulders would be, if shells had shoulders. He gave an upward yank. There was the sound of Velcro fasteners letting go, and off came the big pink head, revealing the smaller, but almost as pink, face of an extremely unhappy Bobby Kemp.

Twelve

LOU TARANT, NOW WEARING BOXER SHORTS, SAT
on the sofa, looking at the TV but really just waiting for the
damn phone to ring. Dee Dee Holdscomb sat next to him,
wearing a purple silk bathrobe and studying her finger-
nails.

"Do you like this color?" she asked, holding her hands
out to Tarant, nails up. "It's like a peach, but with a little
more red in it."

Tarant looked at her.

"What do *I* give a shit?" he said, speaking for the entire
male gender.

"I was just asking," Dee Dee said.

On the TV, the NewsPlex Nine co-anchors were frowning so hard that it looked like their heads were going to im-
plode. Bright red letters in the upper-right-hand corner of
the screen said NEWSPLEX NINE KILLER STORM BULLETIN,
and under that, NEWSPLEX NINE NEWSVAN IN CRASH. The
male anchor was talking.

". . . just received the shocking news that the NewsPlex Nine NewsVan has apparently been involved in a collision on its way to cover the helicopter crash and electrocution deaths in Westchester," he said. He turned to the female anchor.

"Bill," she said to the camera, "from what we've been able to learn so far, the NewsPlex Nine NewsVan, which was carrying our reporter Summer Westfall and cameraman Javier Santiago, apparently collided with a fire rescue vehicle." She looked at him.

"Jill," he told the camera, "this comes as yet another shock to NewsPlex Nine, which, incredibly, has already lost five members of the NewsPlex Nine family to this killer storm, Hector, in a freakish string of mishaps." He looked at her.

"Bill," she said, "we want to assure our viewers that we will continue to keep you informed on these breaking developments, and have dispatched a second NewsPlex NewsVan to the scene."

"Morons," said Lou Tarant.

"Meanwhile," said the male anchor, "expressions of sympathy continue to pour in to the NewsPlex Nine . . ."

The phone rang. Tarant punched the MUTE button as he grabbed the phone.

"What," he said.

"Bad news," said Gene Shroder. "Our boy is on the ship."

"You sure?"

"Yeah. We got a tip."

"From who?"

"He wouldn't say. This guy calls me up, anonymous, got his caller ID blocked, won't say who he is. He tells me our boy went out on the ship tonight, and, get this, he was wearing the shell costume."

"What're you talking about?"

"That shell, from his restaurants, the conch shell, whatshisname, Conan Conch or whatever it is."

"He was *wearing* that?"

"That's what the guy said. So I call the ticket office, and they said, yeah, they got a call from our boy himself, personally, which he never does, saying the shell was going out tonight, and sure enough just before sailing time a limo comes up and the shell gets out and gets on the ship."

"Jesus."

"That's exactly what I said."

"So he's going to try to cut himself in on the exchange? Is that it? This little prick thinks he can fuck with *us*?"

"That's what it looks like. I mean, why else is he out there tonight, in a disguise?"

"All right, listen," said Tarant. "I want you to get Manny on the cell phone right now. I want you to tell him what this little prick is up to. Tell him to take care of it. Tell him I don't care if he wraps a chain around that little prick in his clam suit and throws him off the fucking ship, you understand me?"

"Um, Lou, here's the thing."

"What?"

"There's something messed up with the phones. We called Manny's cell, Eddie's cell, Hank's cell, all the cells we got on there, and we're not getting through to anybody."

"You mean they don't answer?"

"No. It just doesn't go through."

"I just got a call from Hank, his cell, couldn't be more'n fifteen minutes ago."

"I know, we were in contact earlier, too. But all of a sudden, nothing. Could be the storm, some problem with the phone company. We'll keep trying."

"*Shit*," said Tarant.

"Yeah," said Shroder.

Tarant thought for a moment.

"OK, listen," he said. "We need to get on the ship's radio and get hold of Eddie."

"OK, Lou, but everybody can hear the radio. The Coast Guard can be listening to that, the cops, the feds, anybody."

"I know that. You get Eddie on there, and you tell him . . . shit, you figure out some code way to tell him they need to grab the clam."

"It's a conch, Lou."

"I DON'T CARE WHAT THE FUCK IT IS, OK? I just want them to grab it, and warn Manny."

"OK," said Shroder, "I'll call the Chum Bucket and tell them to put me through on the radio. I'll figure out what to say to Eddie, like, watch out for the shellfish, something like that."

"Also," said Tarant, "I want you to tell Stu to get his boat ready, gas it up, and start the engine. And get some guys, the Wookie and that crew, and tell them to meet me at the Chum Bucket in fifteen minutes. Tell them SWAT weapons, OK?"

"You're going out there?"

"You're goddamn right I'm going out there."

"OK, Lou, but, weather like this, it's gonna take you a while to get to the rendezvous point. Plus, I think Stu's boat still has . . ."

"Set it up NOW."

"OK, Lou."

"I'm gonna *kill* that fucking clam."

BOBBY HEMP, PINK HEAD STICKING OUT OF CON-

rad Conch's pink body, waved his pink arms in pink fury.

"What are you *doing*?" he shouted at Tark. "Are you out of your *mind*?"

"Relax," said Tark. "It's gonna be fine."

"Fine? *Fine?* You killed all these other guys, you got your guys running into the ship instead of moving the bags, you're pointing your gun at ME, and I'm supposed to think it's *fine*?"

"Bobby," said Tark, raising his gun barrel, "you don't calm down, I'm gonna *calm* you down, understand?"

Kemp took a breath.

"OK," he said. "OK, I want to know what's going on here. We had a plan."

"We did," said Tark. He knew he was going to enjoy this, maybe even more than he had enjoyed cutting off Juan's nose. "We did have a plan. But now we got a new plan."

Kemp didn't like how that sounded.

"Tark, listen to me," he said. "We don't *need* a new plan. The old plan is working fine, OK? We got the money and we got the product. You didn't need to kill these other guys, but, OK, that's OK. Point is, we load these bags on the boat *now* and we get the hell out of here and go to Venezuela, like we planned, and you get a million dollars. You get a *million dollars,* Tark. You never work again."

"No," said Tark.

"What do you mean, no?"

"I mean that plan won't work."

"What do you mean it won't work? It's already *working.*"

"Bobby, you're a moron, you know that?"

"What're you talking about?"

"I'm talking about, you know the guys you're fucking with here? Whose money all this is? You know what they *do* to people who fuck with them?"

"But that's why we go to Venezuela, Tark. I *told* you. I got some people in the government down there working for me, Tark. *Way* up in the government. We got protection down there. *Nobody* can touch us."

DAVE BARRY

Tark shook his head.

"Bobby," he said, "I bet you need help scratching your own ass."

"What're you talking about?"

"I'm talking about, whatever juice you got with Venezuela, or anybody else, these guys got more. I'm talking about if you went to *Mars,* these guys could get to you. They'd have some Martian working for them, come and cut your balls off. If these guys want you, *you can't get away.* Why the fuck you think they let me carry all this product on this boat in the first place? 'Cause they *trust* me? No, Bobby, it's 'cause they know I know there's nowhere I could go with it they won't find me. If we take this shit to Venezuela, we're dead in two days."

"So what are you saying? You're saying we don't go to Venezuela?"

"That's right," said Tark.

"So what do we do?"

"Lemme explain it slow, so even your dumbass brain can understand it," said Tark. He was really enjoying himself now. "Number one, Lou's gonna know you hijacked his shipment."

"Wait a minute," said Kemp. "They don't even know for sure I'm out here."

"Course they do, Bobby. You think they're stupid as you are? One night, you disappear, same night, there's an ambush. You think they won't figure it out? Plus which, somebody called your friend Gene tonight, anonymous, and told him who's in the shell suit. Plus which, I got two guys heading up to the bridge right now. They're gonna disable the radios, so your captain don't send out any alarms. But they're also gonna let slip that they're working for you, and when he gets back he's gonna tell Lou. So they'll definitely know it's you, Bobby."

"They'll know it's you, too. It's your boat."

"That's true, Bobby. And they're gonna find my boat."

"What are you talking about?"

"I'm talking about, they're gonna find my boat. It has that emergency radio beacon deal that goes off when it hits the water. The Coast Guard'll find it, swamped, with a bunch of holes shot in it, but it won't go down because I got that unsinkable hull. They're gonna find a couple of bags of cash in my boat, and a couple bags of product. You know what else they're gonna find, Bobby?"

Kemp didn't answer.

"They're gonna find *you,* Bobby, in my boat, in your dumbass pink shell suit, all shot up."

"Wait, Tark, we . . ."

"Shut up and listen, Bobby. Best they'll be able to figure it, you set up the ambush out here, maybe working with me. You killed Manny, forced the ship crew to load the cash on my boat. Then when you're pulling away from the ship, a bigass gunfight breaks out, automatic weapons, maybe some kind of doublecross. No way to know what happened, 'cause everybody's shot or drowned. The Coast Guard doesn't give a shit, far as they're concerned it's all scumbags anyway. They get some bags of money, some dope to show on TV, they're happy. Lou and his boys, they're not as happy, because they know there was a LOT more product, a lot more cash. But what the fuck can they do? Looks like it floated away, sank in the storm. They blame you, Bobby, but you're already dead."

Tark paused here, smiling, pleased with the way this was going, the brilliance of his plan, the fact that Kemp was obviously terrified now.

"I know what you're wondering, Bobby," he said. "You're wondering, how does old Tark get out of here?"

"Look, just tell me . . ."

"I'm glad you asked, Bobby, 'cause that's the best part. See that Zodiac over there?" Tark gestured toward the inflatable boat in the recessed deck. "That's how, Bobby. It's a good boat, I've checked it when we been out here before. Won't be comfortable, but it'll get me back to the Bahamas. Course, the Coast Guard'll see that it's missing. But they're also gonna find some pieces of a Zodiac floating out here, same model, which I brought along. They're gonna figure when my boat got shot up, somebody, maybe me, launched the Zodiac, tried to get away, but he didn't make it. Lost at sea, Bobby. Everybody lost at sea. You see, Bobby? You see the kind of plan you can come up with when you got a fucking brain?"

Bobby Kemp figured he had one chance here.

"OK, Tark, please, listen to me. Forget one million. I'll give you three million. *Three million dollars,* Tark."

Tark was loving this.

"Bobby, you stupid little pink shit," he said. "I *got* three million. I got *ten* million. I got *all* of it, Bobby, except the little tip I'm leaving for the Coast Guard. I got the cash here, and I got the product stashed away back in the Bahamas where nobody'll find it. Nobody'll even *look* for me, 'cause I'll be dead. Just like you, Bobby." He raised his gun.

"Tark, man, please," said Kemp. "Let's work something out, man. I got other money, OK? You can have it, OK, Tark? *OK?* Just tell me what you want."

Tark said, "I want you to shut the fuck up," and he pulled the trigger.

ARNIE AND PHIL, ANCIENT HEARTS THUMPING from two sets of stairs, staggered into the first-floor casino and looked around for somebody to tell about the killings out back. The first vaguely official person they saw was Joe Sarmino, at his bartender post. They lurched over. Arnie put one hand on a barstool for support and used the other to gesture for Joe's attention.

"Cahhh," Arnie told him. "Cahhhhh." He had too little breath to get the rest of it out. He motioned for Phil to pick up the narrative.

"Cahhhhh," said Phil.

"You guys OK?" said Joe. "You need some water?"

"Police," said Arnie.

"Police," agreed Phil.

"Police?" said Joe.

"Call the police," said Arnie. "You need to call the police right now."

"What for do you need the police?" said Joe.

"They're killing people," said Arnie.

"Back there," said Phil.

"Who is?" said Joe.

"Some guys with guns," said Arnie.

"And the shell," said Phil.

"The shell?" said Joe.

"It killed that guy," said Phil.

"With a gun," said Arnie.

"The shell did?" said Joe.

"Yes," said Arnie and Phil, together.

"So you got to call the police now," said Arnie.

"We in the ocean," Joe pointed out. "They don't got no police out here."

"Who needs the police?" said Mara Purvis, who had just arrived at the bar to fill a fresh set of drink orders.

Arnie turned to her. "Listen," he said, "we need to call somebody right now, because we just saw some guys killing some guys."

"What?" said Mara. "Where?"

"Out back," said Arnie, gesturing. "They shot them."

"One of them was the shell," said Phil.

"They shot the shell?" said Mara.

"No," said Phil. "He shot the guy."

"The shell did?" said Mara.

"Yes," said Arnie. "The shell killed a guy, and some other guys killed the other guys. With guns. Back there. We need to call somebody. They're on the ship."

"Arnie," said Mara, "are you guys on some kind of medication you're not supposed to take with alcohol?"

"We're not drunk," said Arnie. "I'm telling you, we saw it with our eyes, guys shooting with guns."

"And the shell," said Phil.

Mara looked at Joe and said, "Do you know what they're talking about?"

"I dunno," he said. "But I tell you one thing. Three minutes ago, right before they get here, I see two big guys come out of there"—he pointed to the door at the stern—"and I don't see those guys here before. They was carrying gym bags, and they went up the stairs."

"Oh my God," said Mara. "What's going on?"

"I dunno," said Joe. "Like I say before, sometimes things happen on this boat I don't wanna know nothing about."

"You think they're gonna rob the casino? I mean the cashier on the second deck?"

"Could be," said Joe. "That's the way they went."

"Oh my God," said Mara.

"We need to tell somebody," said Arnie.

"Manny," said Mara. "We should tell Manny."

"Your boss?" said Arnie. "The one was yelling at you before?"

"Yeah."

"You can't tell him," said Arnie.

"Why not?" said Mara.

"He's dead," said Arnie.

"He's the one the shell shot," said Phil.

"Oh my God," said Mara.

"We need to tell somebody," said Arnie.

"Should we go up and warn the cashier?" said Mara.

"If they gonna rob them," said Joe, "they already up there by now. You don't wanna go there."

Mara thought, then said, "The captain. We could tell him, and he could call the Coast Guard or the cops or somebody."

"OK," said Arnie. "Let's go tell him. We'll go with you, tell him what we saw."

"OK," said Mara. "Joe, do you have a phone?"

"I got a cell phone."

"OK, you call somebody in Miami, the police, or the Coast Guard, somebody, and tell them we think there's a robbery, OK? And they should send somebody out here."

"OK," said Joe. "I try."

"OK," said Mara. "C'mon, you guys."

Mara headed for the stairs, followed by Arnie and Phil.

"A nice, relaxing night, you said," said Phil.

"Don't start," said Arnie.

As they disappeared into the stairway, Joe reached under the cash register and grabbed his cell phone. He was trying to decide whether to call directory assistance for the Coast Guard, or just 911. Then he looked at the phone screen: NO SERVICE.

He stared at the phone, trying to decide what to do next. Above him, on the TV set, the NewsPlex Nine co-anchors were looking excited.

". . . first piece of good news in a while," the female was saying. She looked at the male.

"That's right," he said. "We have received word that NewsPlex Nine reporter Summer Westfall and cameraman Javier Santiago have both survived the crash of the News-Plex Nine NewsVan that we reported just minutes ago." He looked at the female anchor.

"According to police radio reports," she said, "Summer and Javier were injured, and are being placed aboard an ambulance now."

"We have no word yet on the seriousness of their injuries," said the male, "but we will, of course, be following this breaking story closely."

"Our prayers are with these two courageous members of the NewsPlex Nine family," said the female, her eyes moistening.

"We've been through a lot tonight here at NewsPlex Nine," said the male anchor, "and if it's not too unprofessional, I think this good news is a good reason for a good old-fashioned hug."

He turned to the female anchor, and she to him, and they held each other in an embrace—an embrace that, to the anchors' spouses, watching from their respective homes, seemed to last just a tad too long.

BREATHE THROUGH YOUR NOSE.

In the transom of Tark's boat, Frank fought yet another wave of nausea brought on by swallowing his own blood. He was worried that if he vomited, he'd choke to death, his mouth sealed tight by the layers of duct tape.

Frank was aware that the boat was tied up to the stern of the *Extravaganza*. He figured, from the number of shots Tark and Kaz had fired, that the ship crew had been taken out. He'd seen Tark and Kaz leave the boat, and then Rebar and Holman, so he knew for now he was alone on the boat. He could hear Tark's voice—the sea and wind were calmer here in the shelter of the big ship—but he couldn't make out the words.

Frank figured now was his best, probably only, chance to do anything about his situation. If he could get his hands in front of him, now bound tightly by the wrists behind him, he could get the duct tape off his mouth, maybe find something to use as a weapon. He knew some people could do this, were limber enough to get their arms down around their legs and feet and then up in front. But he didn't know if he was one of those people. He was a big, stocky guy, and his arms weren't particularly long. But this was his only chance, so he rolled to his side and began working his hands down his back, and right away he could feel how tight it was—*this isn't gonna work, you can't do this*—but he forced himself to keep trying because this was all he could think of and if he didn't get this tape off soon he was fucked.

Swallow. Breathe.

FAY, COMING FAST THROUGH THE DOOR FROM the portside deck, ran directly into Wally, who was on his way outside for one last, desperate attempt to have a non-moronic conversation with her or, failing that, to hurl himself into the sea.

"*Umfh,*" she said.

"Sorry," he said. "Look, that thing about Leonardo Di-Caprio, I was just . . ."

"Shut up," she said. "Do you know where the bridge is?"

"The what?"

"The bridge. The *bridge.* Where the captain steers the ship."

"Oh yeah," said Wally, wanting to punch himself in the face for forgetting what a bridge was. "It's up these stairs behind where we, OK, there's actually two sets of stairs, but you . . ."

Fay grabbed his arms. "Show me where it is," she said.

"Is something wrong?"

"Just *take me there right now,* OK?"

"OK," said Wally, turning toward the stairs to the third deck, clueless about what was going on, but happy that, for whatever reason, she was actually choosing to remain, however briefly, in his company.

Thirteen

TO REACH THE BRIDGE OF THE *EXTRAVAGANZA OF the Seas,* you entered a small hallway at the forward end of the big third-deck salon, the one where the band played. You then climbed a narrow stairway. The bottom of the stairway was guarded by a heavy steel door that said NO AD-MITTANCE AUTHORIZED PERSONNEL ONLY and had an electronic lock with a keypad that required a five-digit code. The door had been installed to prevent hijackings, but First Officer Hank Wilde could never remember the damn code, especially after he'd been drinking, so it was his custom to start each trip by tying the door open with a piece of rope.

And so it was open now as Captain Eddie Smith stood at the bridge, keeping the ship pointed into the wind and drifting with the Gulf Stream, waiting for Manny Arquero to get on the two-way radio and tell him the transfer was complete. He looked at his watch. *Should be any minute now.* His mind was on getting back to Miami now, back to his wife and little boy.

He glanced at the small TV mounted in the control console. On the screen, the male and the female anchors were both looking close to tears; in the upper-right-hand corner the red letters spelled TRAGEDY STRIKES NEWSPLEX NINE AGAIN. Eddie turned the volume up slightly.

". . . incredible turn of events," the male anchor was saying. "We are now getting word that the ambulance carrying NewsPlex Nine reporter Summer Westfall and cameraman Javier Santiago from the scene of the NewsVan Nine crash in the Westchester area has itself been involved in an accident." He looked at the female anchor.

"What makes this all the more unbelievable," she said, "is that, from what we are hearing on the police radio, the ambulance apparently collided head-on with a *second* NewsPlex Nine van, on its way to the scene, carrying NewsPlex Nine reporter Carlosina Verdad and cameraman Doug Pilcher." She looked at the male.

"We are still awaiting word on whether there have been any injuries, or I guess I should say *additional* injuries," he said.

"Meanwhile," the female said, "our thoughts and prayers go out to Carlosina, and Doug, and Summer, and . . . and Summer's cameraman . . ."

"Javier," said the male.

"Yes, of course, Javier, as well as the other members of the NewsPlex Nine family who have been victims of this devastating killer storm, Hector, which has already tragically claimed the lives of . . ."

"HEY! ANYBODY HERE?"

Eddie shut off the TV, shouted down the stairway, "Who is it?"

"It's Ted and Johnny," Ted shouted back.

"Who?" said Eddie.

"Ted and Johnny," said Ted, now clumping up the stairs, Johnny right behind him. "We're in the band."

"You're not supposed to be up here," said Eddie.

"I know, but something bad happened," said Ted.

"You gotta call the cops," said Johnny. "They're shooting back there."

"What?" said Eddie. "Where?"

"In the back of the ship," said Ted. "The shell shot whatshisname, Manny, and then these . . ."

"Manny's been shot?" said Eddie. "You sure?"

"We saw it," said Johnny, nodding violently. "The shell shot him."

"The what?"

"The shell," said Ted. "The guy in the shell shoot. I mean shell suit. He shot Manny, and then these guys on the boat started shooting everybody, and then they came on the boat."

"They came on the ship?" said Eddie. "They're on the ship now?"

"Yes," said Johnny, nodding even harder. "With guns."

"You got to call the cops," said Ted. "Or the Coast Guard."

Eddie turned and stared at the ship's radio, thinking fast. If there was shooting, he needed help out here. But if he called the Coast Guard, they'd find the drugs, the money, whatever it was they were transferring, and there would be no way they wouldn't believe Eddie was involved, and he'd be on his way back to prison, this time basically forever. He'd never spend another night with his wife, another day with his boy. Never.

"Come *on,* man," said Ted. "They're *killing* people back there."

"They're on the *ship,*" said Johnny.

They were on the ship. *They were on Eddie's ship.*

"OK," said Eddie, and he reached for the microphone to call the Coast Guard. He'd have to figure out some way out of this later. Maybe, if there was enough confusion when he got the ship back to Miami, he'd be able to disappear. Back to the Bahamas, maybe. He could contact Luz somehow, try to explain the situation, why he wasn't coming home. But right now, he had to get the Coast Guard out here, because *this was his ship*. He picked up the microphone, and then he heard a new voice on the bridge.

"Hold it, Captain," said Kaz.

LOU TARANT SKIDDED TO A STOP IN FRONT OF the Chum Bucket in his 2002 Mercedes CL-600 coupe, which had a 362-horsepower V-12 engine. It retailed for over $100,000, but Tarant had been able to get it for free, in exchange for not killing the Mercedes dealer's son, who had a gambling problem.

Tarant jumped out of the car without bothering to shut off the engine, knowing that there would be a flunky waiting there to park the car, which there was. As Tarant strode toward the door, he was met by Gene Shroder, who'd arrived a few minutes earlier.

"You reach the ship?" Tarant asked.

"Lou, they don't answer."

"What?"

"We're trying, but they're not answering."

"Fuck," said Tarant.

"Yeah," said Shroder.

"Is Stu's boat ready?"

"He gassed it up, Lou, but he says they need to unload the . . ."

"Is the Wookie here? And the crew?"

"They're all here, Lou. But Stu says before you go he should . . ."

"Tell Stu we're leaving *now*."

"OK, Lou."

*   *   *

JOCK EMERGED FROM THE KITCHEN, ONE ARM around Connie, the grieving divorcée, the other tucking his shirt back into his pants. He expected to find his bandmates tuning up, getting ready to start the next set, but the only person on the far end of the room was Strom Thurmond, on his feet again, dancing to whatever music he was hearing.

Jock turned to Emeril, perched on his stool, and said, "You seen the band around?"

Emeril glared straight ahead.

"Thanks," said Jock.

"What time're you supposed to start playing again?" said Connie.

Jock looked at his watch. "About ten minutes ago. I thought they'd be pissed at me for taking this long."

"So where are they?"

"My guess?" said Jock. He held an imaginary joint to his lips and took an imaginary hit.

"So you got a few more minutes," said Connie.

"Looks like," he said.

"This time I'm on top," she said, pulling him back into the kitchen.

AT THE STERN PLATFORM, TARK WAS PLEASED by how smoothly things were going.

He'd started by creating a crime scene, sticking TEC-9s in the hands of two of the dead crewmen, to make it look as though they'd been shooting. Next, he and Rebar, holding their breaths against the puke stench, had gone into the forward compartment of his boat and hauled out some parts of a Zodiac inflatable boat—a broken piece of fiberglass deck, some pontoon tubing, and some rope. Tark had made these himself by wrecking a Zodiac he'd stolen back in the Bahamas. He and Rebar had tangled the rope up with two *Extravaganza* life vests, then tossed everything into the water, making a nice little piece of easily identifiable wreckage for the Coast Guard to find.

Then they'd hauled the body of Bobby Kemp, his pink costume now punctured by bullet holes, onto the fishing boat, and put his gun—the one he'd used to shoot Manny Arquero—back into his pink hand. Tark had checked on Frank; he'd moved some, obviously been struggling, but he was still hogtied and gagged tight. He groaned when Tark kicked him in the back, so he was still alive; Tark would have liked to mess with him some more, but he had a lot to do, so he decided to let it go.

Tark had leaned over and whispered his farewell in Frank's ear.

"You're a lucky man, Chief," he'd said. "If you can keep from choking long enough, you get to drown."

Then came the hardest part for Tark, at least emotionally: hauling two duffel bags full of cash—man, those things were *heavy*—across the platform and heaving them into the fishing boat. Tark truly hated to part with what he knew was more money than he had made in his whole life until now, but he also knew it had to look real to the Coast Guard and Tarant. He'd also put two duffel bags of product on his boat—one cocaine, one marijuana. The rest of the shipment he'd left stashed back in the Bahamas.

Next, Tark and Rebar had launched the *Extravaganza*'s Zodiac dinghy. It took some effort, as it was a heavy boat, for an inflatable; fortunately, the davits had power winches. They got it into the water, then dragged it over and tied it to the stern platform. Tark tried the engine, which started right away; it had plenty of gas, though Tark had brought an extra can, just in case.

He'd thought of everything, Tark had. No surprise there:
He'd been planning it for almost two years, working it out
piece by piece, detail by detail—how he could stop being
just a delivery boy for a lousy ten grand a trip; how he
could, one time, keep all this money, and all this product,
for himself, and be rich forever.

His big break had come when Bobby Kemp had bought
the *Extravaganza,* Bobby being the perfect combination of
greedy, confident, and stupid. When Kemp had approached
Tark, felt him out about hijacking a shipment, it was like
God or somebody saying, OK, Tark, here you go.

Tark had played clueless, asking a lot of questions, getting Kemp to feed him information about the ship, the security procedures, the personnel. Then, slowly, he started
leading Kemp on, using his questions to feed ideas to
Kemp a little at a time. Kemp ate it up, especially the part
about Kemp shooting Manny Arquero. He *hated* that guy.
In the end, Kemp bought Tark's plan, the whole thing,
thinking it was all his idea, like he was a brilliant criminal
mastermind and Tark was just some dumbass boat jockey
who'd be thrilled to get a whole million dollars. A million
dollars. Shit, that's basically what Tark was gonna throw
away out here, leaving it on the boat with the criminal mastermind, in his pink shell suit.

Tark checked his watch. Kaz and Holman had disabled
the *Extravaganza* radios by now. They'd also set up the
cell-phone jammer—the thing in the metal case—on top of
the ship, where it would have maximum range. Tark had
bought it on the Internet and tested it in the Bahamas. Nobody on the ship could make or receive calls until the jammer's battery died, which wouldn't be for another four
hours. There was no way for anybody on the ship to sound
the alarm.

There'd also be no way for the ship to get back to Miami, at least for a while. Any second now, Kaz and Holman

would put the *Extravaganza* on autopilot, heading north and east, farther off the coast, at a sedate five knots or so. They'd make sure the captain knew Bobby Kemp was behind all this, then leave him bound and gagged on the floor. They'd leave the bridge door locked behind them; besides the captain, the only people who knew the code were Manny Arquero and Hank Wilde, both dead. So by the time anybody in Miami realized that the *Extravaganza* was late coming back, it would be far away, and heading farther, totally out of contact. Search and Rescue would go out, but they'd be looking for a big ship, not Tark in his Zodiac. By the time they found the *Extravaganza*, he'd be back in the Bahamas, with nobody even looking for him.

All that remained now was for him and Rebar to load the rest of the cash into the Zodiac; Kaz and Holman would be down to help soon. In maybe ten minutes, they'd be done. It was a lot of weight for the Zodiac; it would ride low, which meant a wet trip home in these seas. But Tark had no doubt he'd make it. Especially since he'd be going back alone, just him and his money. Because once the boat was loaded, he really didn't need these other assholes.

Fourteen

"PUT THE MICROPHONE BACK, CAPTAIN," SAID KAZ.

Eddie put the microphone back.

"Oh man," said Johnny. "It's the guy from the other boat who . . ."

"Shut up, asshole," said Kaz.

"OK," said Johnny.

Kaz pondered the situation. There weren't supposed to be extra people here. There was just supposed to be the captain. That was how Tark had explained the plan. Disable the radios, put the ship on autopilot, tell the captain this was Bobby Kemp's operation so he'd repeat it to the Coast Guard, tie him up, close the door, get the hell back to the stern. That was the plan.

But now Kaz had these two extra assholes on his hands. He wished Holman would hurry up and get here. Holman had gone up to the top deck, outside. He was supposed to secure the cell-phone jammer in a good spot, where nobody would see it, and where it would have maximum range.

Kaz decided he'd wait and consult with Holman on what to do about the extra assholes. So for the moment, the four of them just stood there on the bridge; Kaz watching Eddie, Johnny, and Ted; them watching him, this big guy with the big gun, smelling of . . . was that *vomit*?

The silence on the bridge lasted a long 45 seconds, ending with the sound of footsteps on the stairs. Relieved, Kaz turned toward the stairwell. His relief turned to concern when two heads appeared at the top of the stairs and neither one was Holman's.

"UH-oh," said Wally.

"Oh, shit," said Fay, recognizing Kaz.

"Get over there and shut up," said Kaz, motioning with his gun for Wally and Fay to go stand by the helm with the other three. Kaz was not liking this. Now he had *four* extra assholes to worry about. *Where the hell was Holman?*

As he pondered, Kaz heard new arrivals in the stairwell. Kaz, pointing his gun at his captives, lifted a finger to his lips. Voices came up the stairway.

"More steps?" said Arnie. "How many steps they got in this boat?"

"We're almost there," said Mara.

"I'm almost dead," said Phil.

"Just a few more . . . Oh my God," said Mara, reaching the top, seeing Kaz, the gun.

"What?" said Arnie, right behind her, then, "Oh."

"What?" said Phil. "Is it more stairs? Because if it's more stairs, I'm . . . oh."

The three of them were stopped on the stairs, looking up at Kaz.

"Get over there with them," Kaz said.

"You're the guy from the back," said Arnie. "With the shooting."

"Shut up, Pop," said Kaz.

"I ain't your pop," said Arnie.

"Pop," said Kaz, "I will blow your fucking head off if you don't shut the fuck up and get the fuck over there *right now*."

Arnie started to say something, but Mara put her hand on his arm and pulled him over with her to the helm, Phil following.

The unexpected-asshole count had now climbed to seven. Kaz glanced at his watch; Tark was expecting him back soon. *Where was Holman?*

Kaz decided, Holman or not, he'd stick to the plan.

"Over there," he said, gesturing with his gun at the eight captives, waving them toward the wall next to the stairwell. As they crowded over, Kaz, keeping an eye on them, moved to the helm. He glanced down at it, locating the communications console, then up at his captives again. The only one he figured could give him any trouble was the captain, who was watching him impassively. The three younger guys looked pretty scared. Kaz wasn't worried about the two old guys, or the two women. Maybe this would work out OK. After all, the point of the plan was to make it look like Bobby Kemp's operation; this way, Kaz figured, there'd be more witnesses to spread the word.

"Anybody moves," he said, looking right at Eddie, "I blow everybody's fucking head off. You understand, Captain?"

Eddie nodded.

"That's good," said Kaz. "Bobby Kemp told me you'd be a good boy, wouldn't give me no trouble."

Eddie frowned.

"Yeah," said Kaz. "Pretty fucking funny, huh? A guy sets up his own ship?"

Satisfied that he'd handled that cleverly, Kaz looked down again at the communications console, a little longer this time, locating the main and backup radios. He looked up again at his captives, then quickly turned and fired a shot—*pop*—into the main radio.

"Oh my God," said Mara.

Kaz looked up again. None of the hostages had moved. Kaz turned away again, located the backup radio, and fired another shot. Then he turned back toward his captives.

Before he got his body around, he realized that he was looking directly into the barrel of a pistol, not three feet from his face.

"Put down the gun," said Fay.

AT THE STERN, TARK AND REBAR WERE HALFWAY done, having lugged ten of the heavy cash-filled duffel bags to the Zodiac and stowed them, which took time because Tark wanted to make sure each one was securely tied in. Tark was looking at his watch every thirty seconds now, expecting at any moment to feel the *Extravaganza* start moving. It was taking a little longer than he'd expected, but he wasn't worried. He had a great plan, a perfect plan, and everybody who could possibly have screwed it up was dead.

THE INSTANT THE LINES WERE CAST OFF, STU Carbonecca's comically overpowered Cigarette boat roared away from the dock next to the Chum Bucket, carrying Stu, Lou Tarant, and six wet, unhappy professional thugs packing enough firepower to successfully invade a Third World nation (or France). Stu was at the helm, with Lou standing right next to him, screaming in his ear to go faster, even though Stu could barely control the boat as it was, what with the bay so rough. Stu had never seen Lou this angry. When Stu had started to suggest that maybe they should unload the boat before they went out, Lou had nearly punched him. So now he was doing whatever Lou wanted. If Lou wanted him to make the boat go faster, OK, he'd make it go faster. Because Stu knew you did *not* mess with Lou when he was angry. He almost felt sorry for the poor bastards out on the ship.

* * *

"OHMYGOD," SAID CONNIE THE GRIEVING DIVOR-
cée. "Yes. Yes. Yes yes yes yesyesyesyesYESSSS. Ohmygod. Ohmygod. OH . . . MY . . . *GOOOOOOOOOOOOOO
OOOOOD.*"

"AAAA*UNHHHHHHHHHHHHH*," responded Jock, and
he meant it. He could hardly believe this was happening to
him for the third time in less than an hour. A personal best.

They were on the floor behind the *Extravaganza* galley's stainless-steel counter. They'd considered using the
counter—which was spotlessly clean, as was the rest of the
galley, since Emeril never cooked there—but they'd have
been too visible if somebody came in. So they'd chosen the
floor, which Jock had gallantly covered with some white
buffet-table cloths. It was romantically dark, as they'd
turned off the lights, with the only illumination coming
from the crack under the door.

Jock lay on his back, Connie's head resting on his chest,
the two of them happy and drained and naked as jaybirds.
For a minute, neither moved, except to breathe, Connie
sounding like she was purring. Then Jock began to stir. He
was not good with time, but it seemed to him that it now had
been a *long* time since the band's break had started. He was
just about to tell Connie that he needed to get dressed, when
the galley door banged open, hard. Jock and Connie, startled,
gripped each other, listening. They first assumed that it was
Emeril, but whoever it was, by the sound of it, didn't know
where the light was. They heard some fumbling around, the
clattering of kitchen implements and bowls falling to the
floor. And then footsteps, coming around the counter.

And then a smell. It was a smell that Jock recognized
immediately, and it struck fear into his heart.

Tina.

Fifteen

FOR AN INSTANT, LOOKING INTO THE PISTOL
barrel, Kaz thought about it.

Fay saw him thinking about it.

"Don't even think about it," she said. "I will pull this
trigger, and the bullet will go through your left eyeball. *Put
the gun on the floor.*"

Kaz put the gun on the floor.

"Now go to the wall, spread your legs, and lean over,"
said Fay. "You know how."

Kaz leaned against the wall. Fay, keeping her gun on
him, slid his gun away from him with her foot.

"Everybody OK back there?" Fay asked, glancing back
at the rest of her group, their faces showing various degrees of incomprehension. Wally was the first to find
words for expressing it.

"You have a gun," he said.

"Yes," said Fay. "Captain, we . . ."

"Oh my God, you have a gun," said Mara.

"Yes. Now we need . . ."

"How come you have a gun?" said Wally.

"I'm a cop," said Fay.

"What?" said Wally.

"Oh my God, you're a *cop*?" said Mara.

"She's a *cop*," said Johnny.

"I heard her," said Ted.

"A nice, quiet evening, you said," said Phil.

"Shut up," said Arnie.

"It smells like puke in here," said Johnny.

"What kind of cop?" said Eddie.

"CGIS," said Fay. "You familiar with that?"

"More than I'd like," said Eddie.

"What is it?" said Wally.

"Coast Guard," said Eddie.

"You're the *Coast Guard*?" said Wally. "But you're, I mean, you're, you're . . ."

"You're wearing a *miniskirt*," said Johnny.

"It's long enough to hide a holster," said Fay. "Listen, I would love to chat more with you boys about my career in law enforcement, but right now we have some guys back there with machine guns to worry about, OK? Captain, we need to contact Miami right now."

"OK," said Eddie, "but it has to be by cell phone. He shot up both my radios."

"My cell phone's not working," said Fay. "Anybody else got one?"

Everybody had one but Arnie and Phil. Everyone checked. Everyone reported: NO SERVICE.

"*Damn,*" said Fay. "Captain, are there any other radios on the ship?"

Eddie thought for a second.

"Not on the ship, no," he said. "But . . ." he stopped.

"But what?" said Fay.

Eddie thought about it, decided he had no choice.

"At the stern, there's a fishing boat," he said. "It's got a radio."

"That's right," said Fay, looking at Eddie hard now, thinking about it, how he'd have to know there was a fishing boat back there, because he was the one who'd stopped the ship out here.

"That's right," she repeated. "OK, I need to get on that boat."

"The guys with guns're back there," said Ted.

"And the shell," said Johnny.

"You saw that, too?" said Phil.

Fay was thinking about it, about the radio on the boat, about the guys with the guns.

"OK listen," she said. "Here's what we do."

"What you do, lady," said Holman, from the stairwell, "is you put down the gun."

"About fucking time you got here," said Kaz.

NOW TARK WAS STARTING TO WORRY. HE AND Rebar had secured most of the cash on the Zodiac—only two more bags to go—and the *Extravaganza* hadn't started moving yet. What the hell were Kaz and Holman doing up there? They were supposed to be done and back down by now. That was the plan. They were supposed to be here, so Tark could kill them, as well as Rebar, and then get out of here, leaving nobody alive who knew anything. What was keeping them?

This is why it's better to work alone, Tark thought. *It's hard to find people you can trust.*

"TINA, PLEASE," JOCK SAID. "PUT DOWN THE knife."

It was a major knife. Tina had found it when she was

looking for the galley lights. She was waving it now in the general direction of Jock's genitals. She was an imposing sight: a very tall, very blonde, very angry, very farty woman waving a very big and sharp-looking blade. Jock was scuttling backward on his butt, with Connie, the grieving divorcée scuttling backward behind him, both of them still buck naked.

"HELP!" Connie shrieked. "SHE HAS A KNIFE SOMEBODY OUT THERE HELP US PLEASE!"

Nobody heard her but Emeril, who was not inclined to get involved. It had been Emeril who, in what was for him a rare moment of human interaction, had pointed to the galley door when Tina, on her break, had come looking for Jock. Emeril was reclusive, but he was also, like so many men, a big fan of tits.

"Tina, just put the knife down," Jock said. "You don't understand."

"I don't understand?" Tina said. "You're naked, she's naked, you're both on the floor, and I DON'T UNDERSTAND?"

The knife flashed groinward then, and Jock, displaying the reflexes that made him such an excellent drummer, was on his feet, over the counter, and out the door, leaving behind Tina, and Connie, and his clothes.

STU CARBONECCA'S BOAT ROCKETED OUT THE end of Government Cut, into open ocean, now getting airborne off some of the waves, the engines over-revving wildly when the props came out of the water. Each time the boat slammed back down, there was a chorus of *FUCK*s shouted simultaneously into the howling wind and rain by the extremely uncomfortable, and now somewhat terrified, cadre of professional thugs huddled in the cockpit.

And still Lou Tarant was not satisfied.

"FASTER," he shouted into Stu's ear.

"BUT LOU WE'RE ALREADY . . ."

"I SAID FASTER GODDAMMIT."

So Stu, a man between a very big rock and a very hard place, shoved the throttles forward yet another notch.

Sixteen

"WHAT THE FUCK TOOK YOU SO LONG?" SAID
Kaz, picking up his TEC-9 and Fay's pistol, putting the
pistol in his pocket.

"The door shut on me," said Holman. "It was locked from
the inside, so I hadda go way the hell to the other end of the
ship to get back inside. What're all these people doing here?"

"I don't know," said Kaz. "This one says she's Coast
Guard."

Holman looked at Fay. "I like the new uniforms," he said.

"Never mind that," said Kaz. "We gotta get going. I did
the radios. You do the other thing."

"What about *them*?"

"I got a plan for them," said Kaz, who'd been doing
some quick thinking. "Hurry up."

Holman went to the helm and started working on the
autopilot. Kaz made a little speech to Eddie, Fay, Wally,
Johnny, Ted, Mara, Arnie, and Phil.

"OK," he began. "I should shoot alla you."

"Oh my God," said Mara.

"But I won't," continued Kaz, "because this is Bobby Kemp's operation, and he don't want a lot of dead people. And we work for Bobby Kemp, so we do what Bobby Kemp says."

Kaz wondered if he was laying the Bobby Kemp thing on a little thick, but he figured better safe than sorry. There was a chance the captain would be dead soon, and he wanted to make sure the rest of these assholes remembered Kemp's name.

"Now," he said, "we're gonna leave you here. You want to not get shot, you *stay* here, understand? We're gonna have a guy with a gun right outside the door downstairs, and if anybody comes out that door, he blows your fucking head off, everybody got that?"

"Done," said Holman. Everybody felt it. The ship was starting to move.

"OK," said Kaz. "Captain, I need you to step over there."

Eddie stepped away from the group.

"Good," said Kaz, and he shot Eddie in the stomach.

Mara screamed. Phil grabbed his chest. Johnny grabbed Ted and said, "Oh *man*."

"Anybody else wants to get shot," said Kaz, backing to the stairway, "just stick your head out the door." To Holman he said, "Let's go."

They clumped to the bottom of the stairs, where Kaz pulled a pocketknife from the pocket of his shorts and began sawing through the late Hank Wilde's rope. As he worked, Holman hissed, "Why the fuck did you shoot him, man?"

"So he can't run the boat," said Kaz. "If we tie him up, they just untie him."

"Oh," said Holman. "Yeah."

Kaz kept sawing.

"Hurry up, man," said Holman. "I'm thinking that fucker is gonna leave us out here."

"No, he won't," said Kaz. "He don't dare leave us here, 'cause we know he ran this whole operation. Plus which, even if he did try to leave, Rebar'd shoot him."

Kaz had no way of knowing that, at that exact moment, a bullet was passing through Rebar's brain, Rebar having served his purpose as far as Tark was concerned.

"Well, hurry up anyway," said Holman.

"OK," said Kaz, as the rope fell to the floor. "Let's go."

At the top of the stairs, the three musicians, the two old men, the barmaid, and the undercover agent heard the heavy steel door slam shut. The captain heard only the roar of his own pain.

TARK FELT THE *EXTRAVAGANZA* START TO MOVE as he hoisted Rebar's body over the transom into his boat. Tark was pleased. All that remained for him to do now was kill Kaz and Holman when the big dumb morons got back with their guns safely tucked away in their gym bags, as Tark had instructed them. Depending on where they went down, he could either put them into his boat with the others, or, if that was too much work, he'd shove them into the sea. Then he'd shoot some holes in the hull of his boat, enough to swamp it. And then he'd be out of there.

A few feet away, the Zodiac, which was now the most valuable inflatable boat in the history of the world, began to bounce and judder in the big ship's growing wake, almost as though it was eager to get going. Tark picked up his TEC-9, stepped back on the platform, where he'd be less visible, and waited for his partners.

FOR MANY PASSENGERS AND STAFF ON THE *EX-travaganza,* the first indication that something might be amiss was when a stark-naked man came racing down the stairs into the second-deck casino, pursued by a tall blonde woman holding a large knife. Both of them were shouting. It was hard to make out the exact words, but he appeared to be making a plea for understanding, to which she did not appear receptive.

Everybody in the casino, except for the really intent slot-machine players, paused to watch as the man sprinted the length of the casino floor and into the stairwell leading to the first deck, with the woman maybe three steps behind, leaving, in her wake, a distinct odor.

The pause continued a few moments after they disappeared, with no sound in the casino except the relentless *bingbingbing* of the slots, as people pondered the meaning of what they had just witnessed. The gamblers decided that whatever the problem was, the casino staff would deal with it. The casino staff decided that, whatever the problem was, Manny Arquero, who always dealt with everything, would deal with it.

So everybody went back to gambling.

BREATHE. SWALLOW. BREATHE. SWALLOW. DON'T puke. Please don't puke. Please.

Frank had his tightly bound wrists way down behind himself now, under his ass, but he was beginning to accept that he couldn't get them any farther. He was too sick now, too weak. He wasn't gonna make it. He felt it coming now, another wave of nausea, and he could tell he wasn't going to be able to fight this one off.

I'm not gonna make it.

STU CARBONECCA'S BOAT HAD TURNED INTO A hellishly rhythmic torture machine. *ROAR* it would blast up the face of a big wave; then *VROOM* the engine would

rev wildly as the boat became airborne and the props broke
free of the water; then *WHAM* it would crash back onto the
ocean, causing the thugs to shout "FUCK!"; then Lou
would scream "FASTER!" at Stu; then the boat would roar
up the next wave, and the cycle would repeat, *ROAR
VROOM WHAM* "FUCK!" "FASTER!" *ROAR VROOM
WHAM* "FUCK!" "FASTER!" *ROAR VROOM WHAM*
"FUCK!" "FASTER!" *ROAR VROOM WHAM* "FUCK!"
"FASTER!" and on and on and on in the unending dark
and hostile sea.

At the helm, Stu, soaking wet and freezing cold, thighs
screaming with pain from constant bracing, eyes half
blinded from the spray, was thinking about when he was
17, and he told his mom that he was going to work with his
uncle Leon in the trucking business, and his mother cried
and begged him to go to St. John's instead like his brother
and become an accountant, and he told her no way he was
gonna spend the rest of his life sitting behind a desk. Stu
was thinking, *I wish to God I was sitting behind a desk
right now.*

Seventeen

FAY WAS TRYING TO REMEMBER HER FIRST-AID training. She was kneeling next to Eddie. The bullet hole was just above his belt, a little to the right of center. Blood was starting to seep into Eddie's white uniform.

Check the victim's responses. That was the first thing Fay remembered. She bent over Eddie's face. His eyes were open.

"Captain!" she shouted. "Can you hear me?"

Eddie moaned.

OK, he's conscious. Now . . . OK, now check the victim's pulse.

Fay felt his pulse.

OK, he has a pulse. Now what? NOW WHAT?

"Does anybody know first aid?" Fay said, over her shoulder.

Nobody responded except Mara, who said, "Oh my God."

Wally thought, *I wish I knew first aid.*

"OK, listen," said Fay. "We need to get him help right now. There has to be a doctor on this ship, or somebody who knows first aid. We need to get somebody up here."

"You mean go outside?" said Johnny.

"Yes," said Fay.

"But that guy said he'd shoot us," said Johnny.

Fay shook her head. "He said that to scare us. They're not gonna stand around up here. They're gonna get the hell off this ship as fast as they can. This guy needs help *now*."

Nobody moved.

"Look," said Fay. "I'll go out the door first, OK? You'll see it's safe. Then I want you guys"—she pointed to Wally, Ted, and Johnny—"to go find a doctor or anybody who knows first aid and get him up here fast. You"—she pointed to Mara—"go to the cashier's cage. They must have a guard in there, somebody with a gun. They might have some kind of alarm or emergency radio. Tell them what's going on. Tell them we need somebody up here right now who can run the ship. You two"—she pointed at Arnie and Phil—"stay here and help the captain."

"Help him how?" said Arnie.

"Put something over the wound," said Fay. "Don't press it hard, though. Try to keep him conscious. We'll get somebody up here to treat him and run the ship. But whatever you do, do NOT leave this man, you understand?"

"I got it," said Arnie.

Fay was on her feet. "Let's go," she said.

"What about you?" said Wally.

"What do you mean?" said Fay.

"Where are you going?" said Wally.

"I'm going to the back of the ship," said Fay.

"Oh my God," said Mara.

"Why?" said Wally.

"Because that's my job," said Fay.

She went down the stairs, followed by Wally, Ted,

Johnny, and Mara. She paused at the steel door, then turned the latch and shoved it open. She stuck her head out. Behind her, Wally winced.

Nothing happened.

"OK," Fay said, stepping into the hallway.

"She has more balls than I do," said Ted.

"Than all three of us," said Johnny.

He's right, thought Wally.

The three musicians followed Fay into the hallway. Behind them came Mara. As she left the stairwell, she let go of the steel door, which closed with a solid *THUNK.*

TARK STOOD WITH HIS BACK AGAINST THE SHIP, TEC-9 at the ready, waiting. He looked around at the scene of carnage he'd created: He had Bobby Kemp and Rebar on the ship, representing one side of the gunfight. Representing the other side were the six bodies sprawled on the platform, Hank Wilde, Manny Arquero and his crew of four, Manny and two of the others holding guns in their lifeless hands. It looked convincing to Tark.

He checked his watch. It had been almost ten minutes since the ship had started moving. *Where were they?*

. . . *ROAR VROOM WHAM* "FUCK!" "FASTER!" *ROAR VROOM WHAM* "FUCK!" "FASTER!" *ROAR VROOM WHAM* "FUCK!" "FASTER!" *ROAR VROOM WHAM* "FUCK!" "FASTER!" *ROAR VROOM WHAM* . . .

IN THE FIRST-DECK CASINO, A CUBAN LADY named Celia sat at a stool in front of a slot machine, one of six machines forming a little nook, three on each side. She reached into her plastic cup, took out yet another quarter, stuck it into the slot, and pushed the PLAY button. She watched the wheels spin and stop, one by one . . . a bell . . . a seven . . . a line.

"Ni agua," she announced, to nobody, for probably the eightieth time that night. *Not even water.*

As Celia prepared to put in another quarter, she felt somebody brush close behind her, into the nook. She turned, and at first saw nobody; then she looked down, and saw a man crouched next to her stool, hiding. He was naked. He was also, Celia could not help but note, good-looking, in a Brad Pitt kind of way, although Celia's heart belonged to Julio Iglesias.

Celia heard shouting, and turned around to see a tall blonde woman, wearing a casino uniform, running along the banks of slot machines, waving a knife. Celia, a smart lady, understood instantly who the woman was looking for. She turned and looked down at the naked man. He looked at her and held a finger to his lips, *shhhh.*

Celia turned back and watched the blonde woman run past. She was shouting, but Celia could not make out any words except "understand." As soon as the woman was past, the naked man jumped and began running in the opposite direction, toward the stern of the ship. Celia could not help but notice that he had a nice butt.

The naked man's path took him right next to one of Celia's friends, Luba, who, already freaked by the lady with the knife, screamed. The scream got the attention of the knife woman, who turned, saw the naked man fleeing, and took off after him, still shouting.

Celia and Luba watched her sprint past. When they had disappeared astern, Luba turned to Celia.

"Vistes eso?" she said. *Did you see that?*

Celia nodded. *"Tremendo cuerpo,"* she said. *Nice body.*

Eighteen

"IS THERE A DOCTOR HERE?" WALLY SHOUTED. "IS ANYBODY HERE A DOCTOR?" He looked frantically around the second-deck casino. A few gamblers glanced up from their slot machines or gaming tables; some even took the time to shake their heads at him. The rest continued to concentrate on losing money. If somebody was sick, that wasn't their problem.

Wally was about to shout again when he saw Johnny trotting toward him, pulling, by the hand, a fifty-ish woman. Ted trotted behind them.

"She's a nurse," said Johnny.

"Ma'am, can you help us?" said Wally.

"I'll try," she said.

"Great," said Wally. "Show her where the captain is, OK?"

"OK," said Johnny, heading toward the stairwell, nurse in tow.

"Go with him, Ted," said Wally. "I'm gonna go see if Fay needs help."

"You're gonna *what*?" said Ted. "Are you fucking *crazy*?"

"Ted," said Wally. "She's down there *alone*."

"You heard her," said Ted. "That's her job."

"I know," said Wally. "But what if she needs help?"

"How're you gonna help her, Wally?" said Ted. "You think she's gonna need a guitar solo?"

"Ted, listen," said Wally. "This is like on nine-eleven, on that one plane, the one they were gonna crash into the White House, where those passengers, regular people, they didn't let it happen. They stood up to the hijackers, Ted. They showed some *balls*. They said, hey, *fuck you*, hijackers, you're not gonna get away with this."

Ted stared at him. "Wally," he said. "All those people died."

Wally was quiet for a moment. "I gotta go," he said.

THE CASHIER'S CAGE WAS AT THE FAR AFT END of the second deck. It was staffed by three people: two cashiers, named Judi and Jennifer, who handled the cash transactions, selling rolls of quarters, turning loose quarters back into cash, and so forth; and a guard named Karl, who wore a revolver on his hip and sat on a chair behind them, watching a small battery-operated TV. All three had been recruited and trained by Manny Arquero, and they answered only to him. If Manny told them to do something—and there had been some highly unusual transactions aboard the *Extravaganza*—they did it, and they did not ask questions.

One of the things Manny had been most emphatic about was what to do in case of an emergency. The procedure was simple: The instant that any of the cashier's-cage personnel had even the slightest reason to think that something suspicious was happening, he or she was to hit one of the two panic buttons, one under the counter and one on the back wall. This would cause a motorized steel shutter to roll down quickly and seal off the cage.

The shutter had a small bulletproof Plexiglas window. If the cashiers saw Manny Arquero in that window, and he made an "OK" sign, they were to push the button that rolled up the shutter. If they didn't see Manny, or if they saw Manny, but he made some other gesture—even a thumbs-up—they were to leave the shutter down. They were not to open the shutter for anybody but Manny. He was very explicit on that point.

So this is what happened:

Karl had his TV tuned to the news. He had just told Judi and Jennifer how, apparently, from what he understood, a TV news truck had rammed head-on into an ambulance carrying some TV news people who got hurt when *another* TV news truck crashed, and it looked like everybody involved was dead, and the male and female co-anchors were now on camera holding each other and bawling like babies.

Jennifer had just gotten up to see this for herself, when Mara came running up to the counter, looking frantic.

"There's been a shooting!" she shouted. "The captain was shot. Hurry!"

"What?" said Judi and Jennifer, simultaneously.

"The captain," said Mara. "He was shot. And some men at the back. The conch shot them."

"The conch did?" said Judi, but at this point, the steel shutter was already descending, Jennifer and Karl having simultaneously pressed panic buttons.

"Wait!" said Mara. "You need to . . ."

BANG. The cashier's cage was sealed.

"Oh my God," said Mara.

* * *

THE THING WAS, KAZ WAS NOT AS STUPID AS
Tark thought he was. Kaz was smart enough to consider
the possibility that Tark would try to screw his partners.
The original deal was that Tark would get half the money,
since it was his plan and his boat; Kaz, Holman, and Rebar
would get the other half, which was a sixth apiece. But it
was a sixth of a huge pie. Plenty for everybody, especially
Tark, who'd have more money than he could ever spend.
But Kaz understood that Tark was capable of trying to take
the whole pie, crazy as that was. Because, as Kaz had come
to understand, Tark was one crazy motherfucker.

This was why, for safety's sake, Kaz had made a slight
alteration to Tark's plan. The plan called for him and Holman to return to the stern with their guns hidden in their
gym bags, so they wouldn't attract attention going through
the ship. But Kaz had decided, just in case, that before he
and Holman emerged at the stern, they'd stop and get their
guns back out, just in case.

Kaz had also worked it out so that Holman would be the
first man through the door to the stern platform. Holman
was not as smart as Kaz.

. . . *ROAR VROOM WHAM* "FUCK!" "FASTER!"
ROAR VROOM WHAM "FUCK!" "FASTER!" *ROAR
VROOM WHAM* "FUCK!" "FASTER!" *ROAR VROOM
WHAM* "FUCK!" "FASTER!" *ROAR VROOM WHAM* . . .

UP ON THE BRIDGE, ARNIE HAD GOTTEN DOWN ON
his knees—this took him almost thirty seconds—and was
peering into the very pale face of Eddie Smith, whose eyes
were now closed. Phil hovered behind Arnie.

"Is he conscious?" said Phil. "She said keep him conscious."

"What am I, Florence Nightingale?" said Arnie. "CAPTAIN? CAN YOU HEAR ME? CAPTAIN?"

Eddie opened his eyes, focused on Arnie's face, three inches away.

"It hurts," he said.

"He says it hurts," said Phil.

"I HEARD HIM," said Arnie. "I'm the one down here. We need something for the wound. Get me something."

"Like a bandage?" said Phil.

"No, like a pastrami sandwich, you idiot. Of *course* like a bandage!"

"I got a handkerchief," said Phil.

"Let me take a look at it," said Arnie.

Phil pulled a handkerchief out of his pants pocket, unfolded it, and displayed it for Arnie.

"You blow your nose in that tonight?" said Arnie.

Phil thought about it.

"Twice," he said.

"It'll have to do," said Arnie, grabbing it.

Nineteen

HOLMAN APPROACHED THE DOORWAY TO THE platform, TEC-9 in hand. Kaz was right behind him. Holman could see most of the platform now, and it troubled him somewhat that neither Rebar nor Tark was visible. He stopped at the doorway, looked back at Kaz, then stuck his head out.

"Come ON, man," said Tark, his voice causing Holman to jerk his head to the left, where Tark was standing, his back against the ship, his gun at his side.

Holman hesitated, not liking this.

"Come ON," repeated Tark. "Let's get the fuck *outta* here. Where's Kaz?"

"Where's Rebar?" said Holman.

"In the Zodiac," said Tark, pointing to the left.

Holman hesitated, then slipped his finger inside the trigger guard, then took a step forward, which was what he needed in order to see over the platform to where the inflatable was tied. It took him only a half second to see that

Rebar wasn't in the inflatable, and to start his turn toward Tark. But that was a quarter-second too long. Tark's three shots caught him—*pop* belly *pop* chest *pop* chest—before he could squeeze his trigger, and in another second Holman had joined the growing population of dead thugs on the stern platform.

Tark didn't watch the body fall. His eyes were riveted on the doorway. Ten seconds passed, twenty. Nothing.

"OK," Tark shouted. "WE CAN SPLIT IT, FIFTY-FIFTY."

Nothing.

Tark *knew* Kaz was in there. "I DID YOU A FAVOR, GETTING RID OF THEM," he shouted. "DON'T TELL ME YOU NEVER THOUGHT OF IT."

Inside the doorway, Kaz almost smiled. He *had* thought of it. Half of the pie. But he'd seen enough of Tark to know there was no chance of a deal.

"OK," he shouted. "YOU GOT A DEAL."

"OK," shouted Tark. He moved quietly to his left, to the body of Manny Arquero. He took the AK-47 out of Manny's stiffening hands and moved back to the side of the doorway. He shouted, "I'M GONNA PUT MY GUN DOWN WHERE YOU CAN SEE IT, OK?"

Tark put his TEC-9 on the platform and shoved it with his foot. It slid in front of the doorway.

"OK," he shouted. "NOW COME ON AND LET'S GET THE FUCK OUTTA HERE."

Thirty seconds passed.

"WE CAN'T STAY HERE ALL NIGHT, MAN," said Tark.

Twenty seconds passed.

OK, Tark decided, Kaz was smarter than the other two. He glanced over at the Zodiac. Four steps and a jump, he'd be in it. If he was quiet, Kaz wouldn't know he'd left the doorway until he had the boat untied and drifting away.

Then he'd make some noise, bring Kaz out. Kaz would *have* to come out, because he'd know Tark was getting away with all the money. But Tark would have the advantage then, because he knew where Kaz would be, and Kaz would have to find him, in the dark. He'd shoot Kaz, start the Zodiac outboard, come back and untie his boat, sink it. It could still work.

And it probably would have worked, exactly as Tark had figured it, except that when he shoved off from the wall, he slipped on the wet platform. And though he caught himself before he went down, the barrel of his gun thumped loudly against the platform. Tark was up again and running in an instant, but Kaz, who had anticipated that Tark would make a run for the Zodiac—What else could he do?—heard the thump, and was out of the doorway in an instant. It was an easy shot, close range, Tark with his back to him and no way to fire back. Kaz, not wanting to shoot the inflatable, took the time to bring his TEC-9 up and aim carefully.

Which is what he was doing when Jock, still naked, still moving fast, came barreling out of the doorway, directly into Kaz, who lurched violently sideways, off the edge of the platform and into the Atlantic Ocean.

JOHNNY YANKED ON THE STEEL DOOR TO THE bridge. "It's locked," he said.

Ted pounded on the door. "OPEN UP," he shouted. "WE GOT A NURSE."

Nothing.

Ted pounded some more, then Johnny took over, then Ted again. They pounded for a full minute.

Nothing.

"What do we do now?" said Johnny.

Ted thought. "We go ask that Coast Guard lady," he said. "She's the one with the plan."

"I dunno, man," said Johnny. "She went back where the gun guys are."

"I know," said Ted. "So did Wally."

"*Wally's* down there?" said Johnny.

"Yup," said Ted.

"Oh, *man,*" said Johnny.

WALLY TROTTED THE LENGTH OF THE FIRST-DECK casino, looking for Fay. He reached the bar at the stern, where he found Joe Sarmino, for probably the tenth time, turning off and then turning on his cell phone, in hopes that this time it would say something besides NO SERVICE.

"Hey," said Wally. "Have you seen Fay? The barmaid?"

"Yes," said Joe. "She go running through here a minute ago, that way, after all those other people."

"What other people?" said Wally.

Joe rolled his eyes.

"You wouldn't believe," he said. "Couple big guys holding bags, then a guy with no clothes on, then a lady with a knife. Then your friend Fay."

"That way?" said Wally, pointing toward the stairwell.

"That way," said Joe, looking at his phone. NO SERVICE.

"Do you have a gun or anything I can use?"

Joe looked up. "A gun?" he said.

"Any kind of weapon," said Wally.

"I got . . . lemme see . . . I got this." He held up a corkscrew.

"Can I borrow it?" said Wally. "It's an emergency."

"OK," said Joe, handing it to him. He was thinking maybe, after this trip, he would go back into the pool-service business.

"Thanks," said Wally. Corkscrew in hand, he took off running toward the stern stairwell, thinking, *A guy with no clothes?*

. . . *ROAR VROOM WHAM* "FUCK!" "FASTER!" *ROAR VROOM WHAM* "FUCK!" "FASTER!" *ROAR VROOM WHAM* "FUCK!" "FASTER!" *ROAR VROOM WHAM* "FUCK!" "FASTER!" *ROAR VROOM WHAM* . . .

"DID YOU HEAR SOMETHING?" SAID PHIL. "I thought I maybe heard something."

"I hear this guy moaning, is what I hear," said Arnie.

"I thought maybe I heard something," said Phil.

"So go look," said Arnie.

"Are you kidding?" said Phil. "There's maniacs with guns out there."

"He's waking up," said Arnie.

Eddie's eyes were open now.

"It hurts," he said.

"I know," said Arnie. "Hang on, we got help coming."

"Where the hell are they?" said Phil.

"Shut up," said Arnie.

Eddie moved his head a little, looked around the bridge. "Who's running the ship?" he said.

"What?" said Arnie.

"It's moving," said Eddie. "Who's running it?"

"Nobody," said Phil, thinking about it. "Nobody's running the ship."

"Shut up," said Arnie, to Phil. To Eddie, he said, "It's under control, Captain. Nothing to worry about."

"A nice, quiet evening, you said," said Phil.

"Shut up," said Arnie.

"I need to see," said Eddie. He turned on his side. He groaned in agony, but kept turning. He was on his hands and knees now.

"Hey," said Arnie, "hey, you're not supposed to move, OK?"

"I need to see," said Eddie. He was struggling to his feet. Phil's handkerchief fell off Eddie's wound and dropped to the floor. It was drenched with blood.

"You're supposed to lie down," said Arnie, struggling to get up, his old knees creaking. "You got shot, in case nobody told you."

"What's he doing?" said Phil.

"I don't know what the hell he's doing," said Arnie. "I'm still trying to stand up, here."

Eddie, groaning with each step, lurched over to the helm. He looked at the instruments for a moment.

"Northeast," he said. "Out to sea."

"I don't like the sound of that," said Phil.

Eddie was leaning over now, left hand on the console, right hand waving unsteadily in front of the autopilot control pad. He punched some keys. Then he groaned again, much louder, and clutched his belly for a moment with both hands. He brought up his right hand, now covered with blood, and aimed it toward the autopilot. Then he yelped in agony and crumpled to the floor.

Arnie, who had just finished straightening up, sighed and started to get back down.

"They never listen," he said.

On the floor, Eddie said, "It's off."

"He said it's off," said Phil.

"I heard him," said Arnie. "I'm right here, remember?"

"What's off?" said Phil.

"How should I know what's off?" said Arnie. "He's the one said it was off."

"The autopilot," said Eddie, fighting to get the words out. "It's off. I was gonna reset it. It's off."

"I don't like the sound of that," said Phil.

"Shut up," said Arnie. To Eddie, he said: "What do we do?"

Eddie was barely conscious now. "Steer," he whispered.

"Steer?" said Arnie.

"He wants *us* to steer?" said Phil.

"Steer west," said Eddie, and closed his eyes.

Twenty

TARK DOVE HEADFIRST OFF THE PLATFORM AND landed on a bed of cash-filled duffel bags in the Zodiac. He turned and squeezed off three quick shots in the general direction of the ship, with no idea who or what he was firing at. He didn't see Kaz anywhere. *Where the hell was Kaz?* He saw somebody getting up off the platform and swiveled the TEC-9 that way and . . . *Jesus, was that a naked man?*

ON THE BRIDGE OF THE *EXTRAVAGANZA,* PHIL PUT his hands on the steering wheel gingerly, as if it might be hot.

"Which way is west?" he said.

"Whaddya mean, which way is west?" said Arnie, who had finally got back down to the floor with Eddie, who was now unconscious. "West is west, for Chrissakes.

You got north, south, east, west. He said go west."

"I *know* he said go west," said Phil. "I'm asking, which way *is* west?"

Arnie sighed. "You got to look at the compass," he said. "You look at the compass, and there's your west."

Phil studied the instruments. "OK," he said. "You know so much, which one is the compass?"

"Christ, do I have to do everything around here?" said Arnie, and he began the slow and painful process of getting back on his feet.

JOCK SPRANG TO HIS FEET. *SHOOTING*. SOME-body was *shooting* at him. His first thought was: *Tina. Tina got hold of a gun.* He swiveled his head around frantically and saw the Zodiac bouncing in the big ship's wake, saw a skinny guy in it, AIMING A GUN AT HIM. *Pop. Pop.* THE GUY WAS SHOOTING AT HIM. Jock dropped to his hands and knees and started to crawl back toward the doorway to the ship. Then he remembered that that was where Tina was. *Pop. Pop.* He could hear bullets zinging over his head. He had to get out of there. For a second or two, Jock, naked on all fours, lunged one way, then another, looking like a giant hairless squirrel caught in traffic on the interstate. Then, seeing what looked like his only hope for refuge, he got into a crouch, sprinted fifteen feet and launched himself headfirst over the transom, into Tark's fishing boat.

. . . *ROAR VROOM WHAM* "FUCK!" "FASTER!" *ROAR VROOM WHAM* "FUCK!" "FASTER!" *ROAR VROOM WHAM* "FUCK!" "FASTER!" *ROAR VROOM WHAM* "FUCK!" "FASTER!" *ROAR VROOM WHAM* . . .

* * *

KAZ HAD BEEN VERY LUCKY, IN TWO WAYS.
First, he'd fallen off the platform close to where Tark's
boat was tied. Second, it had been tied sloppily, and one of
the lines was trailing in the water. Kaz had had the presence of mind to grab the line and hang on, which is why he
was now trailing in the *Extravaganza*'s wake, as opposed
to treading water in the dark rough sea as the ship steamed
off without him. Kaz had no idea what had happened, who
had hit him. For some reason, he had this feeling that it
was a naked man, but that made no sense.

And right now he had more important things to worry
about. Holding the line in both hands, he flipped his body
so he could see the Zodiac. Tark, gun slung over his shoulder, was at the stern, messing with the outboard. It roared
to life. He'd have to go to the bow now, and cast off. That
would keep him busy for a second.

Kaz hauled himself forward on the line to the *Extravaganza,* got one hand on the platform, then the other, and
pulled himself up. Lying flat, he looked to the right. Tark
was working his way forward, over the duffel bags, still
not looking Kaz's way. Kaz looked left and saw that he
was in luck; a few feet away was one of Manny Arquero's
crewmen, his dead hands gripping the TEC-9 Tark had
planted on him. Kaz slid over, yanked it loose, and rose to
his feet.

Shit. Tark had seen him. The bastard was quick: He
was already squeezing off shots. But Tark was at a serious marksmanship disadvantage, perched on a pile of
duffel bags in a bouncing rubber boat. His first shots
missed, and Kaz knew he had him as he squeezed the
trigger and . . .

. . . and heard a scream of fury to his left. He turned to

see a very tall, very pissed-off blonde woman coming right at him, holding aloft a knife strikingly similar to the one that perforated the Janet Leigh character in *Psycho*. He whirled toward her, and she, getting a good look at him, and his gun, screamed and tried to stop. But she skidded on the wet platform, and her momentum was unbroken as she, a woman with a fair amount of mass, slammed hard into Kaz, who fought to hold his balance but could not, and found himself falling, in what felt like slow motion—*This can't be happening*—back into the Atlantic Ocean.

FAY, HEARING THE SHOTS, STOPPED JUST BE-fore the doorway. Directly in front of her, lying on the stern platform, was an AK-47. Fay lay on her stomach, reached out carefully, grabbed the rifle and drew it toward her. She rose and checked to see if it had ammunition, made sure the safety was off. She leveled the gun and, half crouching, moved toward the doorway.

ON THE PLATFORM, TINA STAGGERED TO HER feet, disoriented. She'd thought the dark shape on the deck was that bastard Jock, but as she'd charged him, she'd seen that it was another man, a man wearing clothes. A man with a gun. She was also pretty sure she'd heard shooting. *Shooting.*

She looked to her left and saw where the shooting had come from: a skinny guy, in a little boat, with a gun slung around his shoulder. He was untying the boat, but when he saw her, now standing, he grabbed his gun. Tina whirled to run back into the ship, but then she saw it: a gun barrel, poking out of the doorway. She whirled back: The skinny man was raising his gun. *Pop. Pop.* Tina screamed, turned, sprinted across the platform and dove over the transom, into Tark's boat.

WALLY WAS IN THE STAIRWELL, HEADED DOWN, when he heard it. *Shooting.* Somebody was shooting down there. He turned and started back up the stairs. Then he stopped and said, "NO, dammit." Then he turned back around and started back down the stairs again, now holding his corkscrew in front of him, dagger-style.

Twenty-one

TARK WATCHED THE BLONDE WOMAN IN THE casino uniform dive into his boat, exactly the way the naked guy had. He was furious that, with the bouncing Zodiac messing up his aim, he'd been unable to hit either of them. He wondered who these people were, and why they kept knocking Kaz into the ocean. He also wondered who *else* was going to come through the door.

Glancing up every few seconds, he finished untying the Zodiac, which began to fall behind the ship. Tark clambered back to the stern, where the outboard was idling. His plan now—Tark always had a plan—was to bring the Zodiac back up to the stern of the *Extravaganza*, cut the lines to his fishing boat, then shoot many holes in the hull. With any luck, his boat would take on water fast enough that the naked guy and the woman would think it was sinking, and they'd come out where Tark could kill them.

The waves were getting bigger the farther he drifted from the lee of the big ship. Spray splashed Tark's face as, slinging the TEC-9 over his shoulder, he gripped the seat with his right hand and cranked the throttle with his left, coming back up to the big ship, twenty yards away, now ten, now five. He eased off the throttle and turned the Zodiac sideways, sliding it toward the first of the two lines holding his boat to the *Extravaganza.* He pulled out his knife and . . .

"HOLD IT," a voice shouted. A *woman's* voice.

Tark looked up on the platform and saw a cocktail waitress pointing Manny Arquero's AK-47 at him. *What kind of cocktail waitresses did they hire on this ship?*

"I AM A COAST GUARD OFFICER," she shouted. "PUT DOWN THE KNIFE, AND THEN SLOWLY REMOVE THE GUN."

A Coast Guard officer?

"I SAID PUT DOWN THE KNIFE, AND SLOWLY REMOVE THE GUN," the woman repeated.

Tark put the knife down. He still had his left hand on the throttle. The engine was idling, so the Zodiac was falling behind the *Extravaganza.* It was three yards away from the platform. Now five.

"REMOVE THE GUN AND BRING THE BOAT BACK," said the woman. "OR I WILL SHOOT."

Seven yards, now. Ten. Tark reached down with his right hand, slowly started to unsling the TEC-9. Twelve yards.

"TAKE IT OFF AND BRING THE BOAT BACK NOW," the woman said, and as she did, Tark ducked down and cranked the throttle to full as he yanked it sideways, sending the inflatable into a surging turn away from the ship. Tark couldn't hear, over the engine noise, whether the woman was shooting or not, but he assumed she was. As he raced back into the darkness, the swell of the waves obscuring him from the ship, he felt a surge of elation. *She wasn't going to hit him.*

But in a few seconds his elation turned to alarm as he realized that, although she hadn't hit *him,* she had definitely hit the Zodiac. More than once, in fact, to judge by how quickly it was losing air and settling into the dark water.

"FUCK *ME,*" Tark screamed to whatever dark sea spirits were out there, as he yanked the engine sideways again and turned the sinking Zodiac back toward the receding ship. Having got that out of his system, he began, yet again, to make a plan.

"OH, SEE HERE?" ARNIE WAS SAYING. "THE 'N'? That stands for north."

Arnie and Phil had, after some argument, agreed on which one was the compass. They were now arguing about how it worked.

"I know the 'N' stands for north. I'm just saying, does that mean the 'N' is *facing* the north? Or does that mean when the 'N' is facing us, then we're going north?"

Arnie thought about that. He couldn't bring himself to admit he didn't know the answer, so he said, "They should put directions on this thing."

"Those ARE directions," said Phil. "What do you think north is? It's a *direction.*"

"I don't mean that," said Arnie. "I mean, how it works, they should put on there."

On the floor, Eddie groaned.

"Take a look at him," said Arnie. "See how he's doing. I'll drive this thing."

"Why should *you* drive?" said Phil. "Why shouldn't I drive?"

"Because I'm a better driver," said Arnie. "Fifty-one years I drove, I never had an accident." This was not, technically, true. Arnie had been forced to quit driving when, at age 81, he had driven his car, a 1986 Oldsmobile, into a convenience store, which he claimed had not been there earlier.

"I never had an accident, either," said Phil. This was, technically, true, in the sense that he had never hit anything, but only because for the last few years of his driving career he never went more than fifteen miles an hour, which is the speed he was clocked at on Interstate 95 when he got the ticket that finally persuaded his children to take away his car keys.

Eddie groaned again.

"Will you for Pete's sakes LOOK at him?" said Arnie. "The man is in pain down there, and I can't bend over anymore."

"All right, all right," said Phil, starting, slowly, to get on his knees. "You can drive. For now. But don't go too fast."

"Jesus, what are you, my *wife*?" said Arnie, and he began to turn the wheel.

ON THE FIRST DECK, JOHNNY AND TED TROTTED up to Joe Sarmino. Before they could even ask, he pointed toward the stern and said, "Everybody go that way."

"Wally?" said Johnny. "The guy in the band with us?"

"Him too," said Joe.

"Do you have, like, a gun or something I could borrow?" said Ted.

Joe shook his head. "No gun," he said. "Your friend already ask. I give him my corkscrew."

Ted frowned, then turned to Johnny and said, "Let's go."

They trotted toward the stairwell, both thinking the same thing.

A corkscrew?

* * *

. . . *ROAR VROOM WHAM* "FUCK!" "FASTER!"
ROAR VROOM WHAM "FUCK!" "FASTER!" *ROAR
VROOM WHAM* "FUCK!" "FASTER!" *ROAR VROOM
WHAM* "FUCK!" "FASTER!" *ROAR VROOM WHAM* . . .

FAY, KEEPING THE AK-47 IN SHOOTING POSI-
tion, stood at the edge of the platform, scanning the dark
water. She didn't know if she'd hit the guy, but she knew
she'd hit the boat, she knew it, probably more than once.
The inflatable would probably stay afloat, she figured, but
it would be swamped, and it couldn't get far before the engine would get wet and die. Maybe the guy would risk
turning back.

Fay stared into the darkness, listening for the sound of
an outboard over the roar of the sea and the wind. So focused was she that she failed to see Kaz's hands appear on
the top of the platform, failed to see the big man haul himself onto the platform twenty feet to her right, rise to his
feet and circle around behind her, hesitating as he debated
whether to try to grab her gun, or just shove her off the
platform. She failed to see him as, having decided the
surest answer was to just give her a shove, he stepped forward, hands out.

And she failed to see Wally jump on Kaz's broad back
from behind and drive the corkscrew into his right shoulder
blade.

She did hear it, however; Kaz's scream was surprisingly
high and piercing for a man of his bulk. Fay whirled and
saw Kaz going down, Wally clinging to his back. Kaz
rolled and threw an elbow backward, knocking Wally
sprawling. Kaz started to rise.

"DON'T MOVE," said Fay. He looked up at her, at the gun pointed at him, and stayed on the platform, his left hand going to his injured shoulder.

Fay studied him. This was not the guy with the inflatable. *Where was the guy with the inflatable?* She glanced over at Wally, who was getting to his feet, corkscrew still in hand.

"You OK?" she said.

"Yeah," he said.

"Thank you," she said.

"Any time," he said.

"Is that a corkscrew?" she said.

Wally looked at it. "Yeah," he said.

"Do you think you could handle a bigger weapon?" she said.

"I could try," he said.

"There's a dead guy over there holding a gun," she said. "Why don't you go pick that up?"

Wally, a man who exactly one hour earlier had been playing "My Funny Valentine," pried a TEC-9 from the hands of a dead criminal, this being the second of the two TEC-9s Tark had planted on members of Manny Arquero's crew, back when Tark's plan had been running like a Swiss watch.

"Bring it here," said Fay. She checked to make sure the safety was off, then said, "OK, you pull the trigger, it shoots, got that?"

"Got it," said Wally.

"OK," said Fay. "I'm gonna . . . hold it." She was looking at the doorway to the ship; a head had just peeked out and ducked back inside.

"It's your friend," she said to Wally. "Tell him he can come out."

"IT'S OK," said Wally. "YOU CAN COME OUT."

Ted's head peeked around the corner, followed by the rest of Ted, followed by Johnny. They came over, surveying the scene—the bodies, Kaz, Wally, and Fay.

"Oh, man," said Johnny.

Ted noted the TEC-9 in Wally's hands and said, "That's not a corkscrew."

"Nope," said Wally.

"Did you get help for the captain?" said Fay. "Did you find a doctor?"

"We found a nurse," said Ted. "But we couldn't get back in."

"What?" said Fay.

"The door to the, whaddycallit, the bridge," said Ted. "It's locked."

"We pounded on it and pounded on it," said Johnny. "But they didn't open it."

"Damn," said Fay. Then, "Wait a minute—who's steering the ship?"

"What?" said Ted.

"Somebody's turning it," said Fay. "Look." She pointed to the wake, now clearly angled off toward the left.

"Oh, man," said Johnny.

"OK, listen," said Fay. "You"—she pointed to Kaz, still on the platform—"you stay right there. You do not move. You"—she pointed to Wally—"keep your gun on him, and shoot him if he moves. You can shoot him if you have to, right?"

"I already stabbed him," said Wally. "I can shoot him."

"OK," said Fay. "You two"—she pointed to Ted and Johnny— "get on that boat there"—she pointed to Tark's boat—"and get on the radio. That'll be up in the bridge, near the steering wheel. Get on channel sixteen, remember, channel sixteen, and say we have an emergency on the *Extravaganza,* OK? Tell them we need assistance out here right now. Stay on there and keep telling them, OK?"

"OK," said Ted and Johnny, heading over to Tark's boat. When they got there, Ted looked into the stern and shouted back, "THERE'S MORE BODIES IN HERE."

"Just get on the radio," said Fay.

"Oh, *man,*" said Johnny, as he and Ted climbed over the transom.

Fay turned to Wally. "I'll be back as soon as I can," she said.

"Where're you going?" he said.

"I need to find out who's steering this ship, if anybody is," she said. "I'll be right back."

Holding the AK-47, Fay trotted through the doorway into the ship. She was very reluctant to leave the stern, but figured that right now her biggest responsibility was the hundreds of people on the ship, currently being steered God knows where by God knows who. But as she raced up the stairway to the first deck, the question nagged her: *What happened to the guy in the inflatable?*

Twenty-two

THE OUTBOARD, ALMOST TOTALLY SUBMERGED
now, sputtered, then died, as Tark reached the bow of his
fishing boat. Standing precariously in the now-swamped
inflatable, Tark was just able to reach out and get hold of
the railing running along the deck. With his feet in the Zodiac, he slid his hands along the railing, working his way
along the starboard side toward the stern, where his boat
was tied to the Extravaganza platform.

"OH," SAID ARNIE. "I GOT IT GOING EAST NOW."
"East," said Phil, from the floor. *"East?"*
"East," said Arnie. "Like he said."
"He said *west*," said Phil. "He said steer it *west*."
"Like hell he did," said Arnie, although he suspected
Phil was right. He'd gotten a little confused there, thinking
east because he knew Miami was on the East Coast. But he
was not about to admit that to Phil.

"YES I'm sure," said Phil. "He said WEST."

"OK, then," said Arnie, starting to turn the wheel again. "You don't have to make a federal case out of it."

Phil started the slow process of rising to his feet.

"I'm gonna drive," he said.

JESUS, SAID TED.

"Oh MAN," said Johnny.

The two of them had moved quickly past the three bloody bodies, one of them pink, lying in the stern of Tark's boat. They now found themselves in the main cabin, which reeked of the combined stale vomit of five men. Desperate to escape the stench—but not to go back out with the bodies—they clambered up the ladderway. At the top, they found themselves on the bridge, which was dark. It was also, like the cabin, highly aromatic. But this was a different smell.

. . . *ROAR VROOM WHAM* "FUCK!" "FASTER!"

ROAR VROOM WHAM "FUCK!" "FASTER!" *ROAR VROOM WHAM* "FUCK!" "FASTER!" *ROAR VROOM WHAM* "FUCK!" "FASTER!" *ROAR VROOM WHAM* . . .

WALLY WAS WATCHING KAZ. KAZ WAS WATCHING

Wally.

Wally was thinking Kaz looked like he was getting ready to try something. This was correct. Kaz had decided he needed to make a move now, while the Coast Guard cocktail waitress from hell was gone. He figured his odds were good against this asshole who clearly didn't know one end of a gun from another. He would give it another thirty seconds, wait for something to happen, some opportunity to make a move.

He didn't have to wait thirty seconds.

The opportunity was Tark's head, appearing over the stern on his fishing boat. Tark was climbing over the side, holding the line from the bow of the Zodiac in his hand. His gun was slung over his shoulder.

Tark was planning to quickly tie the Zodiac to his boat—*he must not lose the Zodiac*—then shoot everybody on the platform, cast off, and get the hell away from the ship. When he got out of sight, he'd transfer as much of the cash as he could onto his ship, throw the bodies overboard, and get moving again. He wasn't sure where he'd go, but he knew he'd come up with a plan.

Kaz saw Tark first.

"HEY!" he shouted.

Wally turned for an instant to see what Kaz was looking at. He intended to turn right back, but froze when he saw Tark climbing into the back of his boat, gun slung over his shoulder, holding the line from the Zodiac bow in his hands.

"UUNNNH" was the noise Wally made as Kaz slammed into him from behind. He went down face first, the TEC-9 clattering ahead of him on the platform, Kaz scrambling over his body to get at it.

Tark, forced to decide between cleating the Zodiac to his boat or dropping the line so he could use his gun, correctly chose to drop the line, grab the gun, and start firing. *Pop pop* his first two shots missed but *pop pop pop* his last three slammed home as Kaz, dropping the gun he had just managed to pick up, staggered backward, then sideways. And then, for the third and final time that evening, Kaz fell into the Atlantic Ocean.

Tark then turned and *pop pop pop* fired at the fleeing form of Wally, who, as soon as he'd heard shooting, had started scrambling in the opposite direction, and was just able to dive sideways and up, into the recessed lifeboat deck, as Tark's shots went past.

Tark, seeing his target disappear, whirled to his left. The Zodiac line was gone.

"FUCK," he said. He ran to the starboard side, leaned over, and saw the wreckage of the most valuable inflatable boat in the world disappearing to the stern in the *Extravaganza*'s wake.

"FUCK," he said again, and whirled back to untie the lines to his boat. Which is when he saw Fay—who'd heard shots and turned back—come running through the doorway to the ship. She had her AK-47 in firing position, but she was looking to the left, down the platform to where Wally had been watching Kaz, and where she assumed the trouble was. And thus Tark had the extra second he needed to grab his gun and squeeze off a shot.

Wally saw it. He was on his stomach in the recessed lifeboat deck and had inched his head around the bottom of the opening, where he could see the platform. He saw Tark untying the boat. He saw Fay come running out. He saw Tark fire. He saw Fay turning, looking surprised, and putting her hands up to her head. He saw her stumble forward. And he saw her disappear, both hands still clutching her head, off the edge of the platform.

Tark took a last quick look around for somebody to shoot, reslung his gun, and finished untying his boat. Freed at last from the *Extravaganza,* it began to fall back into the darkness. Tark figured it had been no more than a minute since he'd let go of the Zodiac. It would be close by. He had a good searchlight. He'd find it. He *knew* he would. He'd beaten all these other assholes, hadn't he? He'd find the money, and he'd work out a plan, and all would be well. Tark allowed himself, for the first time in many tense minutes, to take a deep breath.

This is when he felt Frank's arms come down over his head, around his neck.

Frank had finally managed, with a last desperate effort

that felt as though he were ripping his arms from their sockets, to get his hands in front of him and peel off the duct tape, moments before he'd vomited a terrifying amount of blood. He was still bound hand and foot, and he was very weak, very dizzy. As he'd struggled awkwardly to his feet, he'd known he'd have only one chance at Tark.

As Tark felt the arms come down, he'd ducked down and twisted sideways. He almost got out. But Frank, messed up as he was, was still quick, and he got his right forearm into Tark's neck and jerked hard. Tark grabbed Frank's arms but could not weaken the big man's grip. Frantic now, Tark reached down for his gun, trapped between his body and Frank's, and began to pull it out. Frank felt what Tark was doing but could not use his bound-together hands to stop Tark. He could feel the gun coming free. Tark would have it in his hands soon. Frank realized that Tark could bring it up and fire it behind him, into Frank's face.

The gun was out now. Tark was bringing it up. Frank, not really thinking about anything but getting away from it, spun around so that his back was to the transom, bent his legs, and heaved upward and back, hanging on to the choking Tark, the two of them falling backward together into the ocean; Frank almost welcoming this, knowing it was finally over; Tark still struggling, still trying to come up with a plan, as the darkness crept into his brain.

Twenty-three

WALLY FROZE FOR A MOMENT WHEN HE SAW FAY
fall off the platform. She needed help, he knew that. But
there was a guy out there trying to kill him. *But she needs
help right now.*

Wally peeked around the lifeboat-deck opening. The
guy with the gun had untied the fishing boat, which was
falling back into the darkness behind the *Extravaganza*.
The guy was at the stern, but not looking Wally's way.
Wally jumped out and ran to the platform edge.

"Fay!" he shouted. No answer. He frantically scanned
the ship's wake and . . .

. . . *and there she was*. Her body, anyway, a wave lifting
it up, as if to display it to Wally, maybe fifteen yards behind the ship. She was facedown and not moving. And getting away every second.

Wally kicked off his shoes and was about to jump when
he had the smartest idea of his entire life. He turned,
sprinted back to the lifeboat deck, grabbed a life preserver,

turned, sprinted back to the edge of the platform, and leaped into the sea. He went under, came up, looked around, saw the brightly lit *Extravaganza,* moving away. Holding the life preserver in one arm, Wally started side-stroking in the opposite direction, toward Fay, toward the darkness.

. . . *ROAR VROOM WHAM* "FUCK!" "FASTER!" *ROAR VROOM WHAM* "FUCK!" "FASTER!" *ROAR VROOM WHAM* "FUCK!" "FASTER!" *ROAR VROOM WHAM* "FUCK!" "FASTER!"

"LOU," shouted Stu Carbonecca. "I GOT TO SLOW IT DOWN NOW. THE ANGLE OF THE WAVES IS GONNA . . ."

"YOU DON'T SLOW DOWN," shouted Lou. "YOU KEEP GOING AS FAST AS YOU CAN, YOU HEAR ME?"

"BUT LOU," said Stu, terrified of the consequences of arguing with Lou Tarant—*nobody argued with Lou Tarant*—but equally terrified of the consequences of pushing the Cigarette to this insane speed in these seas, "WE ARE GONNA . . ."

He shut up then, because he saw the wave coming, a very large one, at a bad angle. He yanked the wheel to the left, but there wasn't enough time. The Cigarette roared up the face of the wave and launched itself into space, but this time rotating, corkscrewing through the air, staying airborne so long that it rotated 270 degrees, which unfortunately was 90 degrees too little. In the next instant, at 70 miles per hour, it crash-landed on its side, the boys in the cockpit had time for only part of one last plaintive chorus . . .

FUUUUUUUUUUUUUUUUUUUUU . . .

* * *

"OH, LOOK AT THIS," ARNIE WAS SAYING. HE had removed a card from his wallet and was brandishing it at Phil. "This is an official New Jersey driver's license."

Phil took the card, brought it up to the lower lens of his trifocals, studied it for a moment.

"This is *expired*," he said. "This expired in 1989."

"Oh yeah?" said Arnie. "So where's *your* license?"

"I didn't bring it with me," said Phil. "I didn't think I'd hafta drive the boat."

"Well you don't hafta," said Arnie. "I can drive the boat."

"You don't even know which way," said Phil. "You were driving it *east,* for Godsakes."

"OK," said Arnie, "now I got it going west."

Phil looked at the compass.

"It says we're going north," he said.

"Let me see that," said Arnie.

"See the N?" said Phil. "N means north."

"I know that," said Arnie.

"I think I should drive," said Phil, grabbing one side of the wheel.

"NO," said Arnie, grabbing the other.

The two old men bumped against each other, each trying to break the other's grip on the wheel. After a moment, they both realized it was hopeless.

"All right then," said Phil. "Be an idiot."

"All right then," said Arnie. "I will."

And the *Extravaganza* steamed on into the night, Arnie firmly in control of his side of the steering wheel, Phil firmly in control of his.

THE AROMA THAT JOHNNY AND TED SMELLED ON the dark bridge of Tark's boat was a pungent mixture of flatulence and love juices. The flatulence was of course supplied by Tina, who, like Johnny and Ted, had clambered up the ladderway to escape the shooting and the dead bodies and the puke stench. There she had found Jock, and in her terror, she had forgotten her jealous rage and clung to him fiercely. He had clung fiercely back, every bit as confused and horrified as she was by the bizarre carnage outside.

They had huddled in the near-darkness, occasionally hearing shouts and gunshots, not daring to go back outside. In time, Tina's fierce clinging had produced an involuntary reaction in Jock, one that Tina could not help but notice, as he was still naked. One thing had led to another, and pretty soon Tina was naked, too, and they were doing The Deed with the intensity of two people who thought the end might very well be nigh.

"Yes," Tina was saying. "Oh yes. *YES.* Yesyesyesyes*YES.*"

"Yes," agreed Jock.

"Hello?" said Ted.

"AAAIIEEEE," said Tina, leaping up off Jock and scrambling to her feet. There was just enough light from the receding *Extravaganza* coming through the bridge window that Ted and Johnny both could see her entire body clearly for the three seconds it took her to find her blouse and hold it in front of her. They both knew immediately that they would treasure those three seconds for the rest of their lives.

"Oh, *man,*" said Johnny.

"Johnny, Ted?" said Jock. "That you?"

"Jock," said Ted, "where the hell have you *been*?"

"I've been running all over the ship," said Jock. "But listen, there are all these *dead* guys down there, and this guy was *shooting* at . . ."

"We know," said Ted.

"You know?" said Jock.

"You wouldn't believe," said Ted. "We'll talk about it later, but right now we need to use the radio on this boat to call the Coast Guard."

"Why can't the captain call the Coast Guard?" said Jock.

"They shot the captain," said Johnny.

"Oh man," said Jock.

"Yeah," said Johnny.

"So we're supposed to get on the radio, which is up here by the steering wheel somewhere, and call the Coast Guard," said Ted. "We're supposed to tell them to come out here and rescue the ship."

"We're not at the ship anymore," said Tina, who was looking out the window."

"What?" said Ted.

"The ship is way back there," she said, pointing. "We're out here on our own."

"Oh, MAN," said Johnny.

Twenty-four

THE FIRST THING THAT SURPRISED WALLY WAS
that he found Fay, out there in the big waves, which turned
out to be much bigger when he was in them than they had
looked from the ship.

But he found her, found her pretty quickly, and—this
was the second thing that surprised Wally—she was moving. She even had her head out of the water a little, though
in the light from the ship he could see she was struggling.

He sidestroked to her, and she grabbed at him, and right
then he was very glad that he'd brought the life preserver.
Although now he was sorry he had not thought to bring
two.

"It's OK," he said. "It's OK. Hold this. You'll be OK.
Hold on to this."

She had the life preserver now and, feeling it support
her, calmed down a little. She coughed up some water.

"You OK?" Wally said.

"I don't know," she said.

"You'll be fine," Wally said. The *Extravaganza* was getting farther and farther away, sometimes completely disappearing behind the waves. The sea around them was getting darker.

"What happened?" Fay said.

"You don't remember?" Wally said.

"No," said Fay. "I remember I heard shots and came running back, but the last thing I remember was coming out the door."

"When you came running out, the skinny guy shot at you, and you fell off the platform."

"He shot at me?"

"Yeah. And you grabbed your head."

Fay put her hand to her head, felt around, found something that felt wrong on the scalp on the right side. She pulled her hand away and felt that her fingers were sticky.

"He got my scalp," she said.

"Are you OK?" said Wally.

"I think so," she said. "It's bleeding, but I feel OK."

"Good," said Wally.

"So how'd you wind up in the water?" she said.

"I jumped in," he said.

"You *jumped* in?" she said.

"To get you," he said.

Fay thought about that.

"Thank you," she said.

"Any time," said Wally.

A big swell lifted them high. In the distance, they saw the *Extravaganza,* stern toward them, looking much smaller now. The swell passed, and they were down in a deep trough. They could hear the water high on each side of them, but they could not see it, because there was no light now.

"This is pretty bad, huh?" said Wally.

"I'm afraid so," said Fay.

* * *

THERE WAS LIGHT NOW ON THE BRIDGE OF TARK'S
boat; Ted had found a wall switch. Tina, to the disappoint-
ment of Johnny and Ted, was again fully dressed. Jock was
still naked.

"OK," said Ted, "we need to start the engine, so we can
drive back to the ship."

"I don't know that I want to go back to the ship," said
Tina.

"She's right," said Jock. "There's guys shooting back
there."

"Plus," said Johnny, "how're we gonna *find* the ship."

The other three followed Johnny's gaze out the window:
The *Extravaganza* was no longer visible.

"Well, we need to start the engine and go *somewhere*,"
said Ted. "And we need to call the Coast Guard on the radio."

"Let's go back to Miami," said Johnny. "Back to land."

That sounded pretty good to everybody.

"OK," said Ted. "Anybody know how to drive a boat?"

Nobody answered.

"All right, I'll try to start the boat," said Ted. "You guys
work the radio."

"I'm gonna go downstairs and find some clothes," said
Jock. "I don't like being this naked."

"Man," said Johnny, "it smells *awful* down there."

"I know that," said Jock. "But it doesn't smell so great
up here, either." He glanced meaningfully at Tina, whose
back was to him.

"What was *that* supposed to mean?" said Tina.

"Nothing," said Jock, heading down the ladderway.

Tina turned to Ted and Johnny and repeated, "What was
that supposed to mean?"

"Beats me," said Ted, looking busy at the controls. "Listen, Johnny, I'll try to start the engine. And you work on the radio."

"I think I'll open a window first," said Johnny.

"Good idea," said Ted. "Get some fresh air in here."

"THAT'S NOT WEST," SAID PHIL, FROM HIS SIDE
of the steering wheel.

"Yes it is," said Arnie, from his side.

"No it's not," said Phil. "The W is supposed to be pointing straight at us."

"It is."

"No it isn't."

"That's because you're at an angle, you idiot."

"I'm not at an angle. *You're* at an angle."

"Don't tell me I'm at an angle. I know when I'm at an angle."

"Don't call me an idiot."

"Idiot."

"You're the idiot."

"Oh I am, am I?"

"Yes, you are."

"OK, fine, then."

"Fine."

They both shut up then, co-steering the massive ship in silence, each man thinking the same thing:

This was *great*.

THE WORLD'S MOST VALUABLE INFLATABLE BOAT
drifted north, carried by the Gulf Stream, rising and falling with the swells.

Twenty-five

FAY REFUSED TO WEAR THE LIFE PRESERVER.

"You don't have one," she pointed out.

"I didn't get shot in the head," Wally replied.

But she wouldn't put it on. She insisted that they share it, one on each side, holding on. It provided some buoyancy, but not always quite enough for two, especially in some of the bigger swells, when they had to work to keep their heads up.

It was tiring, but they knew they couldn't relax, couldn't sleep. They couldn't do much of anything except hang on and wait for daylight. Although, when they thought about it—which they tried not to—they knew daylight would not significantly improve their situation.

What they could do was talk. Fay was pretty quiet at the beginning—Wally thought maybe she had a concussion, though he didn't want to say it—so at first Wally did most of the talking. He told Fay about his career as a musician, how he'd really thought, for a long time, that because he was as good as a lot of guys who made it—no, he was *better* than a lot of guys who made it—that he was bound to make it, too, to be famous and rich and travel in his own jet. He told her how he'd come to accept that none of that would ever happen, and how he'd come to feel, the older he got, more and more like a loser, still schlepping his guitar and amp around when other guys his age had careers and mortgages, but how he still loved the music, still couldn't see himself wanting to do anything else.

He told her about some of the gigs they'd played, like the private party at a spectacular mansion on Biscayne Bay owned by a billionaire real-estate developer, where they'd played in a living room the size of a tennis court, a bunch of rich people dancing in front of them, and there was a balcony at the back, and the trophy wife of the developer had appeared on the balcony and, looking straight at Jock, removed every article of her clothing, stood there naked for a good thirty seconds, then turned and walked off down the hall, and Jock had stopped the song right there with an improvised drum flourish, then stood up and announced, "Ladies and gentlemen, we're gonna take a short break."

Fay actually laughed at that, out there among the big waves. She laughed again when Wally had told her about the Revenge Song, and how the band had changed its name to Johnny and the Contusions.

She fell silent when he talked about how he'd quit the band and tried to get a grown-up job, so Amanda would be happy with him, and how he'd gone to the office one night and watched her kiss her rich boss. He talked about how he was living with his mom now, and how he loved her but she was driving him crazy trying to make him eat waffles at eight in the morning and telling him over and over and over about the time she saw weatherman Bob Soper buying cold cuts at the Publix.

While Wally was talking about his mom, he realized

Fay was crying. He asked her why, and that was when she began to talk. She told him how, right then, her mom was taking care of her little girl, Estelle, and the last time she'd talked to them, it hadn't gone well because Estelle was crying and her mom was being her usual combination of judgmental and wrong, but she knew her mom really loved her, and she really loved her mom, and she loved Estelle so much that she sometimes felt she couldn't bear the weight of it, and she wasn't afraid of dying so much as she was afraid of dying without ever holding Estelle again, ever kissing her hair, ever helping her act out the Snow White story, moving her little figurines around, making their squeaky little voices.

By then she was sobbing, and Wally put his arm around her and told her not to worry, she'd see Estelle again, they'd get out of this fine, the Coast Guard would come out looking. And Fay had reminded Wally that she *was* the Coast Guard, which had not exactly made her laugh again but at least stopped the crying. And Wally had asked her what was the deal with that, her being in the Coast Guard, and she said she was basically a kind of cop or detective in the Coast Guard, and she'd been doing well in her career until she'd married her dickwad ex-husband, Todd, who didn't like her working, and especially not working in a job that involved carrying a gun and dealing with criminals, and she had stupidly tried to please him, which was how she had Estelle, who was the best thing that ever happened to her, but who had also caused Fay to transfer, after her maternity leave, to a more clerical job, which she hated but which allowed her to be home at regular hours, which was important because she got no help with Estelle from her dickwad ex-husband, Todd, because, as Fay eventually determined, he was busy screwing every living thing that had a vagina, including probably some Labrador retrievers.

This had led to the divorce, and an even worse child-care situation, and money problems caused by her dickwad ex-husband's deep emotional need to file lawsuits. And so Fay, determined to get back on a better career track, had volunteered for the undercover assignment on the *Extravaganza,* which various federal and state law-enforcement agencies were pretty sure was being used for illegal activities. Everybody had thought it was pretty clever, putting a female CGIS agent who happened to be, in addition to smart and well-trained, a pretty hot babe, on the ship as a cocktail waitress. Nobody had considered the possibility that she might end up in a storm at night way out in the Gulf Stream sharing a single life preserver.

The worst of it, Fay told Wally, is that her mom, who was terrified of pretty much everything except certain brands of bottled water, had told her maybe three hundred times that she was crazy to take this assignment, that she could get killed out there, and now Fay would have to admit she was right, and if they ever got back, Fay would never hear the end of it.

If they ever got back.

Then it was quiet for a while, and then Wally, trying to keep things upbeat, pointed out that, hey, this was kind of like the end of *Titanic,* with him as Leonardo DiCaprio and Fay as whatshername. Then they had spent nearly fifteen minutes trying to remember what whatshername's name was, and they couldn't, but they made a pact that they would not drown until they did.

And then Wally said, speaking of Leonardo DiCaprio, he needed to explain what had been going on back there on the ship when he'd stopped her in the casino and started blithering about Leonardo DiCaprio. He told her he'd been rehearsing it so he'd have something witty to say to her. He told her he'd felt like the world's biggest moron. She told him, to be honest, she barely remembered it, because she was thinking about reaching her mom. But in truth she did remember it, and found herself being amazed that this man, floating out here with her now, was the same person as the guitar player back there on the ship.

Then she was quiet for a while, and Wally asked if she was OK, and she said she was feeling cold, and her head hurt. And Wally wanted more than anything to be able to do something for her, but he couldn't think of anything, so he asked if she'd like him to sing, and she said OK, and he said what did she want to hear, and she said did he know any show tunes, and he said as a matter of fact he did, and in fact in the eleventh grade he had played the part of Professor Harold Hill in the Bougainvillea High School production of *The Music Man*. And she said was he kidding, because that was her favorite musical, and he said no he wasn't kidding, and he began to sing it to her, song by song, because he knew them all. Sometimes she listened quietly; sometimes she sang softly along, taking the part of Marian the Librarian. They sang together when they got to the most beautiful love song ever written, "Goodnight My Someone."

> But I must depend on a wish and a star
> As long as my heart doesn't know who you are.

But mostly Wally did the singing, sang the whole thing, his mouth close to Fay's ear, so she could hear the words over the sound of the dark waves.

TED HAD THE ENGINES RUNNING, FINALLY. IT had taken him quite a while to figure out that, in addition to turning two keys, you had to press two buttons. But the engines were running, and now he was working on the controls. There were four levers, and he had figured out that two of them were throttles and two of them were like

gearshifts, making the boat go forward or backward. He
had decided forward was the way to go, but which direction? This brought him to the compass. He wanted to go
back to Florida. That would be . . . OK, Florida was on the
East Coast, so . . . no, wait a minute . . .

Johnny was having his own problems with the radio.
Not turning it on: It was already on. His problem was deciding what channel to use. The Coast Guard cocktail waitress had told him to use a specific channel, but he couldn't
remember which one, and neither could Ted. The radio had
been on channel 24, so Johnny had spent a while on that,
saying "Mayday! Mayday!! Coast Guard!" into the microphone, and then waiting, hearing only static. So after a few
minutes, he'd turned to channel 25 and tried again. Static.
He was up to channel 28 now.

That's what was happening on the bridge of Tark's
boat—Ted looking at the compass; Johnny listening to
static; Tina passing gas—when Jock's face appeared in the
ladderway, smiling hugely.

"You find some clothes?" said Tina.

"A pair of shorts," said Jock. "But I found something
else."

"What?" said Tina. Ted and Johnny were also watching
now.

"You are not gonna believe this," said Jock.

"What?" said Ted.

"OK," said Jock. "The room down here, with the puke?
Well, there's a room in front of it. And guess what I found
in there?"

"WHAT?" said Tina, Ted, and Johnny simultaneously.

By way of answer, Jock pulled up his right hand and
plopped something on the bridge floor. He pulled his hand
away, and there was a wad, a big wad, of fifty-dollar bills.

"Oh, man," said Johnny.

"There's two bags of it downstairs," said Jock.

"What?" said Ted.

"Two bags filled with money," said Jock. "BIG bags."

"Holy *shit*," said Ted, who suddenly found himself thinking, once again, about his 1989 Mazda.

"And that ain't all," said Jock.

The other three said nothing, only watched as Jock pulled up his left hand and plopped something else on the floor: a brick of what would prove, soon, to be very high-grade marijuana.

ABOARD THE *EXTRAVAGANZA OF THE SEAS*, THINGS were degenerating. The staff had figured out that there was some kind of trouble, especially when the cashier's cage shutter came down. But the staff knew that strange things sometimes happened on this ship, and that it was not wise to ask questions. So for quite a while the bartenders, barmaids, and croupiers tried to carry on as normal. And for quite a while most of the gamblers, who generally ignored everything except whatever game they were playing and whatever drink they were drinking, were oblivious.

Eventually, however, it became obvious that something was seriously wrong. By 11:30 P.M., the gambling was supposed to be stopped as the ship got inside the three-mile limit. But it was well past midnight now, and the casinos had not been ordered closed. In fact, Manny Arquero, who always issued that order, and most of the other orders, was nowhere to be seen.

What to do? Some of the croupiers decided to shut down their tables, but with the cashier's cage closed, they had nowhere to take their cash, their chips. Some of the passengers were loudly complaining that they wanted to cash in their winnings. Others were hungry. Many were getting tired, and wanted to go to bed. People were pulling out their cell phones to call Miami and see what was going on, but everybody saw the same message: NO SERVICE.

The passengers hounded the ship employees, but nobody knew anything except Mara Purvis and Joe Sarmino, and they had agreed it was better not to tell anybody about the men with the guns, for fear of starting a panic. One passenger, a nurse, was telling people an alarming story about being grabbed by two guys—she couldn't find them now—who claimed that the captain of the ship had been shot. A group of men decided to go up to the bridge, but they found their way blocked by a steel door with an electronic lock, and nobody knew the code. They pounded on the door, and there was no answer.

One reason there was no answer was that Arnie and Phil did not hear as well as they used to.

The other reason was that both of them had dozed off on their feet. Neither had let go of the wheel, but now, as the ship continued to surge forward in the night, the moans of the injured captain were mixed with the snores of the men at the helm.

Twenty-six

"YOU OK?" SAID WALLY. "FAY?" HE NUDGED HER,
then again, harder. She jerked her head up, startled.

"Sorry," he said. "I just wanted to make sure you're not, I mean, you're . . ."

"I'm cold," she said.

"Just keep talking," he said. "Remember, it's Leonardo DiCaprio who freezes to death. That's me. You'll be fine. You're whatshername."

He was hoping to get a smile, but Fay just said, "I'm cold," and closed her eyes again.

"It'll be light soon," said Wally. "They'll come find us, the Coast Guard. I mean, the rest of the Coast Guard. When it gets light, somebody will come."

He looked at the sky, which was still pitch black, and in his mind he came as close as he had ever come to praying.

Please, please. Somebody come.

* * *

TARK'S BOAT WAS NOW HEADED DUE EAST, THE consensus of the brains on the bridge being that this was how to reach the East Coast. Of course, the brains on the bridge were not functioning normally. Even with the window open, the smell of cannabis mixed with flatulence hung heavy in the air.

Ted was at the wheel. Jock was sitting on the floor, staring at the pile of fifty-dollar bills. Tina was asleep with her head in his lap. Johnny was by the radio, currently tuned to channel 47, but he had given up on reaching anybody, and was concentrating now on making rhythmic clicks by pressing the microphone button.

After a full half-hour of silence, Ted turned to Johnny and said, "OK, I think I see your point."

Johnny looked up from the microphone. "What point?" he said.

"About the Hawaiians," said Ted.

Johnny looked at Ted for a full ten seconds.

"Well it's about damn time," he said.

AS THE FIRST LIGHT OF DAWN REACHED PALM Beach, Wilfredo Hernandez, trimmers in hand, worked his way along a thick hedge, expertly snipping off the occasional protruding sprig, leaving a perfectly flat wall of green. This was his favorite time at the Breakers, the historic, elegant hotel where he worked as a groundskeeper. It was cool and still relatively quiet, as most of the guests were asleep.

Of course, today the sea was rough, with the big waves from Tropical Storm Hector crashing against the seawall about twenty yards away. But the sky was clearing fast, and it would be a nice day—sunny, but with enough wind to keep it from feeling too hot. Wilfredo paused and looked out to sea, admiring the sunrise, and . . .

Ay Dios mio.

Wilfredo dropped his trimmers, turned, and ran toward the hotel, frantically rehearsing the English words he would need to tell somebody what was coming.

Twenty-seven

WALLY HEARD IT, OVER THE SOUND OF THE waves.

An engine. A helicopter engine.

Wally looked up. The sky was a lot lighter now. He hadn't noticed this; he'd been concentrating on Fay, on keeping her head out of the water.

"Fay," he said. "A helicopter. You hear it? Fay? You hear it?"

Fay moaned, mumbled something, but didn't open her eyes.

"Fay, come on, *please*," said Wally.

She moaned again.

Wally strained to hear the engine, hear whether it was coming closer. For a minute or two, he thought it was, *yes, definitely, it's definitely louder now . . .*

But then it was quieter.

And then it was gone.

Please. Please come back.

* * *

FOR WHATEVER REASON—PROBABLY SOME MOVE-
ment of the ship—Arnie and Phil both woke up at almost
exactly the same time. This meant that they saw, simultaneously, that the *Extravaganza of the Seas* was heading directly toward a big wall, behind which was a major
building.

And so Phil and Arnie, without saying a word, decided,
simultaneously, that it would be a good idea to turn the
wheel, which they were both still gripping.

And this was when a miracle occurred, a miracle that,
experts later agreed, definitely prevented a much more serious loss of property, and almost certainly saved some
lives.

Arnie and Phil, without saying a word, both turned the
wheel *the same way*.

TED DID NOT SEE THE ISLAND UNTIL HE DROVE
the boat into it. This was because Ted had become fasci-
nated by the compass, staring intently at the E, for east,
and wondering how it worked, how it *knew*. He understood
magnetism was involved, magnetic rays from the north
pole, and somehow the compass was picking them up. But
how? To him, the compass looked like a plastic ball, floating in liquid; how could a thing like *that* pick up rays from
a pole thousands of miles away? And what happened when
the north pole ran out of rays? Would compasses stop
working?

Ted wanted to ask somebody about this, but Jock was
asleep, and Johnny was in some kind of microphone-click-
induced trance. So Ted was left alone to ponder the issue of
world magnetism depletion, which was why he failed to
notice the island until the boat ran aground, shuddering as

it plowed forward a few yards in the soft sand, then stopped. Incredibly, Ted had the presence of mind to shut down the engines. Then he turned to Johnny and the now-awake Jock and Tina.

"We're here," he said.

Dawn was breaking now, and they saw that they had come aground on a wide, white beach, deserted as far as they could see. Beyond the beach they saw brown, scrubby vegetation, but no trees, no cars, no buildings, no people.

"This isn't Miami," Johnny observed.

"Well," said Ted, "at least it's not the ocean."

Everybody agreed on that.

"Maybe there's a road up there," said Jock. "I could go look."

"I'm going with you," said Tina. "I don't want to stay here with the dead guys."

"Oh man," said Johnny, who had forgotten about the dead guys. So had Ted. Pretty quickly, they agreed that they would all go look for the road.

"What about the other stuff?" said Jock. "There's two bags full of money downstairs, and a *whole* lotta pot."

Everybody looked at everybody.

"All that shit belongs to *somebody*," Johnny pointed out.

"True," said Tina, who, as a croupier, had more experience with financial and legal matters than the other three combined. "But whoever it belongs to is probably dead."

Everybody looked at everybody some more.

"OK, then," said Ted.

Twenty-eight

WALLY HAD GIVEN UP ON TRYING TO GET FAY TO open her eyes. She hadn't spoken in quite a while now; she hadn't even moaned recently. Wally was trying to concentrate on keeping her head up, but he was very tired himself now, and very cold, and Jesus he was *thirsty*. And although he fought against thinking it, it was beginning to creep into the corners of his mind, the thought that it would be so much easier, so much more pleasant if this just *ended*, whatever way it had to end.

As hopelessness and surrender inexorably took possession of Wally's soul, he thought about his mom, wondered why he'd always acted so annoyed at her, a lonely woman who loved her boy, who just wanted to make her boy some waffles. When he'd left for the ship last night, a million years ago, she'd tried to give him her umbrella, which was purple, and he'd brushed it away, saying Mom for God's sake it's *purple,* and she'd said yes but it would keep him from getting wet out there, if he got wet he might catch cold, and he'd said Mom for God's sake I'm not a *baby,* and he'd barged out the door, ashamed to be a man living with his mom, without saying good-bye. *He hadn't even said good-bye.*

And now Wally was weeping, for himself, and his mom, and Fay, and *her* mom, and her little baby girl who liked to play Snow White, and now Wally's weeping had turned to sobbing, and now he hoped that Fay wouldn't wake up, wouldn't see him like this, and he tried to stop but it just got worse, Wally bawling until snot dripped from his nose, bawling so hard that he could not see straight, bawling so hard that he did not hear the noise until it was coming from right there above him, the noise from the big engine of the big helicopter with the man leaning out the side doorway, the loudspeaker saying something, something that Wally couldn't make out. But he knew it had to be good news.

Epilogue

IN THE WEEKS THAT FOLLOWED, TWO STORIES
dominated the news.

One was the aftermath of Tropical Storm Hector. In terms of property loss, it was not that bad: some trees down; some power outages; flooding in the areas that always get flooded.

What made Hector newsworthy was the loss of life, for what was a minor storm: a total of nine deaths. Incredibly, all nine of these were employees of Channel Nine News— four reporter-cameraman teams and one helicopter pilot, all of whom were killed in a freakish cause-and-effect chain of accidents. One of the accidents also injured an ambulance driver, but he was expected to recover.

Ironically, the report that set off this chain reaction— that a boy was electrocuted playing in water near downed power lines—turned out to be incorrect. The boy had in fact slipped, hit his head on a fire hydrant, and been knocked out. He soon regained consciousness and was released after treatment.

The story of the tragic deaths of these nine courageous journalists was to dominate Channel Nine's programming for almost two full weeks. There was the extensive live coverage of the funerals, of course, but there were also numerous special reports, and a major three-hour tribute to what the station called the Fallen NewsPlex Nine, which featured an elaborately remixed and overdubbed version of Elton John's "Candle in the Wind," which resulted in a lawsuit filed by lawyers for Mr. John, who pointed out that their client had never sung any verses involving a helicopter.

As a result of its coverage of this story, Channel Nine News won six TV-news awards, four of them for graphics.

The other major story, which soon became much bigger than Hector, and which produced surprising twists and wrinkles almost daily, was the saga of the casino cruise ship *Extravaganza of the Seas*.

At first it seemed simple enough, although certainly dramatic: Somehow, perhaps because of the bad weather, the ship had gone far off course; at dawn, it crashed into the seawall at the historic and posh Breakers Hotel in Palm Beach. The ship was badly damaged, but fortunately it hit the wall at enough of an angle that it ground slowly to a stop without the violence of a head-on collision, so none of the passengers were seriously injured (although ultimately more than three hundred lawsuits were filed).

It soon became clear that some strange things had been happening aboard the *Extravaganza*. For one thing, the captain, Edward Smith, had been shot in what appeared to be some kind of hijack attempt. Smith was close to death when rescue workers got to him on the bridge, but he apparently was going to pull through. He told police that he had no idea who the men were who shot him, or why.

The story got weirder. With the captain down, the ship's helm had apparently been taken over by two retired men, Arnold Pullman, 83, and Phil Hoffman, 81, who had somehow, with no nautical training, brought it back to land.

But the real attention-getter was the gory tableau found on a platform at the stern of the ship, where some kind of gunfight had broken out. Five men were found, all apparently shot to death: Henry Wilde, the ship's first officer; four members of the ship's crew; Manny Arquero, the casino pit boss; and a William Holman, who police identified as a career criminal, and whose presence on the ship was not explained. Who had shot these men, and why, and what this had to do with the shooting of the captain, was not immediately clear; police said apparently nobody had attempted to rob the casino, or the passengers.

Adding to the mystery was the fact that the owner of the *Extravaganza,* multimillionaire Miami entrepreneur Bobby Kemp, was missing, and a nationwide police manhunt had so far failed to turn him up.

The media were in a frenzy: *What had happened aboard the Ship of Death?* There were rumors that drug trafficking might have been involved, perhaps some kind of rendezvous at sea. The *Extravaganza*'s dinghy was missing, but that mystery was solved when the Coast Guard found the wreckage of an inflatable boat, entangled with two *Extravaganza* life preservers, drifting in the Gulf Stream.

That was not all they found out there, as reported in the next day's *Miami Herald:*

- They found the floating body of a man, John "Kaz" Kazarstsky, who had been shot three times. Kazarstsky, who had an extensive criminal record, was identified by several passengers who said they had definitely seen him aboard the *Extravaganza* that night. But why he'd been there, and who shot him, was not clear.

· They found an upside-down Cigarette boat, with eight men clinging to it, every single one of whom had long been suspected by the feds of being connected with a powerful Miami-based criminal organization involved in, among other things, narcotics smuggling. Incredibly, the boat they were clinging to contained a large quantity of cocaine, which made this an extremely easy bust. Even more incredibly, one of the men clinging to the boat was Louis Tarant, who was believed by the feds to be a very high official in this organization, much too smart to get personally involved in a delivery operation. Everybody assumed that the Cigarette boat had something to do with what happened on the *Extravaganza,* but what? Tarant and his men weren't talking. The only thing that was definite was that they were all going to jail for quite a while.

· Finally, the Coast Guard found, clinging to a single life preserver, two very lucky people who had been working on the *Extravaganza,* a musician named Wally Hartley, and a woman named Fay Benton, who was at first thought to be a cocktail waitress, but who was later identified as a Coast Guard agent working undercover on the ship. Hartley was basically OK; Benton was suffering from a head wound and exposure, but responded to treatment.

When Fay was able to talk, she gave a detailed report to her superiors. There was a lot she didn't know, but she was able to describe Tark and his boat.

This touched off a massive search, and within hours a

boat matching that description was found on a deserted beach on a small, sparsely populated island in the Bahamas. The boat contained a duffel bag filled with cocaine, and something else that made this very big news: the bullet-ridden bodies of two men, one of whom was Bobby Kemp, who, in yet another bizarre twist to this story, was wearing the costume of Conrad Conch.

The media were insane now, reporters from around the world swarming all over the story, reporting everything they heard, most of it not remotely true. Many investigations were launched at many levels; many leads were followed; many theories were devised and endlessly speculated upon. Books were written, and there were two made-for-TV movies.

But in the end, it remained mostly a mystery. Nobody ever did figure out what really happened out there on the *Extravaganza,* because the only person who had known it all was Tark, and his bones were somewhere on the bottom of the Atlantic, with Frank's bones still strangling them. In the end, the authorities stopped actively investigating the *Extravaganza* case, because newer cases came up, and besides, everybody who got killed out there was a scumbag.

LOU TARANT KNEW THAT THERE WAS A LOT OF product unaccounted for, and a lot of money, a *lot* of money. He knew—he *knew*—that it was out there, somewhere. But where? *Where was the money?* He thought about it day and night, in prison. Day and night. It made him fucking *crazy.*

JOHNNY AND THE CONTUSIONS NEVER PLAYED another gig, at least not as Johnny and the Contusions.

Right after the *Extravaganza* crash, Ted, Jock, Johnny,

and Tina each called friends or relatives, saying they were safe in the Bahamas, and they couldn't talk about how they got there, but they would be back soon. They returned to Miami a week later, by private plane, and immediately instituted massive upgrades to their lifestyles—new cars, new clothes, luxury condos.

This is the kind of bandmates Ted, Johnny, and Jock were: They offered to give Wally a full share of the money. This is how Wally had changed: He said no. He knew where the money had come from, and he knew that he could have the money, or he could have Fay. And he picked Fay.

Ted, Johnny, and Jock thought Wally was insane. They were thrilled to be rich. They invested their fortune in, among other things, a South Beach nightclub called Scrotum, the South Florida franchise of a cockfighting league, Enron, and a series of truly astounding parties. They were broke within two years, and went back to gigging, under the name "The Cosines" (don't ask). Sometimes they wished they'd been a little more conservative with their money. But man, did they have some *stories*.

TINA USED HER SHARE OF THE MONEY TO BUY A health-food store, which she ran with great efficiency, but which got surprisingly little repeat business.

ARNIE AND PHIL WERE FAMOUS AT FIRST, THE two old guys who drove the Ship of Death into the hotel. For a while, they were all over the media, culminating in an appearance on Letterman, where they got into an argument when Arnie told Letterman that he would have got the ship back to Miami no problem if Phil had just let go of the damn wheel.

Eventually, the public interest in the *Extravaganza* case died down, and Arnie and Phil returned to their routine at the Beaux Arts Senior Living Center. Eight months after their night on the ship, while they were watching a baseball game on TV, Phil, having just disagreed strongly with Arnie about the umpire's call on a pickoff attempt, died.

Arnie buried his friend, and for a while stayed mainly in his room. After a few months, he started to see Mrs. Krugerman. At first, it was on a strictly pinochle basis, but in time it became more, and finally they got married at a nice ceremony, highlighted by Mrs. Bendocker singing a rendition of "Wind Beneath My Wings" that sent two guests to the hospital.

Arnie was reasonably happy, back in married life. But once a year, he went, alone, to the cemetery, where he placed on Phil's grave a chip from the *Extravaganza* casino, one of the chips he'd had in his pocket that night.

EDDIE SMITH RECOVERED SLOWLY, BUT HE RE-covered. He didn't want to go back to sea, which was just as well, because nobody wanted to hire him to run a ship anyway. But he was more than content to stay on land with Luz and Alejandro, and eventually he got into a nice, successful little business, cleaning pools with his partner, retired *Extravaganza* bartender Joe Sarmino.

MARA PURVIS DECIDED SHE WAS GOING TO DO something more meaningful with her life than be a cocktail waitress. She enrolled in community college, earned a degree in business administration, and got a job at a big South Florida bank. She worked in Human Resources, where her primary responsibility was to help employees fill out claims for medical benefits. In seven months, she quit and went back to being a cocktail waitress.

FAY AND WALLY GOT MARRIED. YOU FIGURED that out a long time ago. They quickly had two more kids, both girls, to go with Estelle. Fay continued her career in the Coast Guard, and did very well, despite almost daily warnings from her mother about the deadly dangers involved. Wally gave guitar lessons part-time. But mainly he stayed home and raised the girls. He loved being a parent, and he discovered he was really good at it. He sang songs to his kids, made up games for them, packed their lunches, told them bedtime stories. The girls loved it, having a stay-at-home dad. One of their favorite things was this: Almost every morning, when their mom had left to go arrest bad people, their dad would take them over to Grandma's house. She made the *best* waffles.

Eventually, Fay and Wally remembered that the name of the actress in *Titanic* was Kate Winslet.

THE HUGE CACHE OF DRUGS THAT TARK HID IN the Bahamas was never found. Eventually, however, some of the packaging began to dissolve, and traces of cocaine, followed by larger and larger quantities, began to show up in the water supply of a major resort hotel. This was good for repeat business.

THE WORLD'S MOST VALUABLE INFLATABLE BOAT is still out there, floating, somewhere.

DAVE BARRY is a Pulitzer Prize—winning journalist for the *Miami Herald*, a guitarist for the legendary Rock Bottom Remainders, and the author of many best-sellers, including *Dave Barry's Complete Guide to Guys*, *Dave Barry Turns 50*, and of course, *Big Trouble*. For a while, his life was even a television series, but then it was canceled. The series. Not the life. He lives in Miami.